Xavier

The Men of Gotham

~ Book Two ~

For my band of misfits,
who make their own unique shapes,
rather than conforming to the world's.

ONE

Him

I can't tell if it's his blood or mine.

But there's an unmistakable metallic taste tainting my tongue.

Not that I care. I barely even notice the rivulets of sweat stinging my eyes and the smattering of bruises I know are slowly blooming against the right side of my rib cage and left thigh.

There isn't time for worrying about the collateral damage.

He is circling me; I'm pivoting on my right leg following him. The air between us is thick, palpable, pulsating with the rhythm of our elevated heartbeats. I'm not looking at any particular part of his body, but rather, focusing on the space around him. The slightest twitch of his bicep, the tiniest shift in the angle of his foot tells me everything I need to know.

So, I wait. And he's not giving anything away.

The thumping in my ears is almost deafening but I'm finding an almost nirvana-level clarity in the chaotic drumming of blood and adrenaline streaming through my body.

One-one-hundred, two-one-hundred, I count silently, *three-one-hund-* and there it is. The toes of his right foot curl into the ground, gripping for traction and I know what's coming. My head tucks into my chest as I duck just as his left leg whips around towards me and I block it with my forearm before hooking my wrist around his ankle and twisting his leg into an inhuman angle; defense and attack both at once.

Just like he taught me.

The jarring of our limbs shudders through my whole body but I hold position until I hear the thud of his chest against the ground. I follow him to the floor, my knee digging into his back, my hand wrapped around the sweat drenched curve of the back of his neck.

Again, I hold and count. *One-Mississippi. Two-Mississippi. Three-Mississippi. Four* – it's almost interminable. And then I hear it. The ding-ding-ding of the bell rings into existence, just as I've been expecting it to.

One hundred and eighty seconds sure is a long time when you're counting them one by one.

My hand relaxes on the neck and I feel my body being pulled into an upright position. It takes a hard slap against my bare back, though, to jolt me back into the moment.

"Holy fuck, man, that was brutal," a raspy voice growls at me from the sidelines, as the hand that slapped my back now steadies me while I take a long, deep breath, the first in minutes. "You trying to get back at him for sleeping with your girl or something?"

I roll my eyes, my drenched palms leaving damp stains on the sides of my shorts as I wipe them before reaching down for my opponent's hand. He turns over onto his back and grips my hand with his giant one and almost drags me down onto the mat with him as I pull him to his feet. My friend and sparring partner for more than a decade. Ram, both in name and in physique. It takes a lot to take him down.

"Please, I wouldn't touch one of his dirty trollops with a ten-foot pole, even though the closest ten-foot pole is right here in my pants," he says, letting go of my hand and patting me on the side of my tenderized torso, making me cringe. He grins in response to my pained scowl, a little consolation for losing the fight. "But yeah, good fight, man. Guess that means I owe you a round at the bar."

"No, man, I'll buy you a round to cheer you up for losing to this little white boy," I say, taunting him back and digging my own hand into his rib cage, making him groan and bend over, clutching his side and letting out a stream of what I can only imagine are the absolute worst cuss words that exist in his native Thai tongue.

I laugh and hand him a bottle of water which he takes, gratefully. "Sounds good to me, but I am on a strict no alcohol diet until after my fight this weekend. It's a big one. I gotta be ready."

"One drink. Come on." I reach out to poke him in the side again, but he's ready for me this time and twists away.

"Nah, you know how I have a propensity to overdo it." He crushes the empty bottle and throws it into the trash can in the corner.

I cock an eyebrow. "'Propensity,' huh? That's a pretty big word for such a tiny brain housed in such a thick skull." I grin at my 6 foot 6 giant of a friend who somehow manages to look a little embarrassed.

"Shut up. My niece gave me some word of the day toilet paper for my birthday."

I laugh, but don't push it. I know how much his niece means to him. She's probably the only one who can reach his heart through all the layers of muscle and protein shakes. "Fine, how about I buy you a vat of boiled pasta and fifteen steamed chicken breasts?"

"You're on. Meet you out front in ten?" Ram's words are muffled by the hoodie being pulled over his head.

"What the fuck? You're not going to shower?" I can feel my face showing my horror.

"Why? Do I need to?"

"My burning nostril hairs say 'in all that is good and holy, fucking hell, yes!'"

"Get fucked!" He lifts his arm and takes, what I can only hope, for his olfactory nerves' sake, is a long, deep, fake sniff. "Mmm-mmm. Like orange blossoms."

"If they were recently fertilized a with truckload of chicken manure!"

"Hey, I'm Thai, we don't have the same propensity for paying for and dousing ourselves in glorified flower water with the names of celebrities printed on the bottle, 'mkay?"

"Jesus. Again, with the 'propensity'? What, you only use one square of toilet paper a day?"

"What can I say, maybe I just have a propensity for 'propensity'?" He grins and gives me a look of pity. "Don't feel bad because I'm becoming more educated than you."

"Yeah, I think my law degree can handle your overuse of one word. Now get your ass in the fucking shower!" I grab our bags and walk to the changing room in the back, satisfied with the sound of his canoe-sized feet dragging behind me.

"Fine, but don't be getting any tawdry ideas when you see my naked body in there. Like I said, I'm on a strict, no pleasure diet until after my fight."

I turn around, just in time to see him whip his shorts and underwear off and twirl them over his head as he tries to run past me.

The last thing I hear as he pushes through the shower doors is the sound of him squealing as the shoe I fling at him leaves a big red welt on his left butt cheek.

***

A gust of wind lifts the flaps of my shirt collar up against my face as I step out of the restaurant and onto the street. Ram jumps into a waiting Uber and waves to me as it drives off. As the car's back lights fade into the distance, I can't help but ponder his last words to me.

"There was something a little too dark in your eyes during the fight. You trying to exercise some demons?" he'd asked, uncharacteristically insightful for someone with a neck that's bigger than his head.

I had brushed it off with a comment about spinach in his teeth but now, walking the streets alone back to my apartment, it's hard to pretend I didn't know exactly what he was talking about. Why today, of all days, I was a little too focused on destruction.

Don't go there, the warning voice inside my head tells me. And I know better than to ignore it. I shake my head, shove my hands into my trench coat's pockets, and turn the corner, one block closer to my destination.

I had refused Ram's offer to share the ride back to my building because I love this time of night. It's not true that New York is a city that never sleeps; it's actually the city that never rests. You can close your eyes, turn off the lights, and even drift off into dreamland. But the heart of the city never stops beating, never stops buzzing with life, with excitement.

Even now, if I look around me, front and back, it looks like there's no one within a hundred feet of me. And there isn't, not on the streets anyway, but the landscape of New York is not two-dimensional. All you have to do is look up. Laughter, tears, broken promises, sweet nothings, rise like hot air, up and up and up, tens and hundreds of feet reaching up to the sky.

Skyscraper after skyscraper. Housing an entire community made famous for its toughness, its tenacity.

I get to another corner and turn. Through the gaps of the other high-rises I can just make out the bright, neon sign spelling out ASH. The headquarters of ASH industries. It's been my true north for almost five years now. I've lived and breathed it, from the purchase of the land to watching the two sides of the inauguration ribbon fall away when it was cut, the ASH building has been my life. And Kaine Ashley, the CEO and founder of ASH Industries, has been my home.

There is a sharp buzzing in my left pocket and I don't have to take it out to know; it's a case of speak of the devil.

"Yes, *boss*?" I answer.

"Quiet." He's not a man of too many words, my best friend.

"What? You're not my boss? Who's the one paying me all this money to be their bitch, then?

"Is that your official title now? Because you're going to have to get new business cards made up."

I can't help but grin. He gives as good as he gets.

"Why are you calling me at 1:13 a.m.? Shouldn't you be in marital bliss?" I ask, knowing his marriage isn't the problem.

"My marital bed is currently occupied by my spouse and my new-born child. There is no room for me," he replies. Seemingly grumpy but the voice is filled with pride.

"No wonder you're calling me. Are there special bitch responsibilities you want me to take on?" I cross the street through a gap in the traffic.

"I need the Kensington contract signed tomorrow. He's wavering, so we've got to lock it down. Address and contracts are in your suitcase. He leaves his house at 6:45 a.m. on the dot every morning. Your car's going to pick you up at 6:20, don't be late." His voice is tense. I know how important this deal is for him.

"What contract in my suitcase? I didn't put anything in there. And who booked the car?"

There is no sound on the other side of the line. But I can imagine some eye rolling.

"Oh." It dawns on me. "Never mind. Patricia. I forget."

"You forget that you have an assistant who anticipates your every need? That's not usually something people should take for granted," he scoffs.

"I guess I'm just that independent."

"Get them signed, Mr. Independent, or the seven-figure loss is coming out of your bonus."

There's a click on the line and I shove the phone back into my pocket just as I cross the last street to my apartment building. From here I can already see Martin, the doorman, at his post by the door even though it's past midnight.

"Hey, Martin," I say, pulling my hand out of my pocket to hold it out to him. "Busy night?"

He takes my hand and gives it a good pump and smiles.

"The busier, the better, Mr. Kent," he says as he lets go of my hand and reaches for the door, pulling it open for me.

Just as I step past him a golden glint catches my eye. My body pivots, involuntarily, following the cab that is hurtling down Second Avenue. I feel my legs move under me, running to follow the cab. *What I doing? I'm just imagining it, it can't be!* But my legs don't listen. They're just a blur against the night, chasing down a yellow New York taxicab at one a.m. As if they're trying to break the light barrier and sprint myself into the past. Ahead, the taxi's back lights glow red and it comes to a stop. I can't believe my luck. I'm gaining. Only another hundred feet ahead. That's all there is between me and...

The door opens and a woman steps out, she flips her hair and for a moment, it's like a golden silken fan over her face. I hold my breath. She closes the taxi door and straightens up, her hair falling down her back.

And I see her.

She is beautiful.

But a stranger.

I trace the lines of her face, comparing. And she comes up short.

I don't realise I'm staring until she frowns, uncomfortable with the inappropriate social interaction.

"I'm... I'm sorry," I say, holding up a hand by way of apology. "I thought... I thought you were someone else." I force myself to look away.

Fatigue suddenly drags through every cell of my body as I slink back to my apartment building. A little older, a little wiser, and somehow, even though I thought it was impossible, a little bit more hopeless.

TWO

Him

I remember the first day I sat behind the desk in my office.

It was a Monday. Of the last week of September. The Manhattan sky was still hanging on to the very last vestiges of an over-extended summer. 80-degree days, that felt more like 90, the heat and humidity stretching long after the calendar pages indicating fall should have arrived. The clouds hung low; from my 30th floor office, it looked like if I jumped out the window, I might be able to land on one and take it for a magic ride around the city.

Not my city of birth.

But my city of re-birth.

There was a black folio waiting on my desk that day, and two pens, both with my name inscribed on them. A small metallic desk clock, with three thin hands ticking away time, sat on the right side of the desk, next to a sleek black phone that had a flashing red button.

I'd pressed the flashing message button and Kaine's voice spoke to me through the small speaker.

"Welcome to ASH Industries. Let's get started."

And that was it.

Short. Succinct. To the point. Just like Kaine. Well, not the short part. I can't help chuckling at the thought of seeing how he'd hold up against Ram in a no-holds barred fight.

"What's so funny?" A voice speaks up behind me, identical to the voice that had greeted me through the phone speaker all those years ago.

"Nothing much. Just thinking of you getting an ass kicking." I spin around in my chair to face my boss. He responds with just the tiniest twitch of his left eyebrow.

"Other than fanciful daydreams, what else have you got for me?"

I slide the envelope on my desk towards him.

"Signed and delivered."

"Not sealed?"

"If you want me to lick something, I'm going to need a raise."

"That would have you getting paid more than me," he growls, picking up the envelope.

"That is completely your prerogative. And still a bargain."

He ignores me, and pulls the documents out of the envelope, flicking through them one by one, meticulous in everything to do with his business.

"What's up for you today?" he asks, as if he doesn't know.

"Ha. Ha." I respond, glaring at him.

"I'm just saying, it doesn't seem as if you remember, considering that," he tilts his chin at me, indicating my blackened eye and split lip.

"Don't worry. I remember."

"Xavier." He says my name like I'm 8 years old.

I can't believe I'm 30 and getting scolded. Not that I don't deserve it. Today's an important day. Not just for the company, but for Kaine, personally. I feel bad about appearing as if I hadn't taken that into consideration before letting Ram pummel me.

"Sorry. Things got a little out of hand at training last night. I'll take care of it."

"See that you do." He turns to leave, then stops. "You want me to send Jade over to see if she can do anything to help?"

"You mean, do I want your wife to come in and put make-up on me? Gee, let me think about it, and get back to you."

I give him what I hope is my most withering look. The effect is minimal; there's a miniscule twitch at the corner of his lips as he steps out of my office. I wait until he's finished saying good morning to Patricia and leaves to make his morning rounds around the office before I call her.

"Patti!"

My assistant strolls through the door, shutting it behind her.

"How'd you know I wanted the door shut?" I ask.

Her look is similar to the one I gave Kaine before.

"I need help. With this," I say, pointing to my face. She holds up a small pink bag she's been hiding behind her back.

"I'm on it," she says, pulling a chair up next to me, laying out on my desk an assortment of torture devices and rainbow-colored palettes.

"No one's to hear about this, got it? Ever." I warn her.

"Trust me. Now shush!" She grins at me as she descends on my face with something that looks like a spongy orange egg. "This isn't going to hurt a bit."

I wish I could believe her.

***

Fuck you, Kaine, I'm thinking to myself 8 hours later as my limo hurtles down 5th Ave. I'm looking forward to tonight the same way I look forward to the part in my annual physical when the doctor lubes up his finger, and something tells me by the end of the night, I'm going to feel just as violated. It's the annual fundraiser for the ASH Foundation, and the aim tonight is to raise the money to build and run two new youth shelters that Kaine has planned.

Not that he needs the signed checks of New York's elite. He could spring for it out of his own piggy bank. But everybody with a fat bank account and a pretty face wants to be seen at these events, and we're happy to give them an opportunity to give. They give us a blank check and we give them more champagne than they know what to do with and the positive publicity. I pat my tuxedo pocket for the list Patti tucked into it before I left the office. A piece of paper with the names of the ten potential donors I'm meant to work on tonight.

The traffic slows and I know we're almost there. Jade was right about choosing the Plaza as the venue for tonight's fundraiser. Why? Because the donors feel comfortable here, it's like home. It's almost like they forget they're in public, dropping their fake smiles and not caring to hide their roaming hands from their spouses. Both husbands and wives, that is. I have had my share of wandering diamond covered fingers slide between my legs.

I take a deep breath and step out of the car, buttoning my suit coat as I look around.

"Xavier Kent," I tell the hostess handing her my invitation and she leads me inside.

"Mrs. Ashley asked me to tell you to please find her once you arrived," she tells me. Her eyes lock on mine a little too long. I take the moment to give her my own once over. Jet black hair, not natural. Tall, slim... too slim. I inwardly shrug and give her a nod to acknowledge her message.

I spot Jade as soon I step into the ballroom. She's gorgeous in a gold fitted Gucci gown. Apparently post pregnancy agrees with her. She smiles and runs over to me, and I can't help feeling my heart swell - both for my affection for her, and how much joy she's brought to Kaine's life.

"Hey there, heartbreaker," she says, leaning in to give me a kiss right on the cheek. No air kisses for her.

"Looking good, Mrs. Ashley. Where are you hiding those track pants Kaine tells me you've been living in since the birth?"

She pokes her tongue out at me, her eyes still sparkling.

"Oh, they're under here, holding in my wobbly belly." She grins as she peers closer at my face. "Wow, good job Patti did. You can barely see it."

My own smile turns into a scowl and I have to bite the side of my cheek to fight the urge to touch my lip or my tender eye.

"Barely see what?" I say, eyes narrowing.

"The Mac foundation stick No.4," Jade says, enjoying it all a little too much.

"I'm leaving! Where's the bar?"

"No, no bar for you! Mingling for you," she says, her voice getting serious. "You got your post-it?"

I pull it out of my pocket and give it a little wave.

"Yes, ma'am."

"Me too. I've got the Gottliebs. Ugh. I'm going to have to hear about how their son is dating some 47th in line to the Danish throne," she whispers as she leans in, dropping her voice.

"Wanna swap? I got Mrs. Rumsford."

"Hell, no. Anyway, it's not what's in *my* pants that's going to get that big fat check from her." She laughs as I curse under my breath. "Go. Do good." She pats me on the arm just as someone calls her name; she turns and disappears in a cloud of orange blossoms and chiffon.

"First stop. The bar," I tell myself. I'm going to need a drink to get through the night.

"Xavier! Xavier, darling!" I hear my name called. Fuck. Mrs. Rumsford.

"Yes? I am Xavier, how can I help you?" I say, plastering a blank look on my face and holding out my hand to the older woman approaching me.

"Oh, silly Xavier. It's me, Charlotte," she says.

"Oh. No, I know Charlotte Rumsford, you can't possibly be her. You must be her gorgeous daughter who I've heard so much about."

"Oh, shush," she chuckles, hitting me on the arm, but clearly happy to accept the blatant flattery. "But speaking of my daughter," she says, turning to the striking blonde standing next to her. "Xavier, this is Miranda. She's just made partner at Hellen and Gunn. *And* she's single."

"Oh, nice to meet you Miranda. Your mother's told me a lot about you," I say holding out my hand. "Are you having a good night so far?"

If there is such a thing as permanent bitch face, this woman has it. She takes my hand, gives it a limp shake, before sighing and brushing the hair off her shoulder.

She's stunning. I'll give her that. But what's the point if she knows it.

"I'll leave you two to chat," her mother tells us, her eyebrows doing a similar dance to Jade's just minutes before. "Come find me after, Xavier. For my *donation*," she says pointedly, as if the size of that donation is contingent on the success of my conversation with her bitch-faced daughter.

"So, can I get you a drink?"

"Champagne," Miranda tells me, with a voice that sounds as bored as I am with her.

I tip my chin to a passing waiter and pull two champagne flutes off his tray.

"You don't seem too happy to be here," I say, handing the glass to her.

The side of her mouth lifts into a sneer, making the whole illusion of her beauty turn ugly.

"Why should I be? I'm just here to make sure my mother doesn't sign off my inheritance to the first boy toy to tell her something like... how she looks so young, they thought she was her daughter."

Touché.

"It's actually for the ASH Foundation, to build some youth centers," I say, though I don't know why. Something tells me she hates charity even more than boy toys.

"Well, yeah, because everyone knows my mother likes them young."

It takes everything I have to not outwardly roll my eyes. As much as I wasn't looking forward to having to deal with the elder Rumsford woman, I'd have taken a whole night of her over this sour puss any day. I take a breath. *For the kids, Xave, for the kids.*

"So, how do *you* like them, then?" I ask, with every last ounce of charm I can muster.

"I don't. I'm single," she says like a warning. She needn't have bothered.

"So, I've heard."

"By *choice*."

"I don't doubt it for a second. Because that'd be *my* choice. Steering well fucking clear of you, Miss Rumsford. Have a good night." I raise my glass to her, enjoying the sight of her jaw dropped wide open, and leave.

The next hour or so isn't as bad as the first encounter, and I'm finding I'm starting to enjoy myself. Or maybe it's that the champagne is working. By the time I make my way around the room and the bell dings for everyone to take their seats at their dinner tables, I'm finding the schmoozing is becoming easier, and the checks in my pocket are getting bigger.

"Table 3," Jade whispers to me as she rushes past me on her way to the stage. What a surprise, I think to myself, scanning my tablemates. A gay couple, three divorcées and a widow.

I'm going to need more champagne.

I make my way back to the bar as the lights dim and the music fades out, calling everyone's attention to the MC.

"Welcome, everyone. To the ASH Foundation for Children."

There's a smattering of applause and I hang back, watching the show play out on the stage as I nurse a scotch.

"Hey," Kaine says, sidling up to me.

This must be worse for him than me. The famous recluse. As much as he's opened up since Jade, I know he's still not completely comfortable showing his face, with its scars, in public.

I tap my glass, and the bartender pours another drink and I hand it to Kaine.

"How's it going so far?" Kaine says before taking a sip.

"Not too bad."

"Think we'll hit our target?"

"Between my ass in these pants and Jade in her dress, we should be okay."

"You make it sound like I'm pimping out my wife and best friend."

"For charity," I tease him. "Relax. I think Jade's the one pimping us out, anyway. And it's fine."

"Jade says we got a lot of good sponsors this year," Kaine says, referring to the businesses who've donated goods and services for the silent auction.

"Yeah. She's good at that."

"You had a look at the list?"

"Why, is there something I might want?"

"I don't know. Do you want sailing lessons?"

"On the boat I don't have time to go out on?"

"What about an Herme's bag?"

"For the woman I don't have time to date?"

18

"Jade says there's an incredible interior designer offering a full house design. Maybe you can do something about that mausoleum you live in."

"It's minimalist."

"You're starting your own movement - emptyist."

"Fuck off. You have me working so hard, I'm barely there anyway."

"And the rest of the time you're at *my* place. Sitting on *my* furniture."

A woman in a cloud of sequins comes rushing towards us. It's Jade's assistant.

"Um, Mr. Ashley, your wife says, and I quote, 'tell my darling husband and his trusty sidekick to get their asses to their tables.'"

She throws her hands up apologetically and then rushes off again.

We down our drinks and wander off to our respective seats.

An hour and a half later and I'm ready to go home. I start to stand up, saying goodbye to my table companions just as Jade takes the stage. Shit. I can't leave now.

"Firstly, I'd like to thank you again, all of you, for joining us and showing your support for us tonight. This cause is so close to our hearts, and you have shown tonight that it's close to yours as well," Jade says, her hand on her chest as the applause rises and falls. "Well, it's come to that time of the night. The announcement of the winners of tonight's amazing silent auction prizes. I'd like to acknowledge the sponsors who donated such generous gifts and their valuable time to help up reach our goal for tonight."

Jade's assistant comes onto the stage and hands her an envelope.

"The first prize we'd like to announce, is the services of Isabella Fountaine. One of Manhattan's up and coming new interior designers. She has just been named as one of Architectural Digest's "designers to watch" and has been so generous as to donate her services to design an entire home for our winner. But even more generously, she will also be donating her time to the design of our brand new youth centers. Isabella, would you like to join me on stage, please? While I make the announcement?"

A spotlight shines into the crowd. Like everyone else, I turn towards it, trying to make out the figure being singled out, and walking to the stage.

Through the bobbing heads, I can just make out a lock of blonde hair.

Something inside me stirs.

No.

The light continues to move but I can't get a clear view.

"Come on," I whisper, willing her to move faster. Once she gets to the steps up to the stage I'll be able to see-

Fuck.

No.

Fuck!

Yes.

It's her.

I watch as she lifts the skirt of her dress and takes the four steps onto the raised stage and floats across it until she reaches Jade.

I'm winded. I haven't moved, but the air is knocked out of my lungs.

It really is her.

"Isabella... thank you against so much," I can just make out Jade saying. Wait. What? She called her Isabella. That's not... that's not her name.

Maybe it isn't her? No, it is. It definitely it.

I watch as she leans towards the microphone and I hold my breath.

"I'd like to thank the ASH Foundation for all the good work you do," she says, and now there's no doubt.

Everything's suddenly a blur as I watch Jade tear open an envelope, smiling and opening her mouth to speak.

"Wait!"

I find myself on my feet.

There's confusion on the stage, and then I feel the heat of the spotlight on me.

"Xavier?" I see Jade mouth.

"I... I'll double it. The bid." I hear myself saying.

"Um, I'm sorry, Xavier, bidding time is over."

"Then triple it. I don't care. Whatever it is." There's a murmuring from the crowd.

"I – uh, well, this is unprecedented. I'm..." Jade says, flustered.

The woman shields her eyes as she looks out into the sea of tables, looking for me. The second our eyes lock, I know. Whatever she calls herself now. I still know. It's her.

"I don't care how much it costs." The crowd is restless, trying to figure out what's going on.

They're not the only ones.

So, I make it clear.

"I want her. She's mine."

THREE

Her

12 years ago

The bell hanging over the door dings as I enter the ice cream parlor two blocks from my high school. The walls, each painted a different color, are covered in faded posters of different types of sundaes and milkshakes.

"Hey, Malynda, I saved you a seat over here," Randi calls over to me, waving me to her table. I wander over, pushing myself through the crowd. It's only mid-April and already the temperature is in the high 70's. The snow has long ago melted, spring has settled in early this year, and Mainers are taking advantage of the sun.

I drop my backpack onto of the pile of bags in the corner and flop down onto my seat.

"I didn't think I'd see you," Randi says, handing me a spoon and pushing her sundae over to me. It looks good. So good, I'm almost tempted to take a bite. But I know better. I promise myself, in one month I can have all the ice cream I want.

"Yeah, I was supposed to have an extra dance training session tonight, but my partner bailed."

"Really? I thought he would've needed it even more than you."

"That's just it, I think he's given up."

I sink back into my seat thinking about Pierre, my partner for the contemporary dance I have planned for the end-of-year showcase. Until I have an acceptance letter to the college of my choice in my hand, I'm not giving up. I know recruiters are still roaming the schools, looking for their next class of freshmen.

Until I have that acceptance, I can't let up. That includes no ice cream.

I reach for the bottle of water in my backpack, looking around. It's 4 p.m. and there's barely anyone here that I don't recognize. The crowd is made up mostly of juniors and seniors from my school.

"Psst. Stalker, 3 o'clock," I hear Randi's voice whisper into my ear. I instantly turn my neck to the right. But I don't see anything but groups of familiar faces.

"What? Where?" I crane my neck to the left.

"Oh, shit, he's gone. A guy was seriously giving me creeper vibes, staring at us."

"You think everyone's staring at you," I say, only slightly envious of her blue eyes and perfect pout.

"Yeah," she grins, "but this time, I said *us*. You included."

"Well, now I know you're nuts. No one ever notices me when you're around."

"Shut up, you're fucking beautiful. And your body looks like your Dad had sex with a cheetah. All sleek and gorgeous."

"Ew. Thanks for that imagery." I shake my head to clear it.

"Shush, there he is again!" she squeaks and points toward the counter.

I look up, just in time to see a pair of deep green eyes staring at me before the gap of talking heads closes in again, and they're gone.

I feel like an entire bucket of ice water has just been dumped over my head; and I keep looking, hoping to catch another look at him.

"Creepy, huh?" Randi says, through a mouthful of ice cream and nuts.

"Um…" 'Creepy' wasn't what I wasn't the vibe I was getting. More like curious, intrigued.

"Do you know him from somewhere? Have you seen him around?" she asks, twirling her spoon in the air.

I don't recognize him from anywhere. But he looked like he knew me. Intimately.

"Er, no." I force myself to turn back towards her, keeping my voice light. "Do you?"

"Nope, but don't worry, we'll protect you. Right, guys?" Randi shouts to the group sitting around the table.

"What? What's going on?" Jack asks, sitting forward in his seat, his unzipped jacket falling open, as if he'd only just noticed us sitting there.

"Some creepster is starting at us, but I just told Malynda that you'll take care of us."

"Oh yeah, hey... don't be scared," he reaches over and lays a hand on my shoulder, and I try not to shrug it off. "I've got you. I promise not to take my eyes off you, babe."

I don't know how I hold back an eyeroll, but I do.

We hang around for another hour and the crowd dissipates, but the owner of the eyes never reappears. It's close to five when we all get up, picking up our bags off the pile in turn. I feel a sweaty hand grip the back of my neck.

"Hey, babe, I'll see you in history tomorrow, okay?" Jack finishes his promise with a wink, thankfully pulling his hand away before I have to push it away. Ever since the one disastrous date we went on a few weeks ago, I've had a hard time avoiding him.

"Um, sure. See ya," I say, keeping my voice as flat as possible.

I hang back, not wanting to have to spend another second in his presence.

"Need a ride?" Randi asks, as she pulls her hair into a ponytail.

I give her a grateful smile. "No, I'm going to walk home, to make up for the missed work out."

"Okay, call me if you want to chat later."

I give her a wave and watch as the door closes behind her.

The silence is calming. It's only me and the owner behind the counter, wiping dry some clean glasses.

I sit and watch as the second hand makes a full turn around the clock, half waiting for Jack to be gone, half hoping maybe if I wait just one more minute, Mr. Green Eyes will make another appearance. The owner throws me a glance, though, that tells me he'd rather I go.

I sigh and push myself to my feet, hooking my hand into my backpack's strap. Just as I reach for the door handle, there's a loud shout from outside, and another one follows it right away, and then a round of yells. I turn to look at the owner, who just shrugs, and goes back to his work. I tug on the door and run outside to see what's going on.

In the parking lot, a crowd has formed in a circle. Just from their backs I can see it's made up mostly of the people I've just spent the last hour with.

"Get the fucker!" I hear one voice yell and then everyone joins in.

"What the...?" I push through the circle, only to come to a complete standstill at the sight in front of me.

It's him.

Green Eyes.

Except now I can see the rest of him.

He's tall, lanky; his hair is dark and pulled back into a short pony tail. A lock of black hair is plastered against his forehead, sweeping just above his eyes.

Those glinting, emerald green eyes.

That are doing their best to avoid mine.

Jack is circling him, arms up, ready to fight.

"What the fuck is happening?" I ask the guy next to me.

"It's that guy, that guy Randi said was perving on you guys. Jack's showing him that we don't take too kindly to that kinda thing around here!"

"But he didn't do anything!" I yell.

"Looks pretty guilty to me. GET HIM, JACK!!! Fuck him up!" he yells, pumping his fist, his eyes dilated, as if high on the anticipation of bloodshed.

At the sound of the growing cheers around him, I watch as Jack takes a half step back and then lunge, swinging his arm around, his fist making contact with his opponent's face. Everything suddenly moves in slow-motion. I hear myself gasp as Green Eyes stumbles back into the crowd. Someone shoves him forward into Jack's swing radius, and another punch lands on the other side of his face. Jack takes the opportunity to push him to the ground, stepping on his back, holding him down.

"Stop it!" I yell, but I can't even hear my own voice over the shouting. "STOP IT!" I scream again, the air dragging against my throat like a razor. I run over to Jack, pushing as hard as I can against his arm, making him sway to the side. "Get off him! He didn't do anything!"

Jack growls, spinning around towards me, his eyes glazed over and red, his arm raised, ready to strike.

"NO!" Green Eyes, jumps to his feet, shoving me over, standing between me and Jack. I trip and almost fall over, but someone catches me, and holds me upright.

Jack blinks; his arm still raised.

They stand there, chests heaving, blood dripping down the right side of Green Eyes' face.

"Oh, so now the pervert is a hero?" The sarcasm drips from Jack's lips. "Relax, I wasn't going to hit her." He takes a breath and steps back, a sneer creeping up his face as he rubs his knuckles. "I would say I don't hit girls but the black eye you're going to sport tomorrow, is evidence to the contrary."

Green Eyes doesn't move. But I can see his jaw clenching, the vein snaking its way down his throat growing thicker. Something tells me, if I don't stop it, someone is going to get seriously hurt.

"Just... just go," I say, glaring at Jack. "Please."

"Great way to thank me, babe."

"There's nothing to thank you for. Just go!" I yell.

Someone squeezes my arm and I realize it's Randi who had caught me. "Hey. You okay?" she asks, softly.

"It's fine. I'll be alright. I'll see you at school tomorrow." I give her a tight smile.

Jack snickers, shaking his head at me. I stare him down until he finally moves, pushing through a gap in the circle, with the rest of the group following behind him. Leaving me with Green Eyes.

It's almost a minute until we're completely alone, but he hasn't moved. The trickle of blood reaches the top of his dirtied collar, and I reach forward, as if to wipe it away.

As soon as my fingertips touch him, he jumps and pulls away, turning his back to me.

"You go, too," he says, so softly I'm not even sure he said it.

"No, please. Let me help you."

"I said go," he says, louder this time.

I take a breath. I don't know why, I can't walk away.

"You're hurt, at least let me help clean the wound. It's my fault. Jack's a jerk."

He doesn't say anything, but I can see him lift his hand, his fingertips gently touching his cheek.

"Does it hurt?"

"No."

"I'm… I'm really sorry. It's all my fault," I repeat. I don't know what else to say.

"Just go."

I stand for a few more seconds, but I can tell he really doesn't want me there. My throat locks as I try to swallow, wishing I could see his face one more time before I leave.

"I go to Langham High, if you need anything. You can find me there." I don't know why I tell him that, I know he won't use the information. But it's the only thing I can think of to say right now. "I'll… see you later," I say, and take one last look at his back, thin, hunched over. Defeated.

When I'm almost fifty feet away, something tells me to turn around. I catch him, standing by the doorway of the ice cream parlor, watching me go. I raise my hand and wave, but all he does is step through the door, disappearing inside.

***

The first time I ever saw someone dance, I thought she was an angel visiting from heaven. It was on TV, a ballerina, decked out in tulle and pale pink tights floating across the stage as if she and air and gravity were separate only in the constructs of our minds.

She leapt from the ground as if lifted by an invisible harness, performing a grand jeté that appeared frozen in time. In that split second of holding my breath as I waited for her to land, I knew I wanted to be a dancer.

There's little that is more persistent than a four-year-old who's got it in her mind what she wants to do for the rest of her life. Even more so, if she is blessed with the knowledge that her parents will do anything to help her fulfill that dream.

I still remember that first time I donned a leotard and slid my hand along that smooth curve of the barre. Probably the single most perfect moment of my life.

That's what I find myself thinking of as I lay here, my damp legs tangled in the sheets, my t-shirt riding up my midriff as I try to cool off in the already too warm nights.

Dreams are funny things.

It seems there is an infinite source of them, but a finite time in which to achieve them all.

As I've grown, so has my desire to do so much.

One month from graduation, and I still don't know what the future beyond the summer break holds for me. There have been acceptances to a few colleges, but not the one I want. And second best is just not something I'm accustomed to. Something I don't want to become accustomed to.

"Fuck this," I whisper and swing my legs off my bed, grabbing my ballet slippers sitting on the chair by the bedroom door as I tiptoe past my parents' bedroom and down into the basement.

My space.

The dance studio my parents decked out for me for my 10th birthday when they finally realized, I was serious about dancing. Nothing special, a wooden floor, a menagerie of collected mirrors propped up against the walls, and a sturdy barre.

That's all I need.

I tuck the wireless earphones into my ears, the music already blaring.

I take a deep breath.

And I dance.

Dance until my feet rub raw in my slippers, my muscles ache from elongation, and my mind tires of running in circles.

And yet, still I dance.

Until the tiny stream of light filtering through the tiny basement window doesn't remind me of strangers' green eyes anymore and I crumple into an exhausted ball on the floor and fall into a dreamless sleep.

***

"So, do you know where I can find him?"

This conversation is going nowhere.

I've spent the last five minutes trying to describe Green Eyes to the ice cream parlor owner, but he either has no idea who I'm talking about, or has even less care.

"I told you, girl. I don't know who you mean. Now are you going to order something? I have to get busy for the after-school rush," he says, annoyed.

"Please. I need to talk to him," I beg.

"Then I suggest you stop bugging me and go find him." He waves a wrinkled dish rag in my face and pushes past me, arranging chairs around the tables, mumbling to himself. I can just make out the words "bloody teenagers."

I sigh and push the door open and step outside.

Coming face to face with him.

He skids to a stop in front of me, an ice cream bucket in each hand. So much for not knowing who he is, I think about the owner.

His right eye and the circle around it is tinged purple and his lip is split. My chest twinges a bit at the thought that I was the cause. I push it away to process at a later time, because right now, he's here.

Say something, you idiot, a voice taunts inside my head.

"Hi." Well, that's a start.

He just blinks and then pushes past me, down the alleyway along the side of the ice cream shop.

It's not what I expected.

"Hey!" I call after him. "Are - are you always so rude?" I ask before I can stop myself.

I see his feet falter, just for a second, before he reaches for a door in the side of the building.

29

***

I come back the next day.

And the next.

I don't know why. I just do.

I'm not always the first one there after school, but I'm always the last to leave. I don't see him much, but there's something about just knowing he's there that brings me comfort. I use the time to finish my assignments, listen to music, run through my final performance dance routine in my head.

As the crowd thins, sometimes he just sits behind the counter, his head deep in a textbook or taking notes. I try to scan the titles of his books from where I'm sitting, but every time he lifts his eyes, it seems like he catches me staring at him, so I stop.

He never says a word to me. Even when I wave goodbye to him, three afternoons in a row, he just ignores me. I don't know what I'd say to him if he ever acknowledged me. Maybe ask him why I'm so compelled by him. But I don't. I just say goodbye.

And wonder why it's so hard for him to say it back to me.

My Thursday dance rehearsal runs long and I'm out of breath as I run to the ice cream parlor, hoping it isn't closed by the time I get there. As I rush past the window, I breathe a sigh of relief as I notice a few stragglers still in the corner booth, and him bent over a table running a cloth over it, collecting the debris in his hand.

There's no time to sit and stare today, though; I'm there for a different reason. Instead of getting up last night to dance, I'd spent it writing a letter to him instead. If he wasn't going to let me say any words to him, then he could at least read them. I woke up this morning to a pile of scrunched up paper at the foot of my bed, but I knew that what I'd written was what I wanted to say.

When he spins around from the table he's just cleaned, I'm there, waiting.

"Hi," I say, my voice breathy from the run and from my nervousness. "This is for you." I pull the cloth from his hand and push the envelope with my note into his palm. Then, before I lose my nerve, I lean over and press a kiss against his bruised cheek and run away as fast as I can.

***

"Thanks, mom. Bye, I'll see you tonight." I give my mom a wave and climb out of the car. I watch as she cuts off another mother as she pulls into traffic, shaking my head at her bad driving.

I pivot towards the school entrance.

And he is there.

"Oh. Um, hi."

He doesn't say anything, just lifts his arm and hands something to me.

It's the envelope I'd given him.

"I left that for you." He doesn't say anything for a moment, just stares at me, his eyes scanning mine with a laser like precision. I feel as if he's seeing everything I've ever seen. Then he reaches over and takes my hand, pushing the envelope into it and walks away, before I can say a word.

"Hey, dipshit! You're here for some more punishment?" I hear a voice yell out to him, and I see Jack standing by the bus stop, his friends cheering him on.

But he just keeps walking.

I turn the envelope over in my hand. It's still sealed. He didn't even read it.

FOUR

Him

Just keep walking.

Don't stop. Don't turn around. Just keep walking.

The urge to turn is almost too much and my walk breaks into a run to distract myself from the temptation.

My feet blur under me, my lungs almost burst trying to keep up with my body's need for oxygen. The muscles strain as they tense and contract, completely unconsciously, like they've done for almost 18 years.

I run until I know that I'm too far for her to catch me.

And then I still keep running.

Until I know that I'm too far for me to fall.

But sometimes, the things we do, are too late.

***

Her

I'm running after him so fast, I can barely feel my feet touching the ground. I'm going to run him down if it's the very last thing I do. He doesn't even turn around to check what's happening behind him, and that both hurts and urges me on. I wonder if he even knows I'm chasing him.

If he thought I would. If he wants me to.

Where is he going?

And why is it so important that he gets there so fast?

I don't even bother entertaining the question that he's running away from something, someone, as opposed to towards.

Running from me.

I'm getting closer. I can tell by the back of his head getting bigger.

Just keep running, I tell myself.

Now is not the time to ponder what it felt like when he took my hand before pushing the letter into it. How my heart jumped when I saw him standing there. How it felt so new and yet like I'd spent my life walking toward him.

Just. Keep. Running.

The street comes to an intersection, and he follows it around the corner. If he makes another turn before I get there, I'm going to lose him. I squeeze my eyes closed for a moment as I gather the strength for a speed burst. I'm used to telling my body to do things beyond what normal people can expect of their bodies, and I feel it respond.

Except, my feet suddenly aren't touching the ground anymore.

"Aw, fuck!!!" I yell, as a sharp pain spreads up my ankle and my shin. I fall to the ground, bracing my fall with one arm, feeling the gravel scratch the outer layer of my skin.

"Shit!" I yell at the traitorous tree roots sticking out from the broken sidewalk, gnarled and wicked, causing my fall.

Everything looks instantly blurry but it takes a few angry wipes of my eyes with the back of my hand before I realize I'm crying.

"Stupid idiot!" I curse myself this time. What the hell do I think I'm doing, chasing a stranger who won't even speak to me? Have I lost my fucking mind? The thoughts are hardly comforting and the hot tears just keep falling. *Asshole*, I glare at the empty street ahead of me as I curse him too.

I brush the dirt from my hands and shake my legs, feeling them out. At least there's no real injury. That would really fucking suck. I take a deep breath, gathering myself, and resolve to never go looking for that asshole again.

Suddenly, something blocks the sun and a hand reaches out to me.

I look up into green eyes.

Something inside me, something stubborn, wants to swat it away, but I push the instinct down.

Taking the hand, I let him pull me to my feet. I drop it as soon as I'm steady, and notice a flicker of something unreadable across his face. I avoid his eyes, shuffling from leg to leg, regaining my balance. There's a gust of wind, and a flash of white catches both our eyes. It's the scrunched-up envelope, making its way down the street. It only takes a few steps of his long legs to catch up with it. He holds it out to me.

"I left it for you," I say, taking it from him, breaking the silence.

His lips tighten for a moment and he finally speaks.

"Why?"

I'm surprised to hear him talk and it takes me a beat to respond.

"Well, read it." I push it back towards him, but he doesn't move.

"No."

"No?" Seriously, what is wrong with this guy? What's his fucking deal?

His shoulders lift in a deep breath.

"No. If there's something you want to say to me, you can say it to my face."

"You haven't exactly made it easy," I scoff.

"Well, I'm here now," he shrugs. "What do you want to say?"

I blink. I feel like I'm permanently being knocked off my feet around him. And not just literally. He's staring at me again, just like he was that first day at the ice cream parlor.

Piercing. Unwavering. Read your soul type staring.

My fingers curl and I feel the paper wrinkle in my hand. I will the words from the paper to seep into my mind. I'd spent hours writing that letter, choosing the right words, the correct phrases. But my mind is turning completely blank.

"I... I just want to say, I'm sorry about what happened, the other day with those guys harassing you. I - I didn't know they were going to. They're just fucking jerks. Anyway, I'm sorry. I didn't want you to think I had anything to do with it."

Not very eloquent, but I hope I'm getting my message across. He stands completely still for a moment and then just nods. Saying nothing.

For so long that it becomes awkward.

"So... um, anyway..." I say, my head hurting with trying to make sense of this strange guy. Strange. Compelling. Unforgettable guy. "That's all I wanted to say."

I take one last look. Something makes me feel like, if he doesn't want to see me again after this, there's no way I'm going to find him. "I... I guess I'll see you around." I reach down to pick up my backpack, swinging it over my shoulder as I turn back towards the school.

"Wait," I think I hear him say and I almost don't stop. But I know I'll wonder for the rest of my life if I don't. "Wait," he says again, loud enough for me to know I didn't imagine it.

And I do.

I feel a soft hand on my shoulder and I spin around.

"Are you game?" he asks. Simple as that.

"For what?"

"For whatever," he replies, his mouth curling up into a smile.

I say the only thing I can in this moment, "Yes."

His hand slides down my arm, the smile growing on his face. "Good. I want to show you something."

***

We run for what seems like hours.

His hand started out wrapped around my wrist, and somewhere along the way, it slid down to meet my hand, our fingers entwining.

I don't know where we're going. And I don't care. I don't notice the city buildings giving way to houses or the houses giving way to trees. I just focus on breathing, and not letting go.

I don't know where we're going, but none of that seems to matter to me right now. Only who I'm going there with.

"How... much... longer...?" I gasp, when my legs feel like they might not last much longer.

"Not long. Just a little way to go."

I save my breath and don't reply.

I've lived in this city all my life, but I have no idea where we are. I can't hear too many cars, but there's a rushing of water, so I know we're near the dam. The path under us is potholed and neglected, grass shooting up between the cracks, reaching for the sun after the long, harsh winter we've just had.

The street is lined with bushes and trees, thick with vegetation. An array of shades of green and brown.

He tugs hard on my hand and pulls me into a sudden gap in the woods. It's instantly dark, the branches blocking out most of the sun. The air is cooler here too.

There's a fleeting moment of wonder - what am I doing following this stranger into the woods?

It passes just as suddenly, as the forest opens up, and seemingly out of nowhere, the lake appears in front of me, in all its glorious decadence.

I stop instantly in my tracks.

What little breath I had is gone.

"Wow." I can't help but sigh.

The morning sunlight dances across the tips of the rippling waves like droplets of liquid silver scattering across the surface, giving it an almost ethereal gleam.

I feel myself reach out, wanting to touch it, but too afraid to shatter the illusion.

"Go," he urges me, stretching my hand forward, and then letting go.

I walk the twenty steps it takes to reach the water's edge, but I don't touch it.

"I've... I've never seen the lake like this before, from here. It looks so different from the bridge," I say, referring to the focal point of the town, the main road that crosses the lake. I can just make out the bridge from here, about a mile away.

It seems like it's a different world over there, people and cars rushing about their business. I turn back and notice him watching me.

"This is amazing. Thanks for bringing me here. Is this what you wanted to show me?"

"Partly. But there's something else." He gestures with his head to the left and presses his finger to his lips. I nod and follow, taking careful steps as he leads me to a tree a few yards away.

He points to a branch about a foot above my head, and I notice a small nest made of twigs and dried grass.

Taking my hand, he helps me take a foothold on the tree stump and I hoist myself up, peering down into the nest.

Three little orange beaks attached to three baby birds reach up to greet me.

"Oh my gosh," I coo, suddenly overwhelmed by the innocence of them. A knot in my throat blocks my voice and so I just stare at them as they squirm around in the nest, keeping each other warm as they wait for their mother to return.

"They hatched about three days ago," he whispers as I jump back down to the ground and step away, not wanting to disturb the infant birds.

"So, so cute. What kind are they?"

"I'm not sure, I think they might be a type of finch. It's hard to tell as babies. But I saw the mother a few times and she had a bit of a red chest," he says, grinning at me.

I grin back, sharing his excitement. "Wow. That's amazing. I've seen a few nests in the trees around my house, but I've never seen any eggs let alone babies!"

He nods, his green eyes glinting, reflecting the sunlight.

"I knew you'd like them," he says. And I try not to die from the thought that he's been thinking of me.

"I did. I do. Thank you. For sharing it with me."

He nods again and we hold each other's gaze for a moment, then he turns away, clearing his throat. I look away as well, giving us both a moment to work out what's happening between us.

XAVIER

I walk closer to the edge of the lake, dipping just the very tip of my shoe into it. It's funny to think that in those depths a whole different ecosystem exists that we can't see from land.

"Do you ever wonder what's happening down there?" he asks, moving over to stand next to me, watching the ripples from my shoe spread out over the water's surface.

"I was literally wondering just exactly that."

He doesn't seem surprised to hear it.

There's a rustling and we both whip our heads around, just in time to catch a glimpse of the mother bird arriving home. Those happy bird babies are safe now.

I scan the area around us and for the first time I notice a small tent set up about 15 feet from the water, in amongst some bushes.

"Oh, hey, look." I point to it, and he looks in the direction of my finger.

"Oh, yeah," he says, then looks away almost immediately.

"Is... is that yours?" I ask, before I can stop myself, before I realize it might not be something he wants to answer. But then why did he bring me here?

"Um. Yeah," he says, still staring out over the lake.

"Do you... um, do you live here?"

He's quiet for a moment and I'm not sure whether he's hoping I'll drop the questions or if he's trying to formulate an answer.

It doesn't matter if you do, is what I want to say to him. *I don't care.* But I don't know if it's what he wants to hear.

"No, not exactly. I just... my house gets a little crowded sometimes. So, I come out here where it's quiet. And I can just read or sleep."

"Where *do* you live?" I can't stop the questions. I want to know everything about him.

"Doesn't matter. I like it here."

I nod. "I do too. It's just so peaceful, I can't believe I didn't know about this place. How did you find it?"

He shrugs and bends over, pulling a weed from the ground. "I like to look for things that other people can't see. Or don't take the time to, I guess."

Something compels me to go into the water. It's urgent. Wild.

My shoes go flying in different direction as I kick them off my feet and wade ankle deep into the lake. The water is cold but bearable. Something about the way it ripples around my ankles makes me laugh.

"Come in here!" I yell at him, and he laughs, shaking his head.

It's the first time I've seen him laugh, and the sounds embeds itself into my sternum.

I kick my leg up and splatter him with cold lake water. He laughs again and lifts his face up to the drops, like I'm baptizing him. I spin around in the water, lifting my arms as I pirouette, the water splashing around me, flicking off my bare toes, as I lift one foot to my leg.

I do another, and another, until I'm almost falling over from dizziness.

I stumble out of the water and flop onto the grass, curling my cold toes into the dirt.

"That was amazing. Are you a dancer?" he asks.

"Well, I hope to be," I admit.

"No, I think you already are."

I shrug.

"You don't sound so sure."

How does he know that? How does he know something I haven't even admitted to myself?

"Right now, I want to dance more than anything. And that I know. But I guess, I guess I think that I may not always want to be a dancer, does that make sense?"

He doesn't pretend it does, but I know he wants to. I want him to understand it, understand me.

"Like, I want to dance, but... I'm discovering there are other things I want to do as well."

"Like what?"

I stand up, and go back to the water's edge.

"Like... that" I point out to the lake. "I want to make something as beautiful as that." Why do I feel so comfortable sharing things with this stranger more than I do with my family, my closest friends?

"Well, I think you dance just as beautifully, if those pirouettes were anything to go by."

"Thank you. I also love color. I *see* color when I hear music, you know. And when I dance, sometimes I imagine I'm painting with my movement onto a canvas. But it's only something I can see, and fleeting. I want to make something other people can see with their eyes as well."

"Do you paint? Draw?"

"Fuck no." I laugh. "I cannot control these damn things," I look down at my hands." I can't make what I see in my head come out through my fingers and onto canvas. I can't explain it. My handwriting's atrocious. You'd know that if you'd read my letter." I poke my tongue at him.

He flushes.

"What about you? What is it you want to do?" I ask and I realize I want to know so bad.

He takes a deep breath. And I know that whatever he's about to say, he's never said to anyone else before. That seems to be the theme of our conversation.

"I just want to find where I belong."

"Wow, I've never heard someone say that before."

"That's because you've been surrounded by people who belong," he says, with no hint of envy or irony.

I nod. I guess there's truth to that. "Probably. Lucky us."

"You have no idea."

I want to ask him more, but it feels like it's too soon. Like he's already given me more than he would give anyone.

The only way I know this is, because I've done the same for him.

"Hey." He stands up, brushing the dirt from his hands. "Come on."

"Come on, what?"

He's grins and holds his hand out again. "You game?"

I take his hand even before I've answered.

"Fuck, yes."

***

We're standing in front of Home Depot.

This can't be right.

But we are, standing here, right outside the opening and closing sliding doors. Into Home Depot.

"Um." I say, once he hasn't given me any idea of why we're here.

"Shush. You said you were game, remember? Well, come on, start walking."

I want to grumble, but the last thing I want is to seem like a brat.

"Where am I walking to?"

"Follow me." He grabs my wrist and drags me through the towering aisles filled with nails and hammers and all sorts of tools that look like medieval torture devices.

This place is huge. I never noticed just how big it was before. Things seem larger when you're being dragged through them by a virtual stranger with no knowledge of the destination.

"Stop," he says as he comes to an abrupt standstill and I bang into him.

"Sorry," I mumble as I look around. We're in the paint department.

"We're here!" he says, with a flourish. He seems to be enjoying this, his initial shyness or whatever it was, seemingly faded into the breeze as we ran.

"Er, and 'here' is where exactly." I turn around in a full circle half expecting to see a prank camera crew jump out from behind a shelf.

"Here. Look." He points to the rows and rows and rows of paint swatches. Perfect squares of color in every possible imaginable shade.

I have to close my eyes for a moment, before taking it all in again. The wall of graduating shades is hypnotizing, the order amongst what could be complete chaos so oddly satisfying.

"You ready?" he asks, as confusingly as ever.

"For what?" I feel a jolt of adrenalin rush through me, I could get used to not knowing. Every surprise has been fun so far.

"Well, you said you like color," he replies as he gestures again to the swatches. "I'm going to give you 30 seconds to grab all the paint color swatches that you like. Okay?" He looks down at his watch.

"Wait! What for?"

"No questions! 5... 4..."

"Why am I doing this?" I grab his arm, yelling at him, the excitement making me giddy.

He ignores me and continues to count through his giant grin. "3... 2..."

"Ahhh!" I scream, turning to the display, frozen to the spot.

"1! Go! GRAB!"

"Holy shit!" I scream, more excited than I can process.

"What are you doing? You've wasted five seconds already!"

"I don't know what I'm supposed to do! I don't know what to choose! Help me!"

He comes up behind me and covers my eyes, leaning in to whisper against my ear.

"Close your eyes and quiet your mind for a moment. Remember those colors you say you love?"

An explosion happens somewhere in the darkest corner of my mind and I see them. The colors.

"Yes!"

"Let them guide you." He pulls his hand away. "Go! You only have twenty seconds left!"

I scramble forwards, grabbing paper strips of color off the wall, handfuls and handfuls. It's like I can taste them. Feel the color through my fingertips. I'm almost drunk on them. I grab some more, and they spill out of my hands and splay into a puddle of dyes on the floor.

In the corner of my eye, I can see him leaning over to pick them up. "I've got 'em! Keep going!"

There's a striking purple, and a neon pink, a royal blue. The more I see, the more I want.

"Five more seconds!" he warns.

"It's not enough!"

It feels like there wouldn't ever be enough time.

"Three. Two. One. And stop!! Step away from the wall!"

I cheat and reach for two more before he laughs and grabs the back of my collar dragging me back through the store, until we're standing where we were just a few minutes ago. I stare at him, panting for breath.

"'Wait here. Don't move." he says, and runs back into the store before I say anything.

I clutch my stack of paint swatches to my chest, already attached to them, despite having no idea what's going on. My whole body is buzzing with adrenaline and anticipation, I can't remember the last time I felt like this.

It feels like an hour before he appears again, but it was probably mere minutes.

"Are you going to tell me what that was about?" I ask.

He shakes his head. "Where's the fun in that? And it was fun, wasn't it?"

All he has to do is look at my face to know that answer to that.

"Let's go," he says. And starts to walk away.

"Now where?" I yell after him.

"You're going to have to trust me one last time," he yells back over his shoulder.

And I do.

We walk in silence. Down along the main street of town and turn into an area I don't know too well. There are abandoned houses and neglected gardens. A little different from the perfectly mowed lawns of the houses near my own.

I move a little closer to him as we walk. He smiles, slowing his step.

"It's okay, you're safe with me. I won't let anything happen to you."

But the way his promise makes a shiver travel down my spine makes me wonder if that's true. I follow him through what looks like an abandoned high school to an empty basketball court.

"Come on, it's over here," he says.

"What is?"

We walk around the outline of the court to a paint chipped wall. He throws our backpacks to the side, as we stand there, staring up at it.

"That. That is your canvas."

"What?" I don't understand what he means.

"Well, you said you wanted to create something beautiful. With colors. Well, you've got everything you need. You're literally holding the colors in your hand. And that is your canvas."

I stare up at the colossus of the blank wall in front of me. It seems like an impossible task. I look down at the giant stack of paint swatches clutched tight in my two fists.

"What's wrong?" he asks, his voice soft.

"I... I don't know what to do," my voice trembles as I reply. I hold my two hands out in surrender. To him. To the task.

He comes up behind me, covering my eyes with his hand again. I shiver at the feel of his hand brushing against my skin, even though the sun is beating down against the side of my face.

"Stop thinking. I can already tell, that's your downfall. Just close your eyes. Remember... remember all those colors you pulled from the wall of paint swatches?"

I don't know how to say that I remember each and every one without sounding like a freak. So I just nod.

"Is there one that stands out to you?"

As soon as he says it, it flashes in my mind. And he knows.

He pulls his hand away.

"Start with that one."

He pulls a paper bag out of his back pocket and hands it to me. It's a pair of scissors and a glue gun. He must've gotten them when he ran back inside the store.

"You've got everything you need. Go. Create."

He steps away and I panic, asking, "Wait, are you leaving?"

He chuckles, "No, I'm not going anywhere, I'll be right over there." He points to a spot in the shade on the far side of the wall.

I nod, comforted and then stare down at the colors in my hand. This is crazy. I started this morning, thinking I'd be handing in an assignment and eating orange jello in the cafeteria and now I'm here with... wait.

"Hey," I call out to him.

He lifts his head from the notebook and, pen in his hand, shielding his eyes as he looks up at me, asks "Yeah?"

"I just realized; I don't know your name."

He grins before answering, "I'm Xavier."

"Nice to meet you, Xavier. My name is Malynda."

FIVE

Her

Present Day

"'Xavier? I'd like you to meet Isabella." Jade turns to me and gestures to the man in front of me, who is so handsome, I turn giddy from breathlessness. But it's not his angled jaw that has me dizzy. It's his eyes. Those shocking green eyes. Eyes I haven't seen in twelve years.

He reaches his hand out to me, his face unreadable.

"'*Isabella,'* was it? I'm Xavier. Nice to meet you."

"Ahem, yes. Y-you, too." I manage to get out, taking his hand. I'm not sure what I expect when our fingers touch, but it's just like any other handshake, and I wonder how that can be.

"Well, I'll leave you two to it. I'm actually really glad Xavier won the auction. He really could use help with the barren space he calls his apartment." With that, Jade rushes off before I can beg her to stay.

I'm not sure how long we stand there gaping at each other. Ten seconds, ten years. Time whizzes by, backward or forward, I can't tell.

"Is it really you?" he finally says, his hand still grasping my hand, and his eyes searching for something in mine. Those emerald eyes. How could I have forgotten those eyes?

"W-what do you mean?" I say, the lightness of my own voice surprising me.

"Malynda..." He says, and it's like I haven't spent the last twelve years trying to forget the name. Something in the way it pricks at my brain makes me remember who I am today.

"No. I'm not Malynda. Anymore."

46

"You are. Your name is Malynda!" he says, a little more forcefully, his forehead furrowing, deep, intense frustration plastering all over his face. I pull my hand out of his, taking a step back.

"My name is Isabella," I say as firmly as I can.

"Not to me, it isn't!" There's a huskiness in his voice that wasn't there twelve years ago. And it's only one of the many changes in him that I'm forcing myself to ignore. He leans in, his lips inches from my ear and I can smell the Scotch on his breath, the cinnamon in his aftershave. "My god, where have you been?"

I can feel my head shake left to right. This wasn't supposed to happen. This was never supposed to happen. "I can't do this, Xavier." I take another step back but he just follows.

"You can't do this? What about... hey, don't walk away from me. Don't you dare."

I can't stand the confusion filling up his eyes and I turn to run. "Xavier, please. I can't..."

"Isabella!" The sound of a man's voice cuts through the tension sphere enveloping us and we spring apart, as if shot through a time portal. "There you are, darling. I was looking all over for you. Jade pointed me over here."

"Oh, wonderful." I can barely speak. I take the glass he hands me and take a sip, hoping he will think the flush on my cheeks is because of the champagne.

"Hello, I'm Cameron," my partner says to Xavier, offering his hand.

"I'm... um... I'm..." Xavier sounds just as flustered as I do. I can't blame him.

"Oh, yes, you're the guy who bid on Isabella's services here. Thanks for doing that by the way, created some buzz. That won't hurt our budding business, will it?" Cameron winks at me.

I just nod, recovering my breath.

"Well, um, I heard she's the best," Xavier says.

"That she is. She's made our place pretty much the envy of everyone."

I feel Xavier's eyes still on me, and I can't focus on anything else.

"Well, darling, we'd better be going. I have an early plane to catch tomorrow morning." Cameron lays his hand in the small of my back, and I try not to push it away when I notice Xavier watching.

"Nice to meet you, um, I'm sorry I didn't catch your name..."

"Xavier. Nice to meet you." He turns back to me and I have no choice but to meet his look. "And um, Maly-er, um... I will be in touch, very soon."

"I'm s-sorry?" I stutter, I can't think of a reason I would put either of us through this again.

"For his apartment design, darling," Cameron says, shaking his head at Xavier and rolling his eyes as if to lament over my forgetfulness.

"Oh, um, yes, of course." No. There's no way. I'm going to have to find a way out of this.

Xavier locks his eyes with mine for one last moment before he flings himself into the crowd, and it's only seconds before he's swallowed up by the bodies in tuxedos and silk.

My breath doesn't return as fast as I hope, but Cameron's hand on my back is now a source of steadiness.

"Hey, he was kind of a strange guy. What were you two talking about?" he asks as we step out into the night.

I take a breath before answering.

"He just mistook me for someone he used to know."

But she doesn't exist anymore.

SIX

Him

"I'm not Malynda anymore."

Her voice loops over and over in my head. The same voice I remember, saying words I don't understand.

What is happening? How did the day turn out to end like this? I lean back, as far as my leather recliner will let me, staring out into the moonlight-washed Manhattan skyline. Has she really been out there this whole time?

I down my drink and reach for the decanter for another.

The burn as it cascades down my throat only gives me a temporary respite from the torturous thoughts in my head.

Where have you been, Malynda? What have you been doing? And with whom?

She can't really be with that... that suit.

My involuntary chuckle surprises me as I catch my own reflection in the glass; as suited up as a man can get.

God, she looked so beautiful.

More beautiful than I could have ever imagined her. More beautiful than I remember.

More beautiful than that first day at the lake.

More beautiful than standing in front of that paint chipped wall, eyes full of possibility.

More beautiful than all the ways I've imagined her since.

"Hey." A deep voice startles me out of my musings. I look up and Kaine is standing there staring down at me, no doubt not too happy with the scene of me hugging a scotch decanter

"What the fuck, man? How did you get in here?"

"Please. Why do you think I co-bought this building with you? So I could come and check on you when you go off brand, like tonight. What the hell was that all about, Xave?"

I empty my glass down my throat before I answer. "It's Malynda," I finally say, emphasizing every syllable.

"What's Malynda?"

"Her. She. It is Malynda." I don't want to say the moniker she's hiding behind. I refuse to. "The interior designer." It takes him a moment, but the pieces finally fit together in his brain.

"Shit. Isabella is Malynda? Are you sure?"

I catch his surprised gaze and let him read my eyes for a moment.

"Shit," he says again and reaches for the scotch decanter in my hand.

"Yeah."

"But... How... Did... Why..."

"Exactly, I've been asking myself the same questions. I don't have the answers yet, if you come across them let me know."

He pours himself a glass and tops mine up. He knows now isn't the time to be curtailing my alcohol intake. "What are you going to do?"

"I could stand up in the middle of a fundraising dinner at the Plaza and declare a woman mine by outbidding everyone else by 300%."

"Well, you've already done that."

I just shrug. I don't know what I'm going to do.

"Don't give me that, you know what you're going to do," he responds to my silent answer.

I laugh into my glass. He wouldn't be Kaine if he didn't know me so well.

"Don't be stupid," he continues. "You don't know what happened to her before and what's brought her here. Give her some time and space. She's probably as freaked out as you are, but she's not going anywhere."

I watch my reflection shake its head.

"I believed that once before. And she did. She disappeared off the face of the fucking earth, man! I don't want to give her time or fucking space! That's all she's had for... for... FUCK! I want here her. Right now! Telling me what the hell happened!" The recliner screeches against the floor as it's pushed back when I jump to my feet, a white-hot rage suddenly rushing through me. Before I can stop myself, my scotch glass flies across the room, smashing against the window. We watching the crystal shatter and fall onto the floor in a pile of glittering shards. "Fuck," I say again, dropping back down into the chair, head in my hands.

"Xavier," Kaine says, I think, but I can barely hear him. My mind already rushing back to the past. "Xavier," he says again. But I'm already lost to my memories.

***

12 years ago

On a perfect late spring day in Maine, you wouldn't want to be anywhere else in the world.

The sun dissolves the clouds that crowd the sky during most of April and May, and the sky hovers like a pristine royal blue canvas over our heads. The rivers and lakes come alive with the awakening of nature around it, refreshed from the deep winter sleep.

There is a scent of hope in the air.

Like today. Today was a perfect late spring day in Maine.

With her.

It's early evening by the time I'm walking home after spending the afternoon after school with Malynda. I'd gone to the basketball courts, not knowing if I'd see her, but there she was, already working on the mural when I showed up.

"Want to see?" she'd asked, after about two hours, coming over to sit by me.

"No. I'll see it when it's done."

"Might be awhile. I don't know if it will ever be done."

"That's okay. I'll keep coming here with you until it is," I'd told her, a promise to myself as much as to her.

She'd given me a hug as we'd separated at Main Street. As always, she'd gone toward the manicured lawns of the west of the city, and me back to my own crowded house, but not before

51

watching her walk away. Until her thin figure was so small, even my squints couldn't bring her back into focus.

She'd hugged me.

Like I said; a perfect day.

I can hear the chaos three houses away before I get home. The door creaks on the hinge as I open it, trying to sneak in without being noticed.

"Xavier! Where have you been?!" my mother yells, barely two seconds after I've entered the kitchen.

I look around, the twins are sitting at the table with their crayons and butcher paper. Brian is lying on the floor in front of the TV.

"I was, er, studying at the library, Mom. Why?"

"I just got called in for an extra shift. I need you to watch the kids." She rushes around, grabbing her bag and the cardigan hanging off the back of the chair.

"But-..."

"Please, Xavier. I'm already late. I didn't have credit on my phone to call you."

"When will you be home?"

"I don't know. It's crazy at work, I might even get a double shift. Oh, and Dairy Joy called, they want you to open for them tomorrow."

"But – Mr. Pritchard said he was going to help me study for a test we have on Friday."

She stops for a moment, looking at me, shoulders dropping.

"I'm sorry, Xavier. I need the help. Look." She points to the letter with the big, red bold writing on the fridge.

"Your choice, honey. You take the shift and we pay the electricity bill, or you... you go study. I'm not going to make the decision for you." She gives me a weak smile and a kiss on the cheek and rushes out the door.

"Where's Mom going?" Michael, the older twin looks up from their mess on the kitchen table.

"Just to work, buddy," I say, sitting down and grabbing a crayon, drawing a sun on the sheet of paper.

"I'm hungry," Brian says, finally looking up from the TV.

"Okay, my specialty?"

"I guess. Not too much peanut butter this time, it makes my mouth feel funny."

"You got it."

My feet drag on the way to the kitchen and I grab the bread and a knife from the drawer. As much as my body feels imprisoned in this house, in this role of big brother, my mind is somewhere else. On a lake, by the water's edge, with a pretty dancer with long blonde hair and hazel eyes.

***

"Hi!"

I look up from the sink the next afternoon, elbow deep in suds and floating puddles of melted ice cream. It's her. Dressed in pink tights and her grey leotard poking out from under the long black tunic loosely wrapped around her body. I'm suddenly more aware of the region just below my stomach than I've ever been. And I'm glad I have a sink to hide it.

"Hi," I say back, feeling my face curl into an involuntary smile. She gifts me with a smile back. "Dance class?"

"Yep, my partner finally decided he can't give up yet. I'm exhausted. I must look a mess!" she sighs as she runs a hand over her messy topknot, pushing back the little wisps of hair escaping the bun.

I want to, but I can't tell her that she looks more delicious than all the tubs of ice cream here put together. I want to bury myself in the crook of her neck and breathe in the scent of her skin. I bet she tastes delectably salty after her workout.

Again, thank god for this sink in front of me.

"Anyway, I was wondering, would you mind going with me to the basketball court after work? I had an idea for my mural I wanted to work on."

"Oh, sure. That's great. But I don't get off until four," I say, shrugging apologetically.

"That's cool, I can wait!" She does a little shuffle on her feet and gives me a grin. There's something so light about her today. I feel like I need to take her hand to stop her from floating away. "I'm going to go sit over there, okay?"

I watch as she bounces away, wishing I could follow her. I give my body a few minutes to settle down and bring a bowl over to her.

"Oh, I can't," she whines, pouting at the sundae I'm holding out to her. "I'm watching my diet for one more torturous week. Then this place better watch out!"

I put it down on the table in front of her. "It's, um, it's just frozen yogurt and some raspberries. Very dancer friendly."

She looks down at the bowl and then back up at me, her eyes round and wide. Her look of appreciation makes me heady. "How did you know...?" A soft breath escapes her nose. "I should stop asking that, shouldn't I?"

"You can ask me anything. At any time," I say, and then return to my station before I say something else as trite and lame.

I can't stop watching her over the next two hours. It's no different to how it was before, my obsession with watching her. The only difference is that now sometimes I catch her watching me back. When I catch her looking she just smiles and gives me a wink. Where does she get that confidence? I could use some. But she already has given me a little; sometimes when we're alone, she makes me feel like I could conquer the world.

"Hey, I dreamt of these ones last night," she says, holding a few paint swatches out like a fan when we're walking to the basketball court later. "It was amazing, I felt like I was floating through an infinite cloud of swirling color. I could touch them, almost taste them. I wish I could recreate it."

I just smile as I listen to her talking, her voice high with excitement, her elbow occasionally bumping up against mine as she waves her arms around, describing her dream.

"What do you think?" She stops chattering for a moment to ask me.

"Oh. Um. I don't know much about art."

"You don't have to, just tell me what you think." Her smile is so warm; as unsure as I feel about giving my opinion about something I know nothing about, I know I can't refuse her anything.

"Well, I think you should stop worrying about *re*-creating it and just *create*. That dream came from you, those images are inside of you. So maybe stop thinking so much, and just trust your instinct. I bet you'll make something that elicits the same feeling you had in your dream."

She doesn't say anything and for a moment I'm worried I've offended her. Then she just sighs and slides her hand into mine, swinging it between us as we arrive, too soon, at the wall.

Then, without needing to talk, we fall into a routine. She gets to work on her mural as I find my spot against the wall, where I can read my books and watch her without reserve.

Her hands work, cutting and pasting shapes onto the wall, her face running the range of expressions, from a furrowed brow in concentration, to excitement at a new idea, to contentment at a square of color placed just right.

Her hair untangles from the elastic holding it up on her head, and the fading sun catches the tips as they whip around her face from a passing breeze. I watch as she absentmindedly runs a finger along the curve of her cheek, pulling at a hair stuck to her lips. Every move she makes entrances me.

I don't know if it's all the years of dance training that has her body moving in shapes and angles designed to capture your attention, or if it's just instinctive to her.

To command every ounce of my attention.

I catch myself holding my breath as I watch her.

She curses at something on the wall and it reminds me to stop staring, at least for a moment and I force my gaze down to the open textbook in my lap. I tell myself to count to ten before I let myself look up but only get to eight before I'm watching her again.

Two hours later she slides down only the ground next to me, pulling her knees in close to her chest, lines of goosebumps jumping up from her arms due to the plummeting temperature.

I take my jacket off and throw it around her. She gives me a look of thanks, pulling it tight around her and then lays her head on my shoulder. It takes everything I have to not lay a kiss on her forehead.

"Thank you," she whispers after a few minutes as a pink hue starts to bleed all over the horizon. And I'm the only one there to hear it.

I don't say "you're welcome" because what I really mean to say is "my pleasure."

"I better be going home," she says once the moon and sun are almost equally visible in the sky, and I'm glad to hear she's as sad about it as I am. "I didn't realize how late it was getting."

I nod and gather my things. "Do you need me to walk you home?" I ask, hoping for an answer I probably shouldn't be hoping for. I'm not sure what this all means to her. Us. Not that I really care, as long as I get to keep spending time with her

"No, I should be alright, it's not too far," she says, fiddling with the zipper of my jacket and pulling it closed all the way up to her throat. "Or, hey, do *you* need *me* to walk you home?" she teases, nudging me with her shoulder.

"Yes! There's a VERY vicious family of squirrels just around the corner from here. If you hear of an attack on the news tonight, you'll know it's because you made me walk home alone." I pout and she laughs and it sounds like every clichéd lovestruck description you've ever heard.

We get to our feet, brushing the dirt from our hands and clothes.

"See you here tomorrow? I have Sundays free," she asks, sliding her arms into the backpack straps.

I nod, "Sure, sounds good."

"What time?"

I bite back the urge to say the earlier the better. "9 a.m.?"

"'K." Then she leans over, and presses a kiss to my cheek before pivoting on her foot and skipping away. She's halfway across the basketball court before I can react, and even then, it's just to press a hand to my face.

***

My father left us almost two years ago, to the day.

He didn't die, he didn't pass away, he wasn't on a sabbatical to find himself.

He *left.*

He packed up his things, folded his clothes, each and every one of his shirts, his two pairs of work pants. Bundled up his socks, two by identical two. Pressed them into the empty pockets of his suitcase, and walked out the door.

In his head I imagine he imagined he looked like the hero shot of a lion walking through a ring of fire, untouched. Except that it was a ring of children he'd selfishly fathered.

Among them, a pair of identical two-year-old baby boys.

"I can't do this anymore," is what he told us.

Like 'doing this,' taking care of your own family, is something you can just wake up to one day and decide that no, it's just not to your taste.

My mother wasn't there the exact moment he walked out. She maintains that he'd been gone long before then and the only difference after was that there was more room in the closet.

For what, I'm not sure.

If I had to draw a picture of her, of how I think of her, she'd be wearing her diner's uniform, in varying degrees of cleanliness.

It makes me sad to think about, so I stop.

I flip over onto my back, the sky still dark outside my window.

Yesterday afternoon replays in my mind like a film reel; every frame, every second, somehow my brain retained it all. Scratch that, it retained everything that pertained to Malynda, everything else is like white noise. Just the background to her shining star.

The film starts with her appearing out of nowhere at work, every inch of her long legs clung to by that pale pink Lycra, making me breathless. My body is already awakening to those images of her, the hem of her tunic only just reaching her upper thigh, hiding the descent of her leotard disappearing between her legs.

Damn.

I'm hard.

I don't know how I can control it when I'm there with her, but right now, my body feels like it's almost bursting with the need for release.

Over her.

I let my hands wander downward as I continue my replay. The way she'd bend and twist, picking up her art supplies from the ground, reaching up on her tip toes, elongating from the tips of her toes all the way to the tip of her index finger as she reached as high as she could on the wall.

Then, when all the exertion became too much, her pulling the tunic from her body, using it to dab at the sweat glistening on her neck before throwing it to the ground by my friend.

The memory makes my hardness twitch, and I grab it, almost out of comfort.

"Fuck."

My eyes squeeze shut, holding onto the image of her against my closed eyelids.

I'm going up to her, my hands on her neck, sliding down her long, slender arms, her skin so soft under my fingertips.

I can almost feel the heat from her against me as I imagine pulling her close, my lips already on her neck, breathing her in.

The hand around my cock grips tight and moves fast.

Too fast for the slow, burning, sensual thought of her in my mind.

The scene jumps, and suddenly it's her hand wrapped around me and my hips thrusting into her fist.

"I want you so bad," I whisper both in and out of my daydream, and I strain to hear her tell me she wants me too.

My breath is ragged in my own ears as I can feel it coming. Me. Coming.

"Faster," I tell her in my head. And she complies, her eyes on mine as I feel my body fall over the edge.

"Oh, fuck. Fuck." I groan as I come. My eyes never leaving hers, making sure she knows it's her that makes me feel this way.

My head falls back onto the pillow, dizzy.

God, I want her.

I want all of her.

All of that sweet, sunshiny, sexy, effervescent, creative body and mind that makes her her.

For all of the ways she makes me me.

***

The hallway light is on when I get up to get a glass of water; there's a flash of a figure running between the kitchen and my mother's bedroom.

"Oh, Xavier! Thank god, you're awake. I have to go into work, Peggy's sick, so I'm taking her shift. I'm so tired but you know I have to take it." She dabs at her face with a sponge covered with something like putty to hide her tired eyes. My heart twinges for her, but also for myself.

"Mom, I've got plans today."

"Honey, I don't have time to discuss this. I need you to take care of the boys. Okay?"

I feel my fists curl into a ball. But I know it's not her I'm mad at. She doesn't deserve me making her feel even worse.

"Yeah, ok. Don't worry about it. I'll... I'll take them to the park or something."

"Oh, thank you! I promised them something fun this weekend, they'd love that."

"I'll think of something," I nod, even while my heart sinks.

She throws me a tired wave over her shoulder as she disappears out the backdoor.

"Has mommy gone to work again?" Brian asks, startling me. He looks so small, hidden in the shadows, rubbing his eyes as he stands in his pajamas.

"Yeah, buddy." I go over and give his shoulder a squeeze.

"But she said she was goi-..."

"She couldn't help it. We'll do something fun today, okay? How 'bout we eat cereal from the box and watch some cartoons?"

His face lights up. "Without the twins?"

"What twins?" I answer and give him a wink and he giggles.

By nine a.m., all three boys are up, breakfasted, dressed, but nowhere near ready to leave the house. I'm not sure what it is, but something about needing to leave the house at a certain time seems to trigger their bladders. By the time the backdoor swings closed behind us, it's almost ten o'clock.

"Fuck," I curse under my breath, checking my watch, one hand on each twin as I yell at Brian every fifteen seconds to stay close as we head to the basketball court.

"You said a bad word," Michael, the younger twin points out.

"No, I didn't." Sometimes it's hard to refrain when they're around.

"You said 'fut' I heard you," he insists.

"Fine, I said 'fut.' Don't tell anyone."

"What will you give me?" he asks, and I realize four-year-olds don't get enough credit for being the master manipulators they are.

"Well, how 'bout I let you say 'fut' one more time, but you can't tell Mom."

He thinks about for a moment, and then nods.

"Fut!" he yells, beaming proudly at both winning the negotiation and getting to curse without repercussion.

"Now, no more, okay? Mom doesn't like us saying naughty words. That was the deal."

He nods, willing to respect the sanctity of his given word.

"Where are we going, Xavier?" Hamish, the youngest of us all, asks.

"You'll see. Now hurry up."

As we half-walk, half-run through the abandoned school yard, I pray that she hasn't left. She's becoming like air. And I'm addicted to the high that breathing her gives me.

I spot the back of her skirt billowing in the wind as we round the corner and into the basketball court, and the tension I didn't know I was holding in my chest relaxes.

"Oooh, are we going to play basketball?" Brian shouts.

"Um, yup. You want me to teach you, so here we are," I say, half-truth that it is.

"YAY!" The three of them cheer. The sound of their voices drifts across the court and she turns around, scissors and glue gun in hand.

"Hey! I didn't know if you were going to make it!" she says as we walk up to her.

"Sorry I'm late. I had to..." I gesture my head to the six eyes staring at her unblinking. "Um, guys, this is my friend, Malynda."

"Hey guys! Nice to meet you!" She shoots them all one of her 1000-watt smiles.

For once in their lives, they're completely mute. I don't blame them. I was like that for the first week of knowing her.

"Guys! Stop staring! Why don't you go over to that hoop and start throwing the ball around and I'll be right there," I urge.

They stare at her for another moment, before Brian finally regains function of his brain and breaks the silence by bouncing the ball. In an instant they're off and running, one in each direction, yelling each other's names.

"Sorry," I say again, shrugging, not wanting to add more to the explanation of why I have three in tow today.

"Aw, shush. Don't worry, I was actually here early anyway, I couldn't sleep. I laid awake thinking about what I wanted to add."

I laid awake in bed thinking of you stroking me, I wanted to say, but don't.

"Okay, well, I'll be here. Keeping guard. And keeping them alive. You create."

She just gives me a bright smile in response.

It takes a toddler yelling out my name to tear myself away from her and to stop myself from pulling her into my arms like I'd dreamed this morning.

Almost two hours later, she turns around to see the four of us walk back from the court to her.

"Hungry?" she asks.

"Starving!" I say, throwing the ball to Brian.

"Who won?"

"We did!" Michael yells out, lifting his arms into the air.

"Well, it was the three of you against me," I clarify.

"Yeah? Can I play next time?" Malynda asks.

Michael splutters, "You're a girl."

"Oh, I get it, you're scared 'cos I'm a girl, I'm obviously better at b-ball than you," she taunts him, winking at me.

My brother's not sure how to respond and she laughs, poking him in the stomach.

"Hey!" he grumbles, swatting her hand away.

"How 'bout this? Me and Xavier, against you three, whoever gets the most baskets in five minutes buys the others ice cream!"

"But we don't have any money," Brian responds.

"Then you better win!" She steals the ball out of Michael's hands and runs toward the basket, whooping as her first throw nets her a clean basket.

"Your girlfriend is crazy, Xave," Brian points out.

"She's not my girlfriend, but yes, she's a little nuts."

"Just like you," Michael giggles as I chase him over to the hoop.

***

"And I want three scoops, double choc chip and with chocolate fudge and chocolate spinkles."

"Mikey, there's no way you're going to be able to eat that," I say, horrified.

"Yes, I will! I never get to order what I want and since Malynda's paying, I can!" he insists.

I gesture to the server at Dairy Joy to make them super small scoops and she gives me a wink. We're pretty used to kids ordering way more than they can eat. We've both also had the experience of being the ones who have to clean up, once the kid discovers just how much they can really fit in their tiny bodies.

"That's not nice, Mikey! Don't take advantage of Malynda's generosity," I scold him.

He pouts, "I'm NOT, I'm taking advana-avtaga, um..."

"Advantage..."

"Advantage of her being bad at throwing baskets!"

Malynda throws us all a look of mock hurt and the boys all dissolve into laughter, clutching their respective ice creams as we follow her to an empty table in front of the ice cream parlor.

It's hot and the ice creams are melting fast.

There's silence for the first time since this morning as we all race to lick up the drops of ice cream dripping down our arms before they reach our elbows.

It's a losing battle for Hamish and before long, there's more ice cream on his arms and legs than left on the cone. He doesn't care, he gives me a big chocolate covered grin as he laps at his treat like a parched dog.

I can only shake my head and grin back, glad that they had some fun today. I take a bite into my own chocolate dipped cone and savor the crackle. I love that sound. It's the breaking of a shell to reveal secrets hidden beneath it.

"Oh. I think... we're losing one," Malynda speaks first, tilting her chin toward Mikey.

She's not wrong, he's struggling under the sheer weight of his ice cream, barely making a dent in the giant dessert he's cradling with both hands, but he's not giving up despite the distinct green color that's creeping up his neck.

"Er, hey, buddy. Why don't you take a break, yeah? We'll take it home and put it in the fridge and you can have it later," I urge him, though I predict it will be in vain.

"No! You guys will eat it!"

"No, I promise it's all yours," I try to reassure him.

"Make Brian and Hame promise too," he begs.

"Guys..."

"I won't eat it, Mikey, I pwomise," Michael's twin says, giving him an earnest, chocolate covered mouth grin.

"Brian," I nudge him with my elbow. But he doesn't say anything, just grins and reaches out to Mikey's ice cream with his finger.

"No!" Michael cries, twisting out of his brother's reach, and taking the ice cream with him. "I told you!"

"Bri!" I yell.

"Fine, I promise, geez. I don't want his germs anyway, he's licked all over that thing," Brian sulks, popping the last of his cone into his mouth.

Michael smiles triumphantly back at his brother, finally letting go of his sundae. I check my watch, and as much as I want to stay, to be with her every second that I can, the twins need a nap.

"Okay, guys, have you thanked Malynda for your ice creams?"

"Thank you, Malynda," they repeat in unison. They've recovered from their initial shyness, but their respective crushes on her are still evident. I don't blame them.

"Thanks guys, but save up those pennies. Next time, you'll be paying for MY sundae and let me tell you, I'm going to ask for EXTRA cherries!"

She says the last word while jumping up from the table and pretends to leap toward them, making them scatter across the front of the Dairy Joy in a chorus of screams. Her laughter penetrates my ears and echoes inside of my brain for a moment, and I forget where I am. Her laugh does things to her face that her smile doesn't. It breaks up the elegant structure of her jaw, her cheekbones puffing out, her eyes crinkling.

"What?" she says, noticing my stare. I thought she'd be used to that by now.

"Nothing. I just like hearing and seeing you laugh."

She reaches out, her hand squeezing my arm. The gesture surprises me. Other than the hug she always gives me before we say goodbye for the day, something about today, maybe because of the presence of my brothers, I think we've both been especially aware of our bodies and their proximity to each other's. I look up into her eyes, her smile softens, and she leans in a little closer to me.

"Hey, lovebirds." A voice speaks up just then and we both turn to see a crowd of kids from Malynda's high school strolling up to us.

The guy who'd fought me is standing at the front of the pack, his face plastered with a smug expression. I feel Malynda's eyes on me instantly, but I keep my gaze locked on him, and remind myself my brothers are there.

"We were just leaving. You can have this table if you want," I say, trying to keep any animosity from my voice.

"Oh, don't leave on my account. In fact, why don't you sit down and join us, you can tell us all about what's been going on with you two," he replies, the sarcasm dripping like melted tar.

"Shut up, Jack," Malynda says, as she presses up closer to me, her hand slowly snaking around my wrist. "Just leave us alone." I can feel her body buzzing, tense. I want to snap my fingers and have us both magically disappear from here.

"Oh, that doesn't sound very nice, babe. I haven't done anything but be nice since I got here. Right? I mean, have you all heard me say anything mean?"

His crowd snickers and says no, almost in unison.

"Let's go," I say softly to Malynda, giving her hand a soft tug before picking up Michael's sundae. She nods and we push past the pack.

"Where are you going?" he says, pushing back, not letting me through. His breath is hot against my face. He's not that much taller than me, but he's big, shoulders stretching far beyond mine.

I know he can throw a punch. My eye has barely recovered from the one he landed on me before. I'm thin, I'm fast. But punch for punch, I can't go up against him. I know that. Best to just avoid it altogether.

"I'm going home. I don't have any beef with you, I just have somewhere to be." In the corner of my eye I can see Brian and the twins coming in behind the group. I give them a shake of my head, but it's too much to ask them to understand to just stay away.

"You might not have a beef with me, but I have a beef with you." With a swipe of his hand he flings Michael's ice cream out of my hold and it goes flying to the side, scattering ice cream and nuts and cherries all over the path in front of the store.

"Oops," he says, his voice flat and cold. "Shouldn't you go clean that, parlor boy?"

"No! My ice cream!" I hear Mikey cry out, and I see Brian grab a hold of his little brother's arm, holding him back.

"What the hell did you do that for?" Malynda shouts, pushing ahead of me and getting in Jack's face.

I can see his jaw tighten as he looks down at her. His fist curling and uncurling.

"Get your slut girlfriend out of my face. Before I make her," he spits and I wonder how he's still alive to take another breath.

I grit my teeth and pull on her arm, calling her name. "Malynda, come on... it's not worth it. He's just a dickhead."

"I'd rather be a dickhead than a fucking peasant who has to live off the scraps his mom brings home from the diner. Come to think of it, maybe next time, I'll leave her a little something extra." He barely has a chance to finish his crude gesture before my arm finishes its upper swing into his solar plexus.

"Xavier! No!" someone yells, as I barrel against him, this time digging my shoulder into his stomach. I feel rather than hear him heave before his arm comes to hook around my neck and he drags me to the ground. Somehow, I end up on top of our pile of swinging arms and kicking legs, straddling him. My fist bears down on his face as I punch him, over and over.

It's all just a blur, my arms swinging down connecting with his face before pulling back to gather momentum again. Die. I just want him to die.

I'm not sure how many times I hit him. The movement is a constant loop, even as I feel myself dragged to my feet and someone, or someones, are holding me back, locking my arms behind me. Someone pulls him up as well, his face torn and bloody, scarlet red dripping from his nose and bottom lip.

"You fuckhead," he hisses and spits, splattering the ground with bloody droplets.

"Don't you ever talk about my mom or Malynda again or I will fucking kill you," I yell back, trying to lunge forward.

"OY!" An older voice breaks in between us. It's Mr. Horsham, the owner. "Get out of here, you bloody kids! And don't come back again!"

My arms are suddenly free and my fists starting to feel the effects of the fight.

Mr. Horsham stands only up to their shoulders, but his gaze is fiery and it doesn't take them long to break formation and walk away. Jack gives me one last threatening glare before wiping his mouth on his sleeve and leaves.

"And you, that's it for you." Mr. Horsham says, pointing his finger at me. "I can't have them coming back here and causing trouble. If you're here, they will. I'm sorry, boy."

I can't believe it. I need this job.

"Mr. Horsham!" I call after him. "Please, no. I need this job! I'll clean this all up right now!" I bend over, grabbing the cup from Mikey's sundae, trying to scoop up the spilled dessert back into it, desperate.

"I'm really sorry, kid. This is my business." He pulls his wallet out from his back pocket and peels off a thick stack of notes. "Here, this is what I owe you and, um, an extra week's pay. You were a good worker. I'll give you a reference." He gives me a regretful smile and steps back inside.

"Shit!" I curse under my breath. What am I going to do now?

Mikey runs up to me, throwing his arms around my waist, his face wet as he sobs over his spilled sundae. My heart breaks for him, but I know I can't afford to get him another ice cream, especially now.

"I'll clean this up. You get them home, they must be exhausted," a soft voice says.

For a moment, I forgot that Malynda had witnessed the whole thing, but now that it's over, I replay it back in my head, seeing what she must have seen, hearing what she must've heard, and utter humiliation is spreading through my body.

"Er, no. It's okay, I can do it," I say, not meeting her eyes. I don't know if she hears me over Michaels wails.

She squats, gathering the scattered remnants of the ice cream into a pile.

"I want to go hooooome," Hamish whines, tugging on my arm.

"Go," she says, looking up at me and giving me a small smile. I see pity in her eyes. "It's okay, I've got it."

I open my mouth and no words come out.

So, I say nothing as she returns to her task.

I just walk away and wish her a goodbye, and a good life, in my head.

SEVEN

Him

Present Day

I turn the key in the door and push. It doesn't move.

I try again, this time with my whole hand, and it budges a little. I sigh, pulling off my suit jacket and take a breath before gathering my strength to lean against the rusted door with my whole body. It opens, reluctantly, each inch a fight. Like the door of a sinking car, the pressure outside bearing against the action.

My cough from the dust echoes around me as I take a step into the abandoned building and look around, flicking a switch that does nothing.

There are paper thin streams of sunlight filtering through the dirty windows, just enough to light the large space. It used to be a furniture display storefront, the main area vast and open, with four or five smaller offices in the back, along with a small kitchen and two bathrooms. Around the back is a warehouse, big enough for a gym or indoor basketball court.

I feel myself nod as I scan the room, as satisfied with this space as the first time I saw it months ago. It's going to make a great youth center up here in Harlem.

Kaine and I had picked out this spot especially due to the proximity to the high school just a block away and also just a few steps to the nearest subway and bus stations. The council approval was a little trickier; not everyone wants a spot where kids will be hanging around. But neither did they want to be seen as turning down the opportunity for an organization to come in and try to do some good.

I wasn't worried. Neither was Kaine when he put me in charge of this project or what he affectionately calls "letting his dog off his leash." He knows I care about these youth centers as much as he does and will fight for it just as hard as he would.

69

How our own teenage years might've have been different if we'd had access to some of the services and facilities we're hoping to provide.

Not that we turned out too badly, I think, as I brush the dust from my Armani suit.

But not every poor child has the luck that we had. Kaine with his adopted father, and then me, in turn, with Kaine. I close my eyes and picture this place once it's finished. Computers, books, games. Counselors and tutors on hand. Then I imagine them all over the city, before I stop myself.

One kid. Let's just help one kid, we tell ourselves when the dreams get too big.

One kid can make the difference.

Never underestimate the effect of a single act of kindness.

In my musings, I almost miss the sound of high heels clicking on the floor. It takes the sound of her clearing her throat before I turn around, her silhouette against the door, tall, shapely. Her name isn't the only thing that changed, I can't help but think. I don't remember her having those hips. Hips that have my fingers itching at my side.

"Oh, um, hi. I was supposed to meet someone from the ASH Foundation here," Malynda says. Is it just me or does she sound a little nervous?

"Well, that would be me," I tell her, wondering if I sound as nervous as she does.

"You? You work for them?"

"I work for ASH Industries and well, yes, the foundation as well." I say each word slowly. Maybe I'm stalling, already not wanting this encounter with her to end. Taking in every detail, things that are different about her, things that are so the same. It feels like we're eighteen again.

She comes up level to me, and I can't take my eyes off her.

Everything about her commands my attention: her body, the way she moves, her eyes, open and earnest looking back at me.

I've missed her so much.

So much; and now she's here, after all these years.

It makes me mad to think about all the wasted time.

"Malynda."

She sucks in her breath. "It's Isabella. Please."

I shake my head. "Don't do that, it's just us here. Don't make me call you... that fake name." I won't bring myself to say it, give life to it. She's Malynda. She's always been Malynda.

"It's who I am now, Xavier." Her voice saying my name strips the years away, and with it, any hope that I'm going to let her have her way.

"No, you're Malynda," I respond forcefully, grabbing her by the wrist. "You're MY Malynda."

She doesn't shake me off, just looks into my eyes. They're closed off now. Cold. Flat.

"'Malynda' doesn't exist. So, whatever you think happened between you and her, never ever existed. I'm not her. And I'm not yours." The cold in her voice stings and I struggle not to let go of her wrist, enduring the frostbite.

"What the hell happened to you? Tell me. You owe me at least that."

"I don't owe you anything." This time she does shake me off, ripping her arm away from me.

I catch her face in my hands instead.

"I know you're in there. Malynda, I know you're in there!" Before I can stop myself, I bury my face in her hair. She still smells the same. Vanilla. Sweet, heady, musky. Driving me insane.

"Stop it, Xavier!" she shouts, and I step away out of shock at how she can be so cold. "I don't know you. And you certainly don't know me."

"You want proof? Is that what you want? You need me to remind you? You want me to remind you of the first time we met? You want me to remind you about my black eye and split lip? The hours we spent at the basketball court? The hours we spent at the lake?" There's a knot in my throat that forces me to stop talking. I take a deep breath and pull something out of my pocket. "Or this – maybe this will prove it to you that I do know you." I take her hand and shove the wrinkled unopened envelope into it.

She looks down, her mouth falling open before she looks up at me again. There's a flash of something nostalgic, vulnerable in her eyes.

"Is this? Is this what I think it is, the letter I wrote you that day? You still have this? How? Why?"

"I found it at the lake after you were there the first time. You must've dropped it. "

"You never told me you saved this."

"No. I thought... I thought it might come in handy one day. Not like this though. I never thought we'd be here like this. Me trying to remind you who we are, what we were to each other." The frustration burns in my chest. This is not how I'd imagined our reunion to be.

She sighs. "Xavier."

"Look, I don't know what happened to you, what happened to us. But if you're so intent on not acknowledging what existed between us in here," I tap myself on the chest, "then that is something that you can hold. Can touch. To help you remember."

She looks down at the envelope again, her fingers running along the crumpled surface of the paper, along the torn edges. I know she's going back to that day, like I have, the thousands of times over the years when missing her.

I watch her eyes soften, the slight part of her lips.

"You remember now, don't you?" I lean in, so close my words move her hair. "Close your eyes," I whisper, like just like I did all those years ago. And for just a moment, like all those years ago, she obeys. "Remember us. How we laughed, how we talked, how we touched each other."

There's a fluttering of her eyelash against her face, then they snap open.

"No," she says. But it's not to me. She shakes her head and says it again, "No." She's talking to herself.

I slide my arm around her waist, pulling her into me before she retreats back into herself.

"Stay with me, Malynda." I tilt her face up to look at me, and tears spring to her eyes.

"I'm sorry, Xavier, I can't. I can't do this." The utter sadness in her voice pierces my skin and I let her go.

I don't know what happened to her. But I will find out and I know I need to give her the space she needs to open up.

"Fine." I say, more brusquely than I mean to and even through the tears, I can see the confusion in her eyes at my change. "Let's get to work."

"Work?" her voice trembles.

"Well, you came here to help ASH Industries with the design of our youth center, right?"

She nods, slowly, unsure.

"Then let's get down to work."

"Xavier, I don't think I can. I can't work with you on the youth center, it's too much."

I nod, hands sliding into my pockets to hide their shaking as I fight to maintain my composure. "That's fine, too. I can get Jade to take point if you want."

There's a look of relief on her face, one that stings almost more than anything else that's happened since she came back into my life.

"Thank you, Xavier."

"No problem. Anything for the youth center."

Her front teeth sink in her bottom lip and she nods. "Okay, then, I guess I'll make an appointment with Jade."

I take a step towards the door, controlling my breath. Thinking of how to deliver the next line. "But, while you're here, I guess we can talk about the other project."

"The other project?"

"Yes, my apartment. I paid to have you help me with the interior design of my apartment, remember?"

She sucks in her breath, before exhaling hard. "I can't do that either, Xavier."

I shrug and force my gaze out one of the dirt stained windows. "Well, okay, no problem. I'll just get Jade to return my check to me. The donation, that I made to Ash Foundation. For your services."

"You're going... to take the money back?"

"Well, of course. You don't expect me to pay all that money for a service I'm not going to receive, do you? It's too bad, though. That's what pushed us to our fundraising goal. Without it..." I make a show of turning around slowly, looking at the space around us and shrugging.

I watch her swallow hard, her fingers wringing each other before she forces herself to speak. "What do you want, Xavier?"

I drag my eyes back to her face, locking my pupils with hers.

"Just what I paid for." I shrug. "You."

EIGHT

Her

Present Day

I was eight years old the first time I realized I loved color. I loved the way the world was essentially just blocks and lines and dots and endless permutations of different colors. Colors shaped our feelings, our behavior, the way we tasted food, the way we heard music.

My mother once served me a slice of ham and pineapple pizza and I refused to eat it because it lacked the speck of black that olives made when scattered over a slice of supreme. Even before I took a bite, I knew it would not have that flavor, what the black represented. That's when I knew my relationship with color was more than just through sight.

Unfortunately, it was also around the time that I realized I could not draw. While even the most simplistic drawings of my classmates would be obvious representations of houses and gardens and their pets, I couldn't put pencil to paper to draw what I saw in my head.

So I gave up the dream of being an artist, and doggedly pursued my love of dance instead.

But I never, ever, not for a second, gave up my love affair with color, or the joy that the perfect shade of yellow on spring's first daffodils could bring me, or the way the rain would intermittently wash out the world and coated it in shades of grey and sadness.

But it wasn't until that day, that day standing in front of the paint swatch wall at Home Depot with Xavier, did I ever think that I could make something with my obsession. I had never thought that there was any room for me in the world as an artist, but that day he awakened something within me.

I pull the crumpled envelope out of my pocket, remembering the first time he returned it to me, pushing it into my hand almost twelve years ago.

How we've changed since then.

He looks almost nothing like the thin, lanky, shy but intense boy from back then; his too long bangs hanging way below his forehead, trying to stay hidden from the world.

But his eyes.

Nothing has changed there.

They're still the same deep, dark green that draws the truth out of me with just a glance.

I wonder what I look like to him. Am I what he thought I'd look like at this age? Is he disappointed with how my body has changed?

And would I react the same way, if he touched me like he did back then?

I push the breath from my lungs, and with it, the thoughts of our past. Whatever he was back then, he's different now.

Hard. Both in body and mind.

"*I paid for you, you're mine*," I can hear him say from our meeting earlier today, confident, in charge. 18-year-old Xavier would never have said such a thing. I guess I'm not the only one who has left that person behind.

"Hey, Isa, I didn't expect you back so soon," Cameron says as he walks past my open office door.

I tuck the envelope into my top drawer and wave to my business partner.

"Yeah, the, er, the meeting was quick." I say, pushing the actual details of the meeting away.

"I brought you lunch from Donnini's. I thought you might not have had time to eat." He lays the small container on my desk.

I thank him for his thoughtful gesture with a smile. Not for the first time, I wonder where I'd be if not for Cam. Not here, that's for sure. But just how much worse off, I don't even want to wonder. His natural business acumen melds perfectly with my desire to just stick to the creative side and work with our customers. Sometimes, I wonder if he's ever considered us in a romantic sense, or if he just knows that I never have and never will think of him in that way. The revolving door of women in and out of his office at all times of the day certainly doesn't scream 'pining for me,' that's for sure.

"How did your meeting go with Ash?" he asks through a mouthful of salad while sinking into the sofa opposite my desk.

"It was fine. Early days there, they still have a bunch of construction to do before it's anywhere near time for us to come in. But I wanted to go in and get a feel for it."

Cameron nods and takes a drink from his water tumbler. "Who did you meet with? Jade? Or the charity director?"

I take a breath, trying to keep my voice light. "Er, no. Not today. I met with their lawyer." I stop short of saying his name.

"Oh, the guy who bid on you on the auction? What's his name again?"

Shit.

"Um, Xavier, I think."

"You 'think'? Didn't you meet with him today?"

"Er, yeah, sorry. I've just got a lot of other stuff on my mind. Yeah, his name is Xavier."

I can feel Cameron watching me, so I busy myself with my lunch, sorting through the salad with my fork before taking a bite.

"Is everything okay, Iz?"

"Yeah." I say, an octave above my normal tone. "Sure, why?"

"Nothing." He gets up gathering his things. "Just that, if you feel uncomfortable working on this project, we can always pull out. I hate to, it's not a good look pulling out of a charity gig, but, hey, we can just write them a big check. It's all these organizations are looking for anyway. Money, money, money."

He shrugs and leaves, closing my office door behind him. I wonder how much of what he said is true.

If they would rather have me, or a big check in my place.

I don't know about the company, but I know what Xavier would say.

***

77

12 Years Ago

It's been over a week since the incident at Dairy Joy with Xavier and Jack, and even though I've shown up at the basketball court every day and left notes on the wall telling him when I'd be there next, he hasn't been there once.

I can't help replaying the look on his face when Jack taunted him about his mother and their home situation. The cracks in his pride showing in those green eyes of his, burning his cheeks red as he tried to push it down. I wanted to tell him, I wanted to yell out that none of those things mattered to me, that it didn't change how I saw him, felt about him.

But I know, I know him enough to know, that he needed time to regroup, to mend his pride, to heal the wounds he'd endured at the ridicule of his peers.

But he's had enough time and I'm going to tell him so.

I go to the one place I know he'll be.

I haven't been back there since the first time he brought me, but I still remember the route, where the gap is in the bushes through to the trail that leads to the lake. To him.

I arrive, backpack heavy on my shoulders, breath held already anticipating the view.

It doesn't disappoint. It's late in the day and the sun is already lagging in the sky. The light reflects off the ripples in a way that makes me instantly sleepy, causing my eyelids to feel heavy, lowering to shield from the glare.

It's breathtaking.

I step to the left and see his tent, and two feet poking out from the flaps.

I wander over and drop to my knees, peering in. He's lying on his back, one arm flung over his eyes, textbook lying on his chest. His chest that is rising and falling with deep breaths. Asleep.

I slide the backpack off and quietly, gently crawl into the tent, laying my body next to his, careful not to disturb his slumber.

The sun must've made him a victim of its sleep spell as well, and he doesn't stir. I watch him breathe, in and out, in and out for a few cycles, before I lie back, and let the sound of the water washing up against the lake edge and the birds singing their last songs of the day lull me into a nap.

***

"AHHHH!" I yell, and jump up, my head coming into instant contact with another one, making us both yell out in pain.

"Ow!" I moan, rubbing my forehead. In the dying light, I can just make out Xavier doing the same, scowling at me.

"What are you going here?" he growls, reaching over and flicking a switch on the lamp, casting a warm yellow light over us and the inside of the tent.

"I came to see you, you boob!" I snap, the dull pain in my head only starting to recede from our impromptu headbutt.

"Why?" he snaps, sitting up and staring at me.

"'Why? Because I haven't seen you in over a week, you double boob!"

"So?" The scowl is deeply embedded on his reddening forehead. I have zero sympathy for him.

"Really? We're back to monosyllabic Xavier? I thought we were over that." I get up on my knees and move to crawl out of the tent.

"Where...?" he stops short.

I look at him over my shoulder. "What?" I snap back, his tone making mine defensive in response.

"Are you leaving?"

I rock back on my heels, staring at him. "Do you want me to?"

There's a tensing of his jaw, then his shoulders fall and he sighs. "No."

"Good, because I'm not. I was just grabbing my backpack." I poke a tongue out at him and he squirms.

I come back into the tent and sit in the spot he's cleared for me. "I came to see you because I haven't seen you for a week, and I decided it's time you stopped sulking."

"I wasn't," he sulks.

79

I bite back and laugh. "Yes, you were. And I get it, you were embarrassed because of what that twatwaffle said, even though you have no reason to be. So, get over it." I lock eyes with him, not giving him a chance to look away, so he can see how serious I am.

He stares back this time and I see something, something defiant in his eyes, that he lets flash and then simmer and fade away. It's a concession I feel like he's making just for me. And no one else in the world. I take advantage of it.

"Hey, grab that blanket and lay it out," I say, while he's distracted by his own thoughts. He does as I say and I unpack the containers from my backpack. Some bread and cold cuts. A fruit salad. Some bags of chips. A container of my special mac and cheese.

"What's this?" he asks when I'm done sorting out the spread.

"It's a picnic. You eat it," I say and grab a piece of bread and make myself a sandwich as he watches. I take a giant bite and chew it, then open my mouth, teasing him with my masticated food.

He shakes his head and then laughs. "So much for the elegant dancer."

"This elegant dancer is taking a one meal break from her diet. So, watch out. Now shush and try my mac and cheese, I put a special ingredient in it."

He follows suit and we eat in silence for a moment before he finally breaks it.

· "How did you know I was going to be here?"

"Well, you weren't at the basketball court, and you don't work at the Dairy Joy any more. I don't know where you live. So I took a chance."

He just nods and crunches on a piece of watermelon.

"I'm sorry... about what happened at the ice cream place. I didn't want you to see that."

"Which part? The guys being a jerk to you or you taking their bait and fighting with them."

"All of it, I guess."

"Don't worry about it. I'm just sorry Mikey didn't get to take his sundae home."

"We, er, it's tight for us. At home, money wise. It's just my mom. She works a lot."

I nod, understanding how hard it is for him to be sharing this with me right now. So, I won't interrupt, not until he's said everything he wants to.

"My dad hasn't been around for... well, since the twins had just turned two. And it's not like we were swimming in it then. So, I've been working as much as I can to help out. They were good to me at the ice cream store. Hired me when I had no experience or references. Gave me as much work as I wanted. Even some times when I know they didn't need it. Understood when I had to take off to take care of the boys when my Mom worked. She's... had it really tough."

He stops talking and takes a big bite of his sandwich and I take the chance to ask a question while the gates might be open.

"What are you reading all the time? Whenever we're at the basketball court, or in quiet times at work?" I point to the upturned book he cast to the side, probably pre-headbutt.

He reaches for it and shows me. It's a law textbook.

"You want to be a lawyer?"

He nods. "Yeah, always."

"Why?"

He thinks for a moment, and I love that about him. How everything he says is measured, considered.

"It think because my life is so messy and there's so much order to law. Almost every aspect of our lives has something that is covered by a rule. But even then, it's so open to interpretation. You can manipulate it. Chaos in order."

"Rather than order in chaos," I say, and he looks at me as if I've spoken exactly what he's thinking.

"That's what dancing is. And art. It can be so chaotic, there aren't rules, there shouldn't be. But dance is about the exact right movement, angle, shape at the right time. And the order of those movements. Dancers spend a lifetime trying to perfect a pirouette, the technical aspect of it, but there is still so much open to interpretation. I think, I think that's why I've been enjoying working on my mural so much. It's all me. And... you. It wouldn't exist without you. Thank you."

He doesn't say anything, just stares out the opening of the tent, watching the pink and orange of the sunset darken into night.

"I can't tell if we're two sides of the same coin, or the same side of different coins," he murmurs.

"What do you mean?"

"Well, we're so different, but the same."

"I don't care. As long as I can be tails on the coin." I say.

"You do have a nice tail." I look at him, and he's grinning. The seriousness of the moment before broken.

"I didn't think you'd noticed."

"Oh, I've noticed... a little too much."

"Well, I've noticed that you have a handsome head," I reply and he takes a deep breath, his eyes on me. I want to be closer to him. As close as I can be. I inch forward, our hands touch on the blanket between us.

The smile fades from his face and it's all seriousness again.

"Malynda. Do you have any idea how beautiful you are?"

I shake my head.

"Beautiful. Stunning. Perfection."

"Even my freckles?"

A flash of a smile dances over his lips. "You mean, these little dots where you've been kissed by the sun?" He lifts a hand and runs a thumb over the tip of my nose and over the side of my left cheek.

A shiver creeps up my spine, thrilling. Something I've never felt before. "Yes, especially those."

"What else?" I ask, wanting to hear more.

His hand slides down to my neck. "You have the most elegant neck. Like a swan. Long, lithe, alluring." He moves closer, I can barely hear him now.

But I can see him.

His face an inch away from mine.

I didn't realize until this very moment that I've been waiting this whole time, my whole life, to kiss him.

"Kiss me, Xavier," I whisper.

And he sucks in the air I breathe out.

His mouth lowers to mine and my lips are touching his.

Everything about it feels right, I push forward, wanting to feel him harder against my mouth, more. I just want more.

He pulls away, and I almost fall into the space between us.

"Malynda," he says, and it scares me the way he says it. Like it might be the last time.

"Yes?"

"I can't offer you anything. I don't have anything. It's why I haven't... I want you to know, I know you deserve more."

I lean forward, my head against his chest, listening to his racing heart beat for a moment, before I look up at him.

"You have the one thing no one else can offer me," I confess.

"And you have the only thing I could ever want," he replies.

We take a breath and in unison we whisper, "You."

NINE

Him

I don't know who moves first but once we break the dam, there's no stopping.

My mouth is on hers and hers is on mine. My hands are tangled in her hair, her fingers digging into my shoulders, like we're trying to grab handfuls of each other to devour.

I'm hard, instantly hard. I've been holding back my want for her for so long that I'm not sure how long I can hold on, at just the thought that I may soon have her.

She moans against my mouth, and my brain short circuits at the thought that it's from me touching her. She lies back on the blanket and pulls me on top of her, her legs wrapping around my hips like they've always belonged there.

It takes everything not to thrust against her. It's not time yet, through two layers of clothing. I hardly want her memory of this being me dry humping her. I pull back, rocking back onto my heels, taking in the sight of her laid out in front of me, her blonde wavy hair wild, like Medusa's, her lips already full and red from my kisses.

"So beautiful," I whisper to myself rather than to her, but the smile she gives me makes my heart skip a beat. Does she really not know how beautiful she is?

She reaches for me and I lower myself back down to her, my lips finding the smoothness of her neck, and I run my tongue along its length. Her skin smells just like I thought it would. Sweet and natural, like dewy flower petals, like sunshine.

"Ohhh," a groan escapes my lips as I feel her hand reached between us and brushes over my hardness. My whole body stiffens as I swallow. "Sweetheart..."

"Shhh... I want it. I want you, Xavier," she says, the words that undo me.

My hand gropes at the side of her thigh, pulling her skirt up to bunch at her hips. She wriggles under me, her legs falling wider apart. I tilt to the side, my fingers reaching along her inner thigh, up higher and higher, until they graze along the hem of her panties.

I take a breath and push them aside. And finally come skin to skin with the sweetest part of her.

She's soft, warm, wet.

She wants me.

Almost as much as I want her.

I tease a finger, following the wetness, and the tip of my finger slides inside her. She squeezes around it, and I feel my hardness twitch.

I can't wait much longer.

But I need to know that she's ready. As ready as I am right now. As ready as I've been waiting my whole life to be.

It suddenly occurs me to ask, and I'm almost afraid of the answer. I kiss her gently, brushing a hair from her face.

"Sweetheart. Is this okay?"

"You're my first, Xavier," she says with a tremble.

And I respond with the gift that she's given me.

"You're my first, too, Malynda," I confess and she wraps her arms around my neck, pulling me down to kissing me deep, hard.

"I'm ready. I didn't know it, but I was waiting for you."

I kiss my way down her body until my face is level with her hips, I gently ease her panties down her legs, breathing her in. Her sweet, salty scent.

I can't wait any longer.

I free myself from my pants and ease myself between her legs.

Running my fingertips along her inner thighs, I position myself against her. She bites her lip and nods, giving me the cue. I hold my breath as I push forward, feeling myself slide into her slowly, inch by inch, until there's nothing left of me.

Her brow furrows for a moment as she takes a sharp breath, and I press my lips against the patch of skin just below her ear.

"Are you ok?" I whisper and she mouths the word "yes." I kiss her gently, as my hips pull back, and I feel every inch of her tighten around me.

Is this heaven?

I ease myself back in and she exhales with me. I do it again; this time her eyes lock on mine and I can't look away. Locked with her, as I slide in and out of her. In and out. Gasping for breath as I feel myself rising and falling both at once.

"Oh, Malynda," I moan, and she closes her eyes for a moment, her head falling back.

I reach between her legs, feeling for the spot I know she must be wanting me to.

"Fuck." The curse falls from her lips when I reach it.

I need to move fast. I want her to come along with me every second of this journey.

My fingers rub in circles over her most sensitive spot as I thrust harder and faster against her. I'm only moments away. Her breath grows as fast as mine, the flush travelling up her neck reaching her cheeks.

"I have wanted you for so long," I gasp, and her hands come up to dig into my forearms.

I slide into her one more time and feel myself explode. My finger doesn't stop on her and she starts to buck under me. I feel her squeeze around me and I know she's coming with me.

I forget where I am for a moment, just that my whole body is releasing. And she is doing the same.

I take sharp, shallow breaths and my arms buckle under me and I fall onto her.

She catches me, her lips on my forehead as I struggle for consciousness.

"I love you, Malynda," I tell her when my lungs permit. She just sighs and holds me until I forget that there was a time before her.

The goosebumps on her arm cast little shadows on her skin, when we both wake up a few hours later. I wrap her tight in the blanket and she just sighs, letting out little giggles against my chest that tickle.

"What's so funny?" I finally ask her.

"Nothing."

"Then why are you giggling?" I poke her gently in the side and she yelps before scrunching her face up at me.

"It's what people do when they're happy."

I make a noise that doesn't sound quite right.

"What was that?"

"That was my attempt at a giggle!" I say defensively.

That makes her laugh outright, so hard it shakes the sides of the tent, and not for the first time I wonder how long we could exist in this space alone.

She reads my mind, and slowly sits up. "I have to go home, it's already past my curfew."

I nod, reaching for a jacket. We crawl out of the tent and walk hand in hand out to Main Street, the moon smiling down at us.

We don't say anything for the twenty minutes it takes to reach her street. I just try to burn the feel of my fingers intertwined with hers into my skin, something to remember when they'll be empty tonight, but with the memory of her in my mind.

We stop outside of a white house, its lawns perfectly cut, two cars in the driveway.

"This is me," she says, turning to me. I pull her into me, memorizing her scent. Her arms come up under my jacket to hug me back. "Basketball court tomorrow? After school?"

I nod to her; she needn't have asked.

"Xavier?" she asks, her voice so quiet, I can barely hear her. I pull away to look into her eyes. "You really were my first."

I lean in to press a kiss against the tip of her nose. "And, Malynda, you will be my last."

I watch until she's inside the house and the silhouette waving to me from an upstairs bedroom fades into the night.

*＊＊

The two weeks after we make love for the first (and first of many) time, is pretty much the definition of idyllic. Every moment we have free is spent together, either at the basketball courts where she works on her mural and I sit and pretend to read while I watch her and wonder when we can next be alone at the lake.

I can't keep my hands off her, and luckily, she feels the same. I feel my body gravitate to her as soon as she is in view, needing to kiss her, to touch her, to be inside her.

She meets my need with her own and we spend hours naked in the tent together, exploring our bodies and what they can do together.

"That tickles," she wriggles, as I run my tongue along the inner thigh of her left leg.

It's the night after her final dance performance and I have just spent the last hour watching her in awe as she embodied the melding of music and movement. And now I want to show her how she made me feel through the mutual exploration of our sexuality.

She's made me, not just my mind and my brain, come alive. She's made me finally understand the use of my body. And that is to bring her pleasure. To make her scream my name in a voice that's husky with lust.

She is my addiction.

I ignore her protestations at my tickling her and I shush her, my voice muffled between her legs as I slide my tongue inside her; her body stiffens and her protests soon fade on her lips. The sweat on her skin is slightly salty, but inside she tastes as sweet as ever

I lap at her, never getting enough and when she comes on my mouth, I drink every last drop.

"You spoil me," she sighs happily when we're done and I pull her against my chest, feeling myself content beyond measure.

"You spoil me by letting me spoil you," I tell her. I mean every word.

The only thing that mars our time together is the worry I see in her eyes as she waits for news on her future. The more time I spend with her, the more I see her pursuit for perfection. She talks about her last performance dance constantly, what had gone right, what had gone wrong, what she could've done differently.

Her rants inevitably turn into talk of our future together. The very thought of ever spending a day apart becomes unbearable. But while her dream seems so much more concrete that mine, she knows I have my own ambitions. Just that I have no way of achieving mine.

"There are ways, Xavier. You will be a lawyer. We will find a way."

I don't tell her there's no money. Not right now. But she's right. I will find a way, and the only way is by her side.

"You know, you told me what you love about the law, but you've never really told me what you want to do with it. Is it so you can afford a giant apartment and a fleet of Rolls Royces?" she asks as she lies with her head on my stomach as I lean against a tree trunk, staring out over the lake. There's the sound of a whistle as a man calls his dog back to his side.

I twirl a lock of her golden hair around my finger and watch it catch the light.

"Well, the law isn't the same for everyone."

"What do you mean? They aren't different laws for different people."

"No, there shouldn't be. But there are different ways to interpret the law for different people. And one of the great differences between the haves and have nots is their lawyer. I want to be the equalizer. I want to help people who can't afford to get good help. Those finding themselves on the wrong side of a law interpreted to benefit just the rich."

She nods and closes her eyes, "That's better than a giant apartment."

"I think so too."

"I mean, maybe you can both!" she giggles, the vibrations travelling up my stomach muscles and into my heart and I can't help but laugh along.

"Maybe, sweetheart. Maybe."

By the time the last day of our high school years comes around, the summer has taken a strong hold of Maine. I walk down the front steps of my school, knowing there won't be a person I'll miss from here. A year from now I'll be surprised if anyone even remembers my name. But I smile as I say goodbye to this part of my life anyway. Because when I think ahead, to today, tomorrow and my future, I know there is one person who will remember me.

She's already there when I reach the basketball courts. Music is blaring from her iPod, and her hips swaying as she stands in front of her almost finished mural.

I try to divert my eyes, as always. As curious as I am to take a close look, take it all in, this was never about me. It was my gift to her. To give her the space to explore this side of her. And when she's ready, she'll share it with me.

I sneak up behind her, this summer's pop hit covering the sound of my footsteps.

In one movement I grab her by the waist, pulling her into me, as I tuck my chin against the hot skin of her neck.

Her squeals are muffled by her lips catching on my cheek as she turns her face to see who's intruded on her time to create.

"Xavey!" She giggles, half because she knows I hate the nickname but won't ever tell her to stop, half because she can't control the sunshine inside her. Even in the cold, dark evenings we've spent huddled in the tent by the lake, I'm warmed just by the smile on her face when she looks at me.

"Happy last day of school, baby," I whisper against her ear. I love that there exists a whole world in the space between her body and mine.

"Happy last day back to you! We're free!" She turns around, throws her hands up and jumps into air. I catch her on the way down and spin her around as she whoops.

Her lips fall on mine as she lowers her face and I kiss her like I've been wanting to do since the minute she left me last night. When we pull apart, she makes a little sigh that thrills me. All the way down to my toes, squeezing her warm body tight against me.

"Too hot! It's too hot for cuddles right now," she laughs and pushes me away, her feet touching the ground again. I grumble and she pokes her tongue out as I wander over to my spot on the wall, cast in shade from the angle of the afternoon sun.

She follows me and waits until I settle on the ground before she settles into my lap, I wrap my arm around her waist and we stare at the basketball court baking in the hot summer sun.

"I thought it was too hot for cuddles," I say, my face against her back.

She doesn't say anything, just sighs and leans back against me.

We don't talk for a few moments, and that's okay with me.

"Xavey?" she whispers a while later as my eyelids are drooping, my hands now resting loosely on her hips.

"Hmmm?"

"I... um, I got a letter today. "As soon as the words leave her mouth, I feel my body tense. And I know she feels it. She twists around and looks at me, even as I try to look away. "I haven't read it yet. I was waiting for you." She slides her hand into the pocket of her denim shorts and pulls out a folded white envelope. Already I can spot the school's address in the top left-hand corner. New York.

Love is a strange thing; it can make you want two opposing things in equal quantity at once.

I want nothing but for her to be happy. But what will make her happy is the exact opposite of what would make me happy. To have her by my side, here.

"Read it," I say, nodding gently, trying to smile.

She doesn't smile back, but slides her finger into an open corner of the envelope, slowly, deliberately, breaking the seal.

She takes a deep breath, a silent prayer on her lips.

"Wait." I stop her before she reads it. Her eyes catch mine, confused.

"Whatever it says, I'm here for you. I'm not going anywhere," I say. Even if you are, I can't help thinking.

She nods and unfolds the single sheet of paper. She closes her eyes and takes another deep breath. Her eyes flutter open and she scans the first few lines of the letter.

She doesn't read it out loud but the instant twinkle in her eyes tells me everything. She drops the hand holding the letter into her lap and grins at me.

"They took me off the wait list. I'm in." She exhales the breath as if she's been holding her breath for months. I pull her to me instantly, hugging her tightly, my heart bursting with happiness for her.

"You're in?"

"I'm IN!" she yells and jumps to her feet. Twirling, her arms outstretched. Feeling everything in the moment.

I drag myself to my feet and follow her, unable to contain the joy I feel for her right now. I don't even need to pretend. This, this is how she should always feel and I'm going to make it my goal in life to guarantee she will.

"You. Are. Going. To. NEW YORK!" I yell, emphasizing every word once the twirling stops and she comes back to stand in front of me.

She grins at my words and launches herself at me, knowing I will catch her.

"I'm going to New York! Oh, my god! I'm going to be a dancer! XAVIER! Can you believe it?!"

"You are a dancer, baby. Now the whole world is going to know it!" I tell her. And mean it. The world is going to know the beauty of my girl.

"You know what this moment needs?" I ask her, my eyes serious.

"What?" she asks, her eyes wide.

"An inaugural swim in the lake."

"Ooooh, you think it's warm enough?"

"I think... it doesn't matter. We're going to do it anyway." I grab her hand and we run, run so hard we can barely keep up with ourselves.

It's almost completely dark when we finally get out of the water. The goosebumps covering every inch of our bodies ignored by us.

I turn on the string of fairy lights I've strung up around the tent just for her and wrap my biggest towel around her shoulders. Her jaw shakes a little as she thanks me, and I can't help but laugh at the tinge of blue lining her lips. She was the one who had refused to get out of the water even when the sky had almost lost all color.

Facing the wall of the tent, I pull off my wet shorts and wrap my towel around my waist, trying not to stare too much at the shadow of her wriggling out of her own wet clothes.

I settle back onto the air mattress on the floor of the tent, watching as she brushes the wet hair off her face and lies down next to me. The blanket is warm and soft on our skin as we shake it over our shivering bodies. She giggles as my hands try to warm her, running up and down her arms.

"Hey," she whispers, her face upturned to mine, the flickering shadows from the fairy lights bathing her in a warm, soft light. I just smile back at her, and drop a kiss on her forehead. "I have to go, you know," she says, and I nod.

"I wouldn't have it any other way." The smallest frown flickers across her face and I run a finger over her cheek. "Shhh, you know what I mean. I'm so happy for you. You are meant to go and study dance in New York and be everything you always wanted to be."

"And you?"

"And I... will be right there, beside you. Watching and cheering you on."

She pushes gently on my chest as she sits up.

"You're going to come with me?"

"You had any doubt?"

"But... how? You have your family and..."

How will we afford it? is what she wants to say. And I don't have an answer yet.

"I'll find a way. It might not work out right away. And it might be hard. Are you game?"

She giggles as she settles in against me.

"More game than ever."

***

It doesn't take me long to find a summer job at a lawyer's office downtown. Lawsuits don't go away, even if lawyers do for vacation. It's menial, mind numbing labor; I file endless case notes, answer phones, hand out mail, and drink in everything I can while I'm there. I find excuses to come into the conference rooms during negotiations and depositions, and take on any job that needs doing. I learn fast and it shows, and I start being assigned tasks beyond my experience.

I sneak away for my lunch hours to the basketball courts and join Malynda, who seems more intent that ever to finish her mural. Before it was just a work in progress, now it seems it's her farewell to this town she grew up in.

But summer comes and goes, and soon just as quickly as early as heat descended on us, so does the crisp fall come encroaching before it is due.

Soon, it's only a few days before it's time for her to leave and for me to still remain.

The job at the lawyer's office pays more than the Dairy Joy, of course, but not by much. My bank account is a leaking bucket, what with helping out at home. But the numbers do start to add up, slowly. I hope that by the spring term, I can join her.

I don't tell her about the schools I've applied to, resolving to only tell her when there's something concrete. Only something good.

It's all I ever want to be in her life.

The good.

"Xavey! Look how big they are now!" Malynda dangles on one leg, half way up the tree branch, peering down at one of the other bird's nests we'd found that had recently hatched.

I look up from the grill I've set up by the lake, fanning the smoke from my face as the charcoal catches light.

"I know, I'm surprised they can still fit in there. Time to move out of home, buddies."

"Nooo, stay there forever. Stay little forever. Don't leave home," she coos at the little chirping, hungry mouths.

"Are you talking to the birds or yourself?"

"I was giving them some of my wisdom," she says, wryly.

"I thought it was some of your cold feet." I pull her legs into my lap and tickle the soles of her feet, making her squirm. "You're going to be great."

"I'm going to miss you so much."

"Good!" I say.

She scrunches up her face and nudges me with her toes. "How long, again?"

"Five, six months, tops."

"Promise?" I answer her with a kiss. "Okay. I guess I can wait four months," she sighs, pouting.

"Five or six! You won't even notice the time go by, I'll be there before you know it."

***

Dear Xavier,

I'm sorry.

I've put this letter off for too long.

Don't come here for me.

I won't be here.

I've met someone else. Another dancer. I'm leaving New York to be with him.

I'm so sorry.

I know it wasn't supposed to work out this way, I didn't expect it to.

I hope you can forgive me someday.

Take care.

Be happy.

x

TEN

Her

Present Day

Ten a.m. is a weird part of the day. Most people are at work already, or, considering this is midtown Manhattan, a lot of people started four or five hours ago. But the crazy chaos of the peak hour is dying down, there are a few stragglers coming in and out of coffee shops, older gentlemen with the Times tucked under their arms and the younger crowd staring down at their phones, a Starbucks in the other hand. Everyone keeping to themselves as the traffic starts to become fluid again after the gridlock of the morning rush hour.

My car stops by the side of the road, arriving at my destination. Normally, I jump right out, ready to start whatever lunch/meeting/appointment I have planned, on the go, never stopping from six a.m. to midnight. Trying to fit as much into my day as possible, which isn't that hard here in New York City. There's always someone perfectly happy to talk work to you at any hour of the day.

But right now, the last thing I feel like doing is stepping out of this car and making my way to my rendezvous.

I want to tell the driver this was a mistake, to turn around and drive. And just keep driving until I forget. Forget what I was here for. Forget his face. Forget his name. Forget like I've been trying to forget for twelve long years.

I should just turn around and walk away. Nothing good is going to come of this. Not for me and not for him. Take the easy way out, write the check, and pretend that Xavier had never come back into my life.

Not that he ever left.

The mind is a terrible thing. It can make you feel like time is no object. Years can go by and yet, you can transport yourself back in the space of a split second. Back to that tent by the lake, sunburned skin kissed by his lips, and your fingernails on his back. Like it was just yesterday and not a lifetime ago.

"Miss?" The driver is antsy to earn his next dollar.

I mumble thanks, gather my bags and linger one last second on the door handle before I step out.

A gust of wind knocks me off my center and I stumble, trying not to drop the black portfolio in my arms, hugging it tightly to my chest. I feel a hand against the small of my back, stopping me from falling.

"Woah. Steady. What've you got in there that's so important?"

I know the voice, but I take a moment to steady myself before I look up.

Into those green eyes.

"Um, hi," I mumble, making a show of twisting and turning, making sure I didn't drop anything, as an excuse to move away from his hand on my back. I'm a little surprised when I notice he already had dropped his hand. Then why could I still feel the heat against me?

"No, really. What's in that thing?" he says, pointing to the folder gripped in my hand.

"It's my portfolio. And some notes. You didn't really tell me what you were looking for, so I don't have a lot of ideas yet."

"Well, that's why we're here. I was just coming back from a meeting. Good timing, you can come up with me." He gestures his head towards the building's entrance, and for a moment I resent him. How can he be acting so normally? Why isn't this harder for him?

Like it's hard for you? my brain taunts me. Every moment in his presence right now, is like walking on nails. I feel like I have to remind myself to do the most basic of things. Breathe, blink, stand, breathe again. And yet it seems like this is nothing to him.

Maybe it is.

I can't tell you if that makes me feel better or worse.

I follow him as the doorman holds open the door for us, almost banging into him when he stops to say something to the doorman that makes him throw his head back with laughter. The doorman gives me a wink as I pass him and I return it with a weak smile.

The lobby is small and quiet. My shoes click against the marble floor as we stand waiting for the elevator.

"What floor are you on?" I ask, just to break the ice.

"31," he says, just as the elevator arrives, waving his key fob over the scanner.

" And how many floors in this building?"

"31."

"So, the penthouse."

"We don't call it that," he retorts, with a shrug.

"Why not?"

"Because we're not rich, elitist, show-offy snobs."

"Touché."

The elevator stops and I hold my breath as the doors open, not quite sure what to expect. This is his home.

Xavier steps out and turns when he notices I haven't followed.

"Well, are you coming?"

"I don't know, yet."

He looks amused. "Well, I don't know if you know this about elevators, but they go down as well as up, and if you don't get off, you're not going to be able to come back up again without me."

Right on cue the doors start to close and I step out, just before they meet in the middle behind me.

"Come on," he says, with a head tilt. "Sorry about the mess." I follow him through the entrance way into the main area of his apartment.

I gasp.

As an interior designer I've seen a lot of homes. Small, medium, large and gargantuan. Some could never be made beautiful, even with the help of some styling, and some are stunning examples of architecture, all on their own.

This is an example of the latter.

It's one big open space. A millionaire's loft. Floor to ceiling windows on all four sides, almost uninterrupted by the bare minimum of walls. Thick white beams hold up the ceiling, strong but elegant. Light streams though the open glass, filling every inch of the space with light. The apartment is completely sparse, but there's a sense of innate warmth.

I spot a king size floor level bed in the far corner of the apartment, beside it a stack of books. I can't help but wonder if he's still reading law textbooks. Scanning the empty space for more furniture, all I find is a leather recliner facing the window and beside it a stocked drinks trolley. I walk over to the kitchen area in the middle of the floor. It's compact and looks unused. I wonder how much time he spends here.

If I had walked into a stranger's apartment and had to sum him up from what I see, I would profile him as three things: bachelor, workaholic, lonely.

And I have to remind myself, Xavier might as well be a stranger to me.

"So, what do you think?" he says, right beside me. And I jump, not realizing how immersed I was in his living space.

I take a breath before answering.

"Eh, I've seen worse. Probably should do something about the clutter."

He grins at me, and I try not to stop my stomach from doing a complete somersault. I don't know if he worked on it, but he seems to have perfected a wolfish grin. I bet women go crazy for it. A flash of white-hot jealousy rips through me, and I fake a cough to turn away, in case he can see it in my eyes.

"So, um, how long have you lived here?"

"Just over two years."

"And you're getting furniture at the rate of one piece a year?"

"Yeah, I'm due for another piece soon. Maybe a key hook or something."

"That's not furniture, Xavier."

"Don't be a snob, Malynda," he says, emphasizing my name. I'm still getting used to hearing it. I'm still getting used to him.

"Hey, stop calling me a snob, I'm not the one living in a penthouse."

Now it's his turn to say it, "Touché."

I poke my tongue out at him. It seems I've reverted back to being a teenager in his presence.

"Anyway, I live here for free," he shrugs.

"Free? Why?"

"Well, my landlord doesn't charge me any rent."

"Who's your landlord?"

"Me," he says and there's that grin again. "Kaine and I have a side real estate venture. This was the second building we bought together. I was going to rent out this floor as well, but I fell in love with it, so I took it. Perks of owning it, I guess."

"What was the first?"

He doesn't answer for a while, walking over to the window and laying a hand on the glass. "The first was the house I grew up in," he finally answers, his voice low, almost inaudible, as he stares at the cityscape spread out in front of him.

I don't say anything. It almost feels like intruding.

Taking a few steps back, leaving him with his thoughts, I take a walk around his apartment again, taking mental notes of what I think I can suggest. I try to separate my personal feelings and try to go through the motions as if it's any other client, and any other job.

There's obviously a reason he's left the place like it is for two years, and I want to be sensitive to that, while still making it into a functional home for him, a place he wants to return to every night.

I can't help wondering what his life is like these days. In most houses, the furnishings and personalized touches tell me what I need to know about a person. In Xavier's case, it's the lack of them.

Is he lonely? Is he just passing through? He seems attached to Ash Industries and this city. I wonder how long he's been here.

All answers I want to know about him, but not willing to answer the same questions myself.

"So, what do you think?" he says, when I come full circle of the apartment and return to where he's standing. He seems to have regained his composure.

"You really want me to do this?" I ask.

He seems shocked by the question.

"Did I ever seem like a kidder to you? Yes, I really want you to do this."

"Fine. Then if we're going to do this, we need some rules."

"Shoot."

"We can't talk about the past."

He doesn't say anything; there's the slightest tension along his jawline but he holds his tongue. So I continue.

"I don't want you thinking that there will be anything past this. I'm doing this to fulfil my commitment to Ash and Jade and their foundation. Once it's finished, we'll go our separate ways." The word 'again' hangs silently in the air.

"Anything else?"

I'm surprised as his brusqueness. "No."

"Well, I'm a lawyer, so, I'm going to need to counter offer. I get one question a day. About the past. No follow ups, just one question. But you have to answer honestly. 100% honestly. Without fear of repercussion. Do we have a deal?"

"What about the last part of what I said."

"About going our separate ways?"

"Yes."

"I'm not going to hold us to something I don't want either of us to want."

"Xavier!"

"Malynda. Whatever happens, happens. Can we just agree on that?"

The words sound amiable, but I know enough of this new Xavier to know, that there's no point in arguing this point. I will just have to be the one who controls what happens.

I nod.

"Let's kiss on it?" he asks with a wink.

"Xavier!" I exclaim, shaking my head as he laughs. "So where do we start?" I lift my hands in surrender.

"With my question for the day." I hold my breath. "Have you been in New York City all this time?"

I didn't know what I was expecting, but I guess I'm not surprised it was this.

"Yes." 100% honesty.

"Wh-" he starts.

I hold up a finger, "One."

He sighs, "I think I was out negotiated. Do you have a question for me?"

"Yes," I nod. "What the hell are we going to do with this place?"

He winks and starts to walk, calling over his shoulder. "What else? We start with the bedroom."

ELEVEN

Him

I can still smell her.

Everywhere I walk in my own apartment, I can fucking smell her.

After twelve years of searching, of whys and where is shes and what ifs, of nightmares and daydreams, she was in my home.

Smelling just like I'd imagined she would.

Lilacs and vanilla. Ice cream. Just like she did all those years ago.

She hasn't changed, at least in that respect.

But I have.

Or have I?

Has she noticed any difference in me? Or am I still the same lanky, love sick dog I always was to her? Does she even care?

No. I know she does. I felt the way her breath would stop every time I came too close, the flush rising up her cheeks giving her away.

Then why, WHY has she come up with these ridiculous rules? Are they to protect her or me?

And her answer to my question.

Yes.

One word. Telling me everything I'd dreaded to hear. That she's been here in New York this whole time. But I already knew that. Or else I wouldn't have spent the last decade the way I did.

Roaming these streets, searching for any sign of her. Reluctant to ever leave in case today would be the day.

Now she is back and as lost to me as ever.

***

A buzz on the makeshift nightstand made of books wakes me up. I sit straight up, jolted out from a foggy dream, the dark horizon telling me it's still early. Earlier than I normally wake up, which is earlier than most people. Who the fuck is texting me at this time? It's either Kaine, wanting to meet me at the office for a dawn work out session, or a text scammer, who will be sorry they ever found my number.

I tap on the screen to check the number.

It's Malynda.

Can you meet me some time today to go over a few furniture choices?

She's kidding me, right? That's what she's thinking about at 5:12 a.m.? And I thought I was a workaholic. I tap a reply.

How about I meet you at the drugstore to get you some sleeping pills? Go back to bed.

The response comes back in less than ten seconds.

Xavier.

It's one word, but I can hear it in the tone it's intended. Hell, I can even see her hands on her hips as she's giving me the eye. Hey, if she has the audacity to wake me up at this hour, then I at least get to have some fun with it.

Shhh, I'm still in bed. But you're welcome to join me.

Xavier!

Yup, I can hear that one, too.

Stop laughing.

Apparently, she can hear me as well.

Fine. Yes, I can meet you. It will be my pleasure.

Don't be expecting any pleasure.

Just that of your company, Malynda.

Isabella.

Yeah, you can bring her too. the more the merrier.

That shut her up. I drag my body out of bed and walk to the bathroom. My apartment might look sparse, but I actually spent a lot of time renovating the interior to some very exact specifications. The first being a bathroom you could have a Roman orgy in. Specifically, an inordinately large shower with a custom-made rainfall shower head and two side shower nozzles and water pressure that could be used for torture by the CIA. It can be also be used as a steam room, with a bench that runs the length of one side of the cubicle. The walls and floor are laid in Pompeii Scarpeletto, a gray Italian natural stone, that is smooth and cooling against my skin. Healing to the touch. And after my sparring sessions with Ram, I need all the therapy, hydro or otherwise, that I can get. While others prefer to layback in a whirlpool tub, I prefer that the soreness is massaged out of my muscles by shower jets.

This is my sanctuary. I return here in sickness and health.

The lights turn on as soon as I walk into the bathroom.

"On," I say, and the audio system starts up. A playlist of nature sounds I've curated to switch my mind and body into gear every morning.

I abhor the onslaught of TVs at Ash Industries' gym that Kaine had built for his employees. Kaine insists on having all news channels up at once in the morning, so he can absorb everything.

My morning ritual requires serenity before the inevitable chaos of my work day.

I make sure the small screen in my shower is hooked up to my phone's Bluetooth and I press the button on the touch pad to turn the water on to my morning shower program. The jets scald my back for 30 seconds before it switches to ice cold, shocking my body awake.

There's a beep and a glance at the screen tells me Malynda's replied.

I don't bother to stop the instant grin spreading across my face, completely resigned to the fact that she has turned me into a giggling school boy. I haven't felt like this in years. Twelve, to be exact.

"What time?"

"Quippy!"

"What time, Xavier?"

"12? For lunch?"

"2. AFTER lunch."

"Fine. Make me eat my PB&J by myself."

"2 it is. I'll send you the address later."

"Okay, I'll be the one looking sad and hungry."

The emoji I get back is ruder than I expected and the echo of my laughter in the shower cubicle lasts long after her message is sent.

Then I lean back, my hand reaching for hardness, trying to think of her in all the ways I've missed her.

***

"Holy shit. I want that one!"

"No." She grabs the front of my shirt and pulls me past the race car bed display and down toward the back of the store. "And anyway, I don't remember you liking Ferrari's."

"Maybe I've changed. Maybe I like fast cars now. And anyway, I'm pretty sure you're supposed to listen to my ideas."

"You didn't pay all that money for us to be listening to your ideas. You paid for me, so you're going to get me."

I stop and look at her, one eyebrow raising.

Her brow furrows for a moment and then her eyes roll.

"You know what I mean. You paid for my services."

Now I feel my other eyebrow raise as well.

"Oh shush, come on. I have other clients to meet. You're not my only appointment today."

"Oh, so we're really not having lunch together."

"I already had lunch."

"Oh? With whom?"

"Cameron."

It's like a splash of ice water over me, and it takes me a few seconds to recover before I shake myself out of it.

"What do you think about that?" She points to a bed.

It's fine. I don't care. I tell her so.

"You're supposed to care. It's your home."

I shrug. "Have you seen my home? Does it look like I care?"

"Then why am I here, Xavier?"

My eyes wander for a moment over her face before resting on her eyes. "You know why."

She takes a moment and then looks down at the list in her hand, clearing her throat.

"Fine, that bed it is. You'll like it. It won't take too much away from your minimalist aesthetic. I'll have it delivered by the end of the week."

She gives me a look and starts to walk away.

"Wait," I grab her by the wrist before she can get too far. She stops, and I drop her hand. "My one question."

Her shoulders lift as she takes a deep breath, bracing herself.

"OK. What is it?"

"The letter you sent me. You... you said you'd met someone else. Was that true?"

"Xavier. What's the point of all this? It's not going to change anything. Let's leave it in the past and move on..." She meets my eyes, and they tell her that there's no moving on. Not for me. Not without knowing. "No. It's not true."

"Oh my god, Malynda, then what happened?"

She holds up her hand, stopping me. I can't see her face.

"No more questions, Xavier. This was a mistake. I knew we couldn't do this."

I block her as she moves to run past me, and I know the only thing stopping her is the look in my eyes.

"I need to know what happened, Malynda. If you didn't meet someone else, then why did you stop me coming to New York? We had our whole lives together, a future ahead of us. It was all planned!"

"Sometimes things just don't go to plan, Xavier. Sometimes, they just don't."

TWELVE

Her

"Another drink?"

"I think the one martini that's already gone to my head is plenty, thanks, Jade," I say, shaking my head.

"It's on Ash Industries, we could have ten bottles of Dom and they wouldn't notice."

"I'm pretty sure they'd notice us showing up singing Broadway musical numbers in the lobby. Again." Harriet, Jade's best friend and assistant, laughs.

I can't help but laugh along. The two ladies have a hilarious rapport and have had me in stitches all afternoon. They have that gift of showing their closeness without ever making me feel left out. I can't remember the last time I had such an enjoyable meal.

"Just a sparkling water for me," I tell the waiter still standing by our table. He nods and carries my empty salad plate away with him.

"Anyway, back to the plans, Isabella, these are just amazing. And you really think it can be done with the budget we set?"

"Yes, in fact, probably a little less. I mean, see the way I've used these boards here? That'll cut down on some of the cost, but still look good. And be sturdy enough for whatever you've got planned for the center."

"The sturdier the better!" Jade laughs.

"Got it."

"Well, I'll run these by Kaine and the committee, and we'll go from there."

"Sounds great." I'm pretty sure I'm beaming, and not just from the martini. I'm thrilled that she's happy with what I've presented to her so far. I'm fast becoming attached to this project.

"Did I just hear my name taken in vain?"

We turn to see Kaine coming towards us. He's wearing an Armani suit and it's hard to look away.

That is, until I notice who's coming up behind him.

It's Xavier, looking no less commanding, in just black shirt and slacks. He certainly grew out of his lanky frame, I can't help thinking. His biceps threaten to bulge right out of his shirt sleeves and I have to force myself to look away before anyone notices I'm staring.

"Hello, Isabella. My bride here tells me that you are going to make us the envy of the downtown area." He looks directly at me, and I feel warmed by his crooked smile. I wonder how Xavier came to work for him.

"Oh, not at all! I'm still in the ideas stage and Jade has been kind enough to look over them."

"Mind if we have a look?" He reaches for the portfolio before I can even respond. I guess he's not used to having people refuse. I steal a glance at Xavier, but he's looking at the plans. I can't tell if he's actually engrossed in them, or just avoiding me.

We didn't leave things on a good note at the furniture store with me walking after refusing to answer any more of his questions. It's been a long week of radio silence from the both of us, and I guess I should be glad.

There's a buzz on my phone, and I pull it from my bag, welcoming the chance to focus my attention on something other than Xavier. I glance at it, then look up to see Jade watching me.

"It's just my partner. He's outside and wanted to know if I needed a ride back to the office."

"Oh! Tell him to come in and have a drink with us," she offers.

"Oh, um, no, I'm sure you have a lot to do, you've already spent so much time with me."

"Oh, please. She's relishing having conversation with people who won't expect her to change their diapers after," Harriet says and waves the waiter down, asking him to bring another chair.

"Okay, sure, I'll ask," I cave, and quickly tap a few words into my phone.

It's only seconds before I hear my name called out.

It's Cameron, a bunch of flowers in one hand, his phone in the other. He leans in and brushes a kiss on my cheek before turning to Jade and Harriet, giving them a wide smile. With a flourish, he pulls two roses out of the bunch and hands one each to the two women and then holds the bouquet out to me, with a wink. I laugh and take it from him, making a show of burying my face in it and fluttering my eyelashes.

Kaine reaches out his hand and Cameron takes it, giving it a solid shake. I know Cameron has a small spot of hero worship for Kaine and his business acumen, and it shows in the giant grin on his face.

"Cameron, you remember Xavier from the other gala?" I say, a split second before I notice the stormy look on Xavier's face.

"Of course, you're one helluva bidder, did wonders for getting our firm's name out there!" Cameron says, holding his hand out. It takes a second too long for Xavier to take it, who looks down at the offered hand like he'd rather not touch it, and there's instant tension in the air. I tug gently on the sleeve of Cameron's jacket, pulling him back into a chair, giving him a reassuring nod as a look of confusion crosses his face.

"Cameron, what's your poison?" Jade asks.

"Oh, just an espresso for me, please. Need something to knock some life into my brain at this time of the afternoon most days."

"Xavier, what about you?" she asks and is met with stony silence.

What the hell is wrong with him?

"Three double espressos," Kaine says, waving the waiter off, before throwing a look at Xavier.

"So, Kaine, what do you think of Isabella's plans for the youth center?"

"Well, from what I see, I think Jade's right, you are really going to brighten up that old warehouse. You've got a real eye, Isabella. I think you're going to make that place open right up, and yet still give it a warm, cozy feel for the kids."

I blush from the compliment. I'm never quite used to telling people what they should do with their homes, their offices.

"She's a star all right, I like to think I discovered her," Cameron boasts, giving me a wink.

"Pffft, please," I hear Xavier mumble under his breath, and hope I'm the only one.

"Well, it's just a rough proposal, things will change once all the interior repairs have been done and we can really know what we're working with. Even then, plans can change."

"No shit, Sherlock," Xavier scoffs, this time, not so quietly.

"Sorry? I'm not quite sure what you mean." Cameron asks Xavier directly, and I hold my breath. He's sweet and charming, but there are no doormat tendencies to Cameron. He's as tenacious under that smile as anyone I know.

But he doesn't faze Xavier, who just shrugs. "I just mean plans, apparently, can change. Dramatically. It almost seems like a waste of time making them. Isn't that right, *Isabella*?" He says my name like it's cyanide, and he needs to spit it out before it poisons every last cell in his body.

"Hey!" Cameron says, his hand coming up to touch my shoulder. "I'm not really sure I appreciate your tone, buddy."

Xavier pushes himself out of his chair, ignoring the clang as it topples onto the floor. His biceps bulge and I follow the line of his arms down to scrunched up fists. For a moment, it looks like he's going to face off with Cameron, then he exhales and pivots, storming out of the restaurant.

"What the hell was that?" Harriet asks, and the look on Kaine's face tells me he knows more than he's letting up. He gets up to follow but I give him a weak smile and shake my head.

"No, I think it should be me."

It almost looks like he doesn't want to give in, but Jade touches his arm and he relents.

"Go. But go fast. He won't hang around for long."

I pick up my purse and squeeze a confused looking Cameron on the arm before I run after Xavier. He's hailing a cab as I step outside and I run up to him.

"What the fuck was that, Xavier?"

"Go away, Isabella."

"Not until you tell me what's wrong!"

"You know, I have recently learned that you're a liar, and a promise breaker, but I guess maybe I should add clueless to that list! Who knows? Maybe a gold digger as well?"

I rip my palm across his cheek before either of us can stop it.

"You have no fucking right to talk like that to me!"

He just stands there, hand print on his face growing redder by the second. I can't read his eyes, but there's a look of contempt I never thought I'd see in them. And I say what I should've from the start.

"We shouldn't have done this. We can't be in each other's lives. Goodbye, Xavier."

I spin around before the twisting in my stomach makes it too hard.

But before I can walk away, there's a hand on my wrist, pulling me back.

"Do you think this is easy for me? Seeing you. With him? With anyone?"

"What are you talking about?"

"I spent twelve years, TWELVE fucking years looking for you, Malynda. Not knowing what happened to you, to us. Using every resource at my disposal to find you. Not even really knowing if you were alive. It got to a point I hoped that you'd fallen in love with someone and were living your dream of being a dancer in Europe somewhere. And then, after all this time, I find out, you've been right on my doorstep this whole time. You just changed your name, been living it up on the upper east side with your businessman, and what? Playing dollhouse for fun? What happened to dancing? What happened to your dream? What happened to you?!"

There's a crowd building around us, but I don't care. I can barely see out of my blurry eyes to focus on his face.

"You... you don't know me, Xavier. You knew me for one summer, twelve years ago. You don't know what I've been through. You don't know what got me here. So don't you lecture me about my life. I'm not the only one that's living it up on the upper east side as you put it, playing dollhouse in your penthouse. Maybe I should ask you what got you there. Last I heard helping the poor didn't put you in designer suits. All this tells me is, our past is just that, in the past. We have no present, and definitely no future."

I stare at him, daring him to respond. I don't know what to expect, don't know what I want him to say. Just that, for all my bravado, I don't have the strength to be the one to walk away.

"Malynda," he finally says, in a sigh as long as the day. His eyes still on mine, he reaches out slowly, taking my hand in his. I ignore the way my fingers twitch instantly at his touch. "I'm sorry. You're right. I don't know what's brought you here. But I want to know. Don't you understand that? Don't you get what it's been like for me all this time?'

Any contempt we felt in the heated moment is gone. All that's left in his eyes are questions. That he's hoping he can get answers to from me. But I have none. Nothing that can help him. It's better to wonder sometimes. He doesn't know, I'm holding back for his sake.

"I'm sorry too, Xave. I don't... I can't give you the answers you're looking for."

He lets go of my hand, and it drops to my side. I look down at the ground, grey pavement worn down by countless footsteps of countless New Yorkers.

"Fine. If that's the way you feel, I'm not going to pressure you about it today. But you're wrong about one thing. We can. We can be in each other's lives."

I open my mouth to protest but he stops it with a look.

"We can. I will try to make it easier for you to be around me. Okay? I'd rather have you in my life, giving me grumpy looks and scolding me every few minutes for pushing you too far, than not at all."

I roll my eyes, and a little of the tension in the air dissipates. The truth is, I can't imagine him not being a part of my life, now that he's back in it. However wrong it might be.

"You deserve the scoldings," I say, accusingly.

He bows low, with a flourish of his arm. "I will accept them obediently, ma'am."

I snort, louder than I mean to, and it makes him grin. That fucking grin. Where did he learn to do that?

"Friends?" he says, holding out his hand.

I take it, my hand feeling delicate but safe in his. We shake.

"Friends."

"With benef-.."

"XAVIER!"

"Just testing the scolding feature. It works," he chuckles.

He's still holding my hand and I give it a squeeze and then pull it back.

"I can't talk about the past, Xavier. I need you to understand that, if we're going to be friends."

He nods, his lips tightening for a split second, like he's holding back the barrage of questions I know he has. But he doesn't say anything more.

"So, friend. Can I get you that espresso?" He gestures with his head back toward the restaurant.

"And an eclair. And a scoop of vanilla. And some mac and cheese."

"Some things never change," he mutters as we walk back to our waiting friends.

***

"You're here late," Cameron says around 9 p.m. as he walks past my office, pulling his suit jacket on.

"Yeah, I'm way behind, probably been spending too much time on the youth center." I look up from my desk from the first time in hours to see that the sky over Manhattan is dark. I can't remember how long I've been sitting there.

"Hey, about that." Here it goes, I knew this was coming. "You sure you're okay working on that project."

"What do you mean," I answer, wondering if he'll fall for my look of confusion.

"Iz, I only let you play dumb because it puts the clients at ease. It doesn't actually work with me."

I poke my tongue out and he responds in kind. "No, really, what are you talking about?"

"Xavier. He's an ass. I don't know what's going on between you two but I'm not sure it's a good thing."

"It's nothing, a misunderstanding," I say, with a wave of my hand. "Just... we didn't agree with an idea for his apartment."

Cameron isn't convinced, but he keeps it to himself.

"Need a ride home? Or maybe some dinner?"

"No, I think I'm going to finish up here and stretch my legs a bit and walk home."

"You know, one of these days, you'll realize what a sexy hunk you have for a business partner, and you won't be able to resist me."

Right on cue, there's a buzzing of the phone in his hand. He glances at it and then looks at me sheepishly.

"Yeah, you're really lacking for company."

"Guy's gotta eat," he shrugs before coming around behind my desk and giving me a kiss on the cheek. "You know I just want the best for you."

I nod. I do know. I'm just not really sure what that is anymore.

THIRTEEN

Him

"Is there a name for the face you're imagining on that punching bag, or is it just your time of the month?" Ram grunts as he hugs the bag, absorbing the leftover shock from my kicks with his body. I've punched that torso of his, I'd rather take my chances with the bag of sand.

"Cameron." I pant and give the bag one last kick before I drop to the ground, catching my breath.

"Sounds like one of your snooty lot, rather than mine."

"He's not 'my lot'," I growl.

"Well, you're not going to see a lot of Camerons around here."

"I wish I didn't see any Camerons anywhere," I sulk.

"Ah, it's a girl thing. Gotcha."

I don't answer, just throw my sweaty glove at him as I make my way to the bench press.

She said I had to be nice to her. She never said anything about her partner.

***

Malynda is completely engrossed in a pillow when I get to the store. Holding it right up to her face, she stares at it for a moment before rubbing it against the side of her cheek, eyelids closed. I can almost hear her sigh from 100 feet away.

I'm not really sure what she's doing, but I'm wishing I was that pillow right now.

She opens her eyes and lays the pillow back down on the bed, running her fingertips along the seam, a soft smile on her face.

I am probably going to have to skip any meeting where she wants to discuss my bedroom design. Even after the energy depleting workout last night, I'm not too tired to imagine throwing her on that display bed right now. And showing her just how much I've missed her all these years.

As if she can hear the impure thoughts running through my head she turns, sees me, and waves.

"Hi, what about these?" she says as I walk up to her, holding out a sheet set for me to look at, but all I see is her.

"Er, yeah, great."

"No, you have to feel them. They feel like liquid silk, ugh. Amazing." She grabs my hand and pushes it over the bed spread. Liquid silk. That's how I would've described her. Being inside her.

"Mmm," I force myself to say, as I beg my cock to behave. "Very nice."

"Ugh! this is wasted on you. Might as well go get you a sheet set from Walmart."

I can't help but laugh. Truth is, my apartment IS sparse, yes. But my bed linens are of the highest quality. When you sleep naked, you tend to care about what you're sleeping on.

Even if, right now, I'm more focused on who I want to be sleeping with.

She's wandered over to the lighting section and looks like she belongs there. Reflections off the tousled blonde bun on her head hit me like sun rays, lighting up her face like a spotlight.

She gestures impatiently to me and I take three steps to catch up with her.

"What about these?" she says, pointing to a set of wall panels with a LED light behind them. It disperses the light while emitting a warmth that wouldn't look out of place in my apartment. "We can get them in a darker color, red oak, maybe. I think that'll suit you better. For the entryway, where the elevator opens to."

She's right. She's always had that impeccable sense of color. For a moment, I cringe, remembering what I said to her yesterday. The truth is, I think this is the perfect job for her. But I can't take back what I said. I can only apologize.

"Hey, you're the boss," I say, as I do every time she suggests something.

"Xavier! You're the one who has to live there and look at this stuff. You're going to regret letting me choose everything."

"I really don't care. You have a good eye. I trust you." The words come out of my mouth before I can stop them. And the way she looks away tells me, she caught it too.

"Fine," she clears her throat a few seconds later, "but please look over some of the fabric swatches I sent over so you can be prepared to give me an opinion next time."

"Yes, I will tell you exactly what shade of puke I want for my tablecloth."

"Puce!"

"That's what I said."

"Ugh," she grumbles and waves her hand at me.

I follow her as she wanders over to another stack of sheets.

"So, um, what are you doing tonight?" I ask.

She frowns, "Why?"

"Just making conversation."

"Well, I have a late meeting, but then, I actually have quite the romantic night planned."

I swallow the burn of white-hot jealousy. "Oh, yeah?"

"Yup, I bought a special outfit at Victoria Secret just for tonight."

Don't think about it, don't think about it. "Oh. Ok. Wow. Lucky guy."

"Yup, it's a flannel pajama set with matching slippers. I'm going to slip into something very comfortable and eat my special mac and cheese, with a glass of wine and Netflix." She makes a show of fanning herself and winks dramatically at me.

If she could read my mind she'd see the sheer relief flashing across it. "Well, sounds like you're in for a night to remember!"

She giggles as I take the basket from her and walk her to the checkout.

"So, hey, these pajamas of yours, any chance flannel comes in see-through?"

"Xavier!"

FOURTEEN

Her

I admit it. I was slightly disappointed when Xavier asked my plans and then left it at that. What did I want? Did I want him to ask me out for dinner?

No. No! Because then I would've had to say no, and I don't know that I could've.

But now here I am, in my office, last meeting of the day finally over, and the prospect of mac and cheese alone in my apartment is actually making me feel more lonely than I have felt in years.

The stack of catalogues on the side of my desk are seemingly mocking me as I reach out to pack them into my work bag, knowing that I'll be spending tonight of all nights with them.

"Shush. I like my work," I tell them, and try not to cringe at the pathetic way my voice sounds as I try to defend my hermit lifestyle to a stack of papers.

I flip the switch on my desk lamp and pull the coat off the back of my chair. I contemplate calling Jade before I realize she's probably busy bathing or feeding her baby.

Alone it is.

"Hello?"

I jump as a man wearing a candy stripe uniform and a bunch of helium balloons wanders into my office. It's the last thing that I expected to see right now.

"Um, yes, can I help you?"

"Are you Malynda?"

I roll my eyes. Sent by Xavier.

"I guess. What's up?"

"I have a delivery for you." He holds out a box and ties the balloons to one of the desk legs. "Have a good night."

I'm too engrossed in the big white box to notice him leave.

What is this, Xavier? I wonder, but not for long. My curiosity gets the better of me, and I tear off the ribbon on the box and fling the cardboard lid across the room. I rifle through the layers and tissue paper until I get to the main part of the gift. Then I can't help but guffaw.

Inside is a pair of flannel pajamas. With goldfish on them. Where did he even find them?

I lift up the flannel top and a small card falls out.

"Put these on and I'll meet you downstairs in 15 minutes. Don't argue. And don't be late!"

I hug the card to my chest, something tickling inside my stomach. A deep breath doesn't make it go away.

"Fuck it." I push myself up away from my desk. "I told you I'm not a loser," I say to the stack of catalogues and pull the blinds closed as I slip out of my skirt and into the pajamas.

I've been downstairs for about 5 minutes, when I hear the faint tune of Happy Birthday. I step out onto the road peering down Madison Avenue and see a limo coming toward me with a bunch of balloons floating out from its roof. It's only about twenty yards away when I realize there's a head bobbing around amongst the balloons, one that belongs to my high school sweetheart.

"Hey! You're not appropriately dressed," is the first thing he says to me when the limo comes to a stop outside the building.

I can barely breathe from laughing to respond so I just open my jacket, flasher style, to show him what I'm wearing underneath.

"Yay! Now we match," he exclaims.

He ducks down and disappears for a second before jumping out of the limo. He's dressed exactly like I am, except he has something I don't. A pair of Nemo slippers on his feet.

"Oh my god, Xave!" I squeal pointing at them with one hand, the other holding onto his arm as I hug my cramping stomach.

"Don't worry, I brought you a pair as well!"

He kneels down and lifts my foot, throwing my stiletto off, flinging it onto the street before sliding a Nemo slipper onto my foot.

"Xavier! Those are Jimmy Choos!"

"Choos Shmoos! These are TARGET! Way more comfy, right?" He wriggles his eyebrows at me as he slips my other foot into the second slipper. My toes instantly curl into the plush insides of the slippers. It feels heavenly after a day of being in those pointed torture devices.

"Don't worry, I'll get you another pair," he says as he gets to his feet, taking my hand and leading me into the limo.

"I want Dory next time!" I shout.

"I meant the Jimmy Choos."

I giggle and shrug. "I know, but I'd rather have the slippers."

He looks at me, his pupils open, warm and friendly. He holds my gaze for a moment, before asking, "Would you really?"

I shrug again, "Well, yeah. Choos don't go with flannel pajamas, Xave." I give him a wink and climb into the limo. He follows, closing the door behind him. The limo pulls away from the curb and into traffic.

I take a moment to look around me and burst out laughing again. How is this happening right now? I push the thought away. Fuck it. Jump now. Deal Later.

"I can honestly say I've never done this."

"Ridden a limo? I doubt that."

"Not in pajamas and slippers!"

"Only way to do it!" He stretches his body out, his long legs spreading out in front of us, his hands locked behind his head. "You hungry?"

My stomach growls in response.

"I guess so," he laughs and reaches across me over to the drinks bar and hands me a glass of champagne. "Drink this, it'll tide you over until we eat."

"This is going to go straight to my head," I say pointedly, then take a long sip anyway. "Where are we going?"

"Out."

I give him a look, and then finish the champagne.

"Where out?"

"Out out," he winks, knowing how much I hate not knowing.

"Xavier."

"Malynda."

I know better than to argue. I haven't forgotten how stubborn he used to be, how impossible it was to get him to talk about anything he didn't want to. Hell, he didn't say a word that first week I was trying to get to know him. Something tells me, while some things are different, how much more confident he seems now, flirty, in command, um, muscly, other things have stayed just the same.

I lean back into the leather seat, enjoying how comfortable I feel. Usually when I'm in a limo I'm zipped up tight into a dress, my hair pinned within an inch of its life, my feet pinched and blistered.

My eyes flutter closed and there's the unmistakable sound of New York City traffic whizzing past my window while I'm cocooned in here. With Xavier.

A sigh escapes my lips before I can stop it, and I open my eyes to see him staring at me.

He doesn't bother to look away so I'm the one to who breaks our gaze.

Careful, Malynda, I tell myself, and am a little surprised at my use of my old name. From the moment I changed it, I'd been careful to never think of it again, even just in my own head. Until now.

The rest of the drive is in silence. Quiet but not awkward. The stress of the day slowly seeps from my bones, and I feel my muscles loosen and relax. When the limo finally stops I peer out the window and am surprised where we've arrived.

"Um, Xavier?"

"Yup?"

"This is The Barn."

"Yup again."

"Like, one Michelin star, top 100 best restaurant in the world, Gourmet's best new chef, Jaxon Sinclair's place, The Barn."

"You've heard of it, then. Good." He shuffles forward in his seat.

I blink at his response. "Heard of it?! I've been DYING to go here."

"Well, we're here, let's go. I'm starving too." The limo door opens and he starts to climb out.

"Er, no. Nope." I sink as far back into the leather seat as I can.

"What? Why?"

"I'm... wait, no, *we* are in pajamas, Xavier."

"So?"

"No." I shake my head and sink deeper into the shadows.

He laughs and takes my hand. "It's fine, come on!"

"There are dress codes in these places, Xavier."

"And you are in keeping with the code. Trust me. Come on, we'll be late." He ignores my protests and drags me out of the limo. I stumble out onto the footpath and Xavier pulls me close against him, so close I can feel his heart beat against my cheek. "Come on, I got you," he whispers and pushes me through the restaurant entrance, ignoring the groups of people glaring at us as we skip the queue.

It's dark inside, and it takes my eyes a moment to adjust. There's a little waiting area, a hostess's podium just to the right. We're the only ones standing here, even though I can see the restaurant is full and buzzing over Xavier's shoulder. He gives me a quick wink and lets go of me as a guy I recognize from his profile in the Times comes over to us.

"Xavier. Buddy!" The men hug and Xavier turns to me.

"This is the guest of honor, Malynda. Malynda, this is Jaxon," I take the hand offered to me, voice completely lost.

"She's a little bit starstruck. Apparently, you're a big deal," Xavier says and Jaxon just grins.

"You guys ready? I have your table all set."

I pull my jacket tighter around me, hoping no one will notice the slippers in the dark as Jaxon leads us through his restaurant. I try not to drool as I watch the plates being carried past us, and colorful cocktails being concocted at the long bar, stretching the length of the dining room. He takes us through a door that leads us through a bustling kitchen and then another door and it's instantly quieter.

"Where are we going?" I whisper to Xavier as Jaxon presses on a button by what looks like a freight elevator.

"Up."

"Where up?"

"Up up."

I bite back a growl and just glare at him instead. Before I can ask another question, the elevator doors open and Xavier ushers me inside.

"Have a great night! My guys will take care of you," Jaxon says, not following us into the elevator.

"Wait... where..." I start but don't get to finish as the doors close.

"He's not coming with us. He has a restaurant to run. Apparently, it has one Michelin star and is on the World's 100 best restaurants list," Xavier mimics me, and I punch him on the arm like I've been wanting to do since he made me get out of the limo in pajamas. "Ow! Meanie!"

"Don't you forget it!"

He just shakes his head and holds out his hand to me.

"Come on, time to eat."

"Where are we going?"

"We're here," he whispers and tilts his chin.

I spin around and see, we're on top of the world.

"Happy Birthday, sweetheart," he whispers, his lips grazing my ear as he gently pushes against my hips and guides me forward onto the roof of the building. My mouth is open and silent as I take in the view in front of me. There, with the backdrop of the Empire State Building, is a single table set up in the middle of the roof, with a vase of sunflowers and an ice bucket with a bottle of champagne.

"Wow."

"Yeah, this place is reserved only for private parties. And by private, I mean people who know Jaxon on a first name basis."

"And how is that you?"

"Well, it gets boring calling each other Mr. Sinclair and Mr. Kent when you're doing business together."

"You and Jaxon?"

"Yup."

"Business? How?"

"Kaine and I own the building."

I shake my head. Who is this Xavier? This business mogul. He's all grown up now, I guess. It makes me sad that there's so much I don't know about him. But then who's fault is that?

"Come, I can hear your stomach rumbling from here."

He pulls out a chair and sits down. I can't stop touching the plate and the silverware. It's all so beautiful. And then I remembered what he said.

"You remembered." I don't even have to tell him what I'm talking about.

He smiles, pulling the napkin out of the wine glass. "Of course. You didn't think I'd forget your birthday, did you?"

"I don't remember yours," I admit, my cheeks flushing. Or maybe it's the effects of the champagne.

"Well, we never spent my birthday together."

He grins and I fall into a wormhole that takes me back twelve years ago. He'd spent some of his hard-earned money from working at the lawyer's office and taken us to an Italian restaurant in Portland.

"Remember the bus trip up to Portland?" he says, his eyes twinkling.

"Most romantic bus trip in the history of bus trips," I laugh. "I love being ogled by a guy wearing a Futurama T-shirt and sucking on the same YooHoo for two hours."

"Hey, I was eighteen and poor."

"No, really," I reach out and squeeze his hand. "It really was so romantic. The whole night was," I say, not laughing so he knows I mean it.

He nods, "Well, I thought so. Even when you made us Lady and the Tramp it with the spaghetti."

"You made a great Tramp."

He nods as if to accept the praise. "You weren't so great a Lady though."

"Hey!"

"You hogged the spaghetti; you know you did! You're supposed to meet in the middle, not hoover up almost the whole thing!"

"I was hungry!"

"Speaking of which," he points behind me, and I glance over my shoulder to see a parade of waiters carrying dishes come out from the elevator and lay them out in front of us.

I bite my tongue waiting for them to leave before I give into the laughs.

"Oh my god. What. Is. That?" I point to the piled plate in front of me.

"It's penne e quattro formaggio e truffle a la Jaxon Sinclair."

"It's MAC AND CHEESE!" I cackle, so loud I'm sure they can hear me on the streets.

"I told him he had to use some sort of orange cheese or else you wouldn't eat it. 'It has to look like it came out of a box' is exactly what I said, if you must know."

"Oh my god, what must he think, us showing up in PJs and now you requesting mac and cheese.'

"He's thinking 'Gee, Xavier, thanks for cutting this month's rent bill in half' is what he's thinking!"

"Xavier. You didn't!"

"Shut up and eat. Your mac and cheese is getting congealed. Or whatever orange cheese does."

I fill up my fork with the delicious smelling food and cram it into my face.

"Ohmyeffingod," I moan through a mouthful of creamy pasta.

"Yeah," Xavier nods, his mouth just as full, "this almost beats Kraft."

"Yeah, almost, if Kraft could get their hands on cheap truffles. Ughhh, this is so good," I mumble through another mouthful.

There are a few quiet minutes as we both enjoy our dinner. The pasta is creamy and unctuous and cheesy and decadent. My plate is almost empty when I see Xavier reach across the table with his fork and try to stab one of my penne tubes.

"Wow, hey, stay on your side!" I pull my plate closer to me.

"Rude! My plate was the same size as yours!"

"So?"

"I'm bigger, I should get more. You owe me anyway!"

"Nuh-uh!"

"Yuh-huh, *Lady!*"

I growl and roll my eyes. I spear one of the penne tubes and lift it towards Xavier's mouth. He grins and opens wide.

Just as he clamps down, I pull the fork away and pop the pasta into my mouth.

"Mmmmmm, yummy. Isn't it funny how the last piece is always the best?"

"Bitch," he hisses and stares down at his plate, forlorn.

I giggle and reach for the half-filled wine glass. The swirl leaves ribbons of liquid claret on the bowl of the glass and I watch them slide down toward the stem. I take a small sip and I close my eyes, savoring it. When I open my eyes, Xavier has moved my empty plate away and replaced it with a small cupcake, speared by a single candle.

"Where did that come from?"

"It was under that cloche," he says and points to the metal dome on the side table. "You didn't notice it because you were too busy ogling the melted cheese."

"Mmmm, it was very sexy," I nod. "But this looks delicious too."

"I don't have a lighter, I'm sorry. You can just pretend to blow the candle out."

"Do I still get a wish?"

"Er, hang on." He pulls his phone out of his pocket and starts tapping at it.

"Um, now who's being rude?"

"Shush, I'm finding out if your birthday wish will still come true!"

"Oh, and?"

"Um, there's nothing about unlit candles, but someone suggests to make a wish that you want to die. And then you should tell someone that was your wish."

129

I laugh at the ridiculous idea. "What the hell? Why?"

"Because your wish doesn't come true if you tell someone!" He says this with his eyes lit up like the rows of fairy lights around us. "Wow. The internet really is a treasure trove of useless information."

I bat his phone away, impatient. "Can I eat my cupcake yet?"

"Did you make a wish?"

"Well, you didn't sing Happy Birthday to me yet."

"Fine." I sit with my hands in my lap like I'm waiting to open a big present. He clears his throat and sings. Loudly. And badly. Very, very badly.

"Happy birthday to you. Happy birthday to you," he warbles. A car alarm goes off somewhere in the distance and I'm not convinced it's not because of his singing. I try to keep a straight face right up to when he lingers on the last line and gets up and presses a soft kiss to my cheek and sits back down. "Happy Birthday to youuuuuuuuuuuuuuu."

"'Wow. Um. Thank you, Xavier."

"No problem. Now you can have your cupcake. Are you going to share it with me?"

"No. One does not share their cupcakes," I say and pop the entire thing in my mouth.

I make a show of rubbing my stomach and licking my lips even though it's hardly pretending, it's delicious. He sits and watches, mouth open. Once I'm done, he gets up and carries another cloche covered plate over and sits it down in front of him.

He smirks and lifts the dome with a dramatic flourish; revealing a much bigger cupcake under it.

"My turn!" he exclaims, and lifts the cupcake to his mouth.

"No! HEY! It's MY birthday, you have to share!"

"Oh no, someone once told me, 'one does not share their cupcakes!'" He lifts it up and waves it in front of me. I reach out and grab it, tearing half of it off and stuffing it quickly into my face. Xavier gasps and jumps up off his chair and runs over to me. Before I can move away, he pushes what's left of his cupcake against my face.

"No! Help! Cupcake attack!" I yell and run from the table, brushing the crumbs and frosting off my face. He chases me down and grabs me by the hips, spinning me around to face him.

Those eyes.

Those deep green eyes.

How could I forget what it was like to lose myself in them?

Our laughter fades into the night, and my breath stops completely as he lowers his mouth onto mine, kissing me deep.

He tastes like red wine and chocolate.

Or is that me?

I don't know. All I know is I can't stop kissing him.

My fingers run through his hair and my chest is pressed against his, feeling every hard inch of him.

"Oh, Malynda," he whispers against my mouth.

And for a moment I forget that's not my name any more.

His tongue grazes against my lower lip, and his cheek is deliciously rough against mine.

Need for breath forces us apart, finally. My fingers instantly coming up to touch my lips.

They feel different already.

He leans forward again, but this time, I stop him.

I shake my head, and hope that that's enough.

He sighs and rests his forehead against mine, waiting for our breath to steady before he pulls away and stares out into the night, resting his hands on the wall's edge, keeping us from falling off the roof.

"There were more stars out last time. On your birthday. It's almost like it's a different sky."

I look up, aware that our arms are still touching, my skin raising into goosebumps.

"Same sky. Different city. Too much light here, I guess. It's not Maine."

"Have you been back?" he asks.

And I answer honestly, "No. You?"

"Not once." I hadn't expected that. I didn't know what I was expecting. "Not even when my Dad died and he was buried there."

"Can I ask you something?"

He nods.

"Why did you buy your old family home?"

"Because I could."

I'm not surprised. Xavier has never been lacking in pride. I understand that more now than back then how hard it must have been for him to live in the circumstances he did.

"Is that where your mom still lives?" I ask, not sure how much he wants to talk about it.

"No. She lives here now. She's been here for about seven years. I moved her here as soon as I could. "

"And the boys?"

"All here as well. Well, Brian's serving."

"Wow. Things *are* different," I sigh.

He turns to me, brushing a hair off my face. It sends a shiver through my body. "What about your parents?" he asks. And he has every right to.

"Um, they moved."

"I know."

I must look confused, so he explains. "I went to them first, when I got your letter, when you changed our plans. They didn't know anything. And trust me when I tell you, I hounded them. It took me a long time to believe them. And, er, then when I looked them up again a few years later to see if there was anything new they could tell me, they had moved. Didn't leave a forwarding address. I couldn't find them. I tried. I tried everything to find you."

I just nod. I don't know what else to say. I don't know how to tell him that I'd kept my secrets from them too, that it took me years to get back in touch with them. That my life has been a complete and utter mess. And since I left Maine, I haven't been as happy as I am right this very moment.

We're quiet. Each lost in our own memories.

"So, um, why didn't you go back more often?" I wonder.

"Honestly?"

"Why not?"

He faces me, and I know what he's about to say might hurt me as much as it hurts him. "I never left because I didn't want to miss running into you. From the moment I got your letter, I've been looking for you. I didn't know where you were in the world, but if it was here, then I wasn't ever going to leave in case today was supposed to be the day I'd find you. And I was right."

"You've really been here all this time?"

"Yeah, I mean, I roughed it on the streets for a while after I used up all my savings. Then a guy I met took pity on me and took me in, trained me up and got me a job as a bouncer. I kept getting into fights, though and one particularly bad night Kaine came across my sorry ass, scooped me out of the gutter, cleaned me up and put me in law school. And here we are"

"Good thing you met him then."

"He saved my life."

"I'm... I don't know what to say, Xavier. I didn't know that this is what would happen."

He shrugs. "I was lucky. I met good people."

Lucky him, I think. Luckier than I was.

"So, do any of my confessions buy me some of yours?"

"Not tonight, Xavier. Please. Just let me enjoy this. Enjoy you. Us."

He nods.

"Can I just ask one question? You can reply or not."

"You can."

"Do you miss dancing?"

I tell him the utter truth. "The only thing I miss more than dancing is you."

Somewhere out there, it's time for someone to finally go home, and a light turns off on the Empire State Building.

"I guess I should go home," I sigh.

"Okay, let me call the car," he says, giving in easier than I thought he would.

I stare down looking at the lines of cars on the street as he dials his phone.

All this time, we've been just circling this city, never meeting. I don't know what I would've done if I'd known he was here the whole time. I honestly didn't think he would be. I guess it was fair to think he might've come to look for me. But I thought he would've left, once he couldn't find me, that he would just give up.

But he stayed to find me. And he did.

Was it fate? Serendipity? Pure luck?

I may never know, but I can't help but think that it's better we found each other now than then. He wouldn't have wanted to find me twelve years ago. Then it wouldn't have just been my life that was ruined, but his as well.

"Car's just around the corner," he says, coming back over to join me, taking a sip from his wine glass and handing it to me.

I take it from him, our eyes locking over the glass rim.

My last birthday's memories with him sustained me for twelve years.

I wonder how long it will be before I would forget this one.

FIFTEEN

Him

She doesn't say anything the whole way home.

She does let me take her hand though, in the limo, and somewhere along the trip she leans back, her side against my chest, as she stares out the window.

I breathe more than I need to, long deep breaths, taking in her scent, her warmth.

She's the same but different.

There's something in her eyes that wasn't there all those years ago, but I can still hear the Malynda I knew in her laugh, her silly jokes, the way she wears her emotions on her face. How she points at things that make her smile and laugh; and it's almost always tied to something that ignites her creativity.

I didn't know what to expect from tonight, I just couldn't imagine her on her own on her birthday. Why she wasn't spending it with her boyfriend, Cameron, I don't know. But I was going to take every chance to show up for her, when he wouldn't.

She sighs gently and I look down at her.

The lights from the city catch on her eyelashes, framing her face with a soft glow.

Twelve years I waited for this.

But I feel more clueless than ever.

She's here, but where has she been? What happened? And when can I kiss her again like I did on the roof?

The limo swerves, parks, and she sighs again before sitting up.

"This is me," she murmurs, as if she's telling herself.

"I'll walk you up."

"No, it's okay."

"Relax, I'm just making sure you get to your apartment, okay? I won't ask to come in. I won't pretend to need a glass of water. I won't even smile and I promise to waddle bow legged so you don't get tempted by my sexy manwalk." She doesn't say anything but I can see the corners of her mouth twitching hard, so I go in for the kill. "But hey, if you don't think you can resist me in all my flannel manliness, I understand. I wouldn't want to make you do something you'll regret. You're right. It's settled, I'll stay here."

"Bastard! Come on, then, sheesh. Stop before you hurt yourself."

She climbs over me to get to the open limo door, mumbling, and I have to bite my tongue from getting hard at the feel of her body across my lap. Something tells me that she knows exactly what she's doing, though, and that revenge was in order.

I exhale and follow her out of the car and to her building's entrance. There's no doorman so I open the door for her and she brushes past me.

Vanilla. I'm drowning in the scent of vanilla.

"What floor?" I ask, when we get into the elevator.

"Not the penthouse," she shoots back.

"That doesn't mean it's not the top floor."

"Fifteen," she says and rolls her eyes. I try not to laugh, she's being awfully cute in her pretend standoffishness, so I have no reason to make her stop.

The elevator stops.

"Good night!" she says, pushing past me through the opening doors.

"It *was* a good night," I say, as I follow her down the hall.

"What are you doing?" she says, her hand pushing against my chest.

"I'm walking you to your door, just like I said."

"I'm fine, Xavier."

"Good, I'm going to make sure you're fine all the way to your door."

"I don't remember you being this testosterone-y."

"I'm hurt. I remember being very testosterone-y around you. How could you forget?" I waggle my eyebrows at her, and she doesn't look impressed.

She mutters something under her breath that sounds like, "Remembering isn't the problem."

We come to a stop outside apartment 1506.

"Xavier," she starts, and I have a feeling I don't like what's coming. "Thank you for tonight."

Well, that wasn't too bad,

"But," she continues, "it's probably not a good idea we see each other too much."

I don't say anything for a moment, to give use both time to think.

"Why?" I finally respond.

"Because, nothing's going to be able to come of this. And... I don't want you to be holding on to some hope for a future for us."

I nod.

I hear her, I do.

And it's time, she heard me.

I take a step forward and she backs herself against the wall. My hand comes up to rest against it, over her head, my body looming over her. All she can see is me.

"Malynda, tonight was the happiest I've been since the last time I saw you, getting on that bus to New York."

She opens her mouth and I press my finger against it. It's my time to talk.

"I've felt like... I've been living in some kind of suspended state, for twelve years. And during that time, all I ever wanted, was to see you one last time. To tell you all the things I never got to tell you when we were together."

She blinks, slowly, and I know the words are penetrating.

"So, whatever does or doesn't happen, this isn't going to change. I love you. Like no man has any business loving another person. Like it's all that matters to me, and there's nothing else. So you can tell me not to hope, that's your prerogative. But it has no meaning to me. Because I live one day at a time. And each of those days, I wake up thinking of you and I fall asleep thinking of you. So until you're in my arms, and I know that's where you'll be for the rest of my life? I'm living my life the same way. Fighting for you.

There is no yesterday and no tomorrow. Just today. I'm not chasing the past. I'm not living for the future. Right now, I'm just trying to survive each day without you."

SIXTEEN

Him

It took me about two months to completely run out of money when I first arrived in New York to look for Malynda. All the money I'd saved over the summer so that we could have a deposit down on our own place once I followed her, was spent on scouring the streets of Manhattan for any sign of her.

I went to her dance school; all they could tell me was that she had dropped out. I stood in the hallways asking everyone who passed by me if they knew her, had heard anything from her. All people could tell me was that she was there one day and gone the next. She hadn't made a lot of friends while she'd been there, apparently, and her footprint faded with the first few rains of November.

Here one day and gone the next.

Not once though, did it occur to me to go home.

My only home had been with her.

With nowhere to go at night, I stayed out there, on the streets. Showing her picture to anyone who would stop long enough to look.

I knew, I knew no matter what that letter had said, she had not fallen for someone else and left. I was more inclined to believe that she'd murdered someone in cold blood, than betray me.

Now twelve years later, my gut instinct has been proven right though it feels like now there are just more questions. And she's unwilling to give any answers.

The kiss on her birthday told me everything I need to know, though. That she's still in there, the girl I knew. And that she's just waiting for me to coax her out.

"Xavier! Watch out!" Gabriel shouts at me from across the warehouse and I move just in time to get out of the way of the guy in the hard hat and his wheelbarrow filled with broken bits of wall.

We're deep into the renovation for the youth center now, the inside of the warehouse being gutted so that we can construct some new partitions and office areas. Gabriel, Jade's brother, is in charge of overseeing the day-to-day operations at the warehouse as it's converted. He's done well staying clean since coming out of his stint in rehab a year ago. With a seemingly renewed purpose in life, this dedication to the youth center seems to be giving him something concrete to build his life on.

"Thanks, man!" I yell across the room and he gives me a thumbs up before turning back to the foreman and the plans laid out in front of them.

"Um, hello. Is Jade here?"

The voice makes the hair on the back of my neck stand up and I don't need to turn around to know who it is.

"No. What do you need?" I say, my voice flat as I address Cameron.

He waves a roll of paper in his hand. "Isabella asked me to drop this off here."

"I'll take it." I reach out and Cameron pulls his hand back.

"I'd really rather it go directly to Jade."

His petty tone riles me up even more. "Seriously? Because I can direct you exactly where to go."

"Woah. What's your problem, man?"

"Nothing. Just give me the damn thing. I'll make sure she gets it." I rip it out of Cameron's hand and stare at him, daring him to protest.

"Fine," he shrugs, "saves me a trip uptown." He holds up his hands and backs away. Just as he's almost out the door, he spins around and faces me again.

"You know, I'm just trying to work with the Ash Foundation here. If you don't want that, maybe you should tell them they can find someone else, willing to provide all this service for free."

Great. Threats. Where did Malynda find this asshole?

"It's not you whose services we require. It's Isabella's." I hiss.

"Well, she and I are one." He stares me down

Don't fucking remind me.

"As I understand, you're the paper pusher, and she's the one who does the work that we're actually looking for. So, maybe next time, she can come down here herself."

He tilts his head, tapping on his mouth like he's thinking. Well, think faster asshole, and fuck off. "You know, I've known Isabella for almost twelve years now."

The twitch at my jaw is the only thing that gives away how much I want to wail on this guy right now. I just stare at a point just an inch above his forehead. Breathe, Xavier. Just breathe. He's not worth it.

"What I mean by that is, I know her. Better than anyone else in the world. And that's just to say, I'm pretty sure if she wanted to come down here, where she knows you'd be, she wouldn't have sent me. Just something to think about. Have a good day. Send Jade my love."

SEVENTEEN

Her

Somehow I've managed to stay away from Xavier for almost a week. One of the longest weeks of my whole fucking life.

I didn't see him, I didn't call him, I didn't text. All questions for his apartment, I send through to his work email address and someone nameless replies. But I don't think it's him.

After the bombshell he left me on my birthday, it was probably best that we had some time apart. Truth is, after he kissed me, I wasn't quite sure if I could stop him if he wanted something more.

Of course, he wants something more. If I'm honest, so do I.

He isn't the only one living in a perpetual state of suspension. From the moment I saw him again at the fundraiser, it feels like there are parts of my body, my mind, that has come out of hibernation. Even apart, we seem to have been living parallel lives.

But you can't do this, you can't be with him. There's a reason you pushed him away then and nothing has changed that reality. Don't do this to yourself.

It feels like I've been telling myself that on loop for the last five days. And apparently, I don't listen.

The doorman opens the door and tips his hat. He's used to me coming in and out the last few weeks as I've worked on Xavier's apartment. I use the security keycard Xavier gave me to have access to his apartment to let myself and the delivery men in and press 31 on the panel.

I run my hands down my red dress as the elevator creeps up to his floor. I don't even know what I'm doing here. I don't have any business to discuss with him. I just couldn't stand another day of not seeing him.

I take a deep breath and step into his living area.

Someone crashes into me, knocking me to my feet, temporarily winding me.

"Oh! Shit! Sorry!" She holds out her hand and I take it, letting her pull me to my feet.

The woman is striking. Tall, redheaded, dressed in a pantsuit that looks like it was custom made for her. Every inch of her perfect body.

She's holding an overnight bag in her other hand, a Burberry coat flung over her arm.

"Fuck, sorry, I'm such a mess. I'm late and just in such a hurry. Hope you're okay!"

"Oh, um, yeah, I'm fine, no harm done."

"Xavier! I'm on my way out!" she yells over her shoulder as she rushes over to the still open elevator. I can't help wanting to flee with her but the last thing I want is to be stuck in an elevator with Xavier's overnight guest. Especially one looking like that.

She's long gone by the time he comes out of the bathroom, wearing just a pair of track pants, drying his hair on a towel.

It's the first time since we reconnected that I've seen him without a top, and I'm almost speechless by what I see. His body is ripped, his chest and stomach look like they've been sculpted out of marble. Hard. Chiseled. It's a long way from the tall and lanky Xavier I remember.

"Oh, um, hi," he says, stopping when he sees me. "I didn't expect to see you. Did we have an appointment?"

The combination of seeing him half-naked and running into his lady friend has my mind turning and twisting in ten different directions all at once.

"No. We didn't." I snap at him. "Just... nevermind, forget it. I'm going."

"Whoa, whoa, whoa," he says, blocking me from leaving. "Malynda, why did you come here?"

"I don't know." The words come out before I can stop them and I try to focus on anywhere but his body.

"Malynda," his voice drops and he reaches out for my arm.

"No!" I push him away and almost run to the elevator. I can barely breathe. I need to get away from here.

"Hey! Malynda! What's going on?!" He says, following me,

I can't face him. "I... I... I shouldn't have come. I thought... after the other night..."

"Yes?"

"But I was wrong. Sorry to bother you, I didn't mean to run into your... girlfriend."

"Whoa. What? My what?"

Still facing the wall, I wave my hand towards the bathroom, as if that explains it.

"Yeah, I need more than that." He grips me by the shoulders and spins me around. "Look at me! Who are you talking about?"

A force myself to breathe before I yell. "That... fucking... supermodel! The redhead. Your girlfriend or lover or... whatever."

His brows wrinkle. "Who... wait. You mean Patricia?"

"I didn't ask her her name, Xavier. She just knocked me over and ran off. Anyway, I hope you enjoyed the new bed we bought for you." I'm being a petty bitch, but I can't see to stop myself.

But it doesn't get past Xavier. He shakes his head and pushes me back against the wall, his hands still on my shoulders, staring me directly in the eyes.

"Are you jealous?" he asks.

I just close my eyes, trying to block out his face, trying to stop him from reading me.

I feel his hand let go of my shoulder and grip my chin.

"Open your eyes, Malynda."

I obey, I don't have the energy to fight him.

"I'm asking you, are you jealous, Malynda?" Each word makes me flinch. Makes me realize what I am feeling.

I glare at him. If he wants me to say it, I will.

"Fuck you, Xavier. Yes!" I yell, almost spitting in his face, "Is that what you want to hear? Yes! I'm jealous at the thought of you fucking her!"

He shakes his head and pushes away from me.

"Unfuckingbelievable."

144

I move to pull away from the wall, but he's back, pressing his bare chest against me, making me feel every inch of his body on mine.

"That is Patti, she's my assistant. You've been emailing with her all week. To avoid talking to me directly." He stares at me, watching his words sink in. And then he continues, "And no, I'm not fucking her. I told you. I told you, Malynda, that you were my first, and that you were going to be my last. And unlike you, I keep my fucking promises. Every single one."

His face is barely two inches from mine.

He's whispering but it feels like a storm in my mind.

What is he saying? No. He doesn't mean it.

"A-Are you telling me you've never slept with anyone else?" It can't be. Not all this time. Not looking like he looks.

His answer is short, abrupt. "Yes."

"I don't believe you." I hiss at him. Even though I know it's true. *Oh my god.*

And that's the last thought I have before he closes that two-inch gap between us and his mouth is on mine.

His tongue is instantly in my mouth and I feel myself involuntarily suck on it, a heat rising up into every part of my body. I push against his chest but pull him in by the shoulder all at once. His hands are in my hair, against the back of my neck. Strong, hot, commanding. Controlling.

"Fuck, Malynda," he groans against my mouth, and then we're kissing again. His hand moves down over my back, cupping my ass, grinding his hardness against me. I'm putty in his hands, giving in to him. I barely know how I'm standing.

He pulls away for a breath, and in that moment, my brain tells me. Stop.

He leans in again and I push hard against his chest.

"I can't. Xavier, we can't do this!" I gasp.

He stops, but doesn't take his hands off me. "Why? Tell me why and I'll stop right now. But you have to tell me why."

"I don't know! I don't know why!" I cry. Because I don't want to stop. Something just tells me it's better this way.

He lifts a hand to my cheek, cupping it, dragging his thumb over the single tear that falls.

"I love you. I promise you, I've never, ever slept with anyone but you, Malynda. You're the only one I've ever wanted. Ever. Do you really think that us being together could be wrong?"

I feel my knees buckle, a physical manifestation of my resolve wavering. I can't say no, to him. He's the only one I've ever wanted as well.

"Xavier."

"Yes?"

"I've never... I never slept with anyone else either"

He frowns. It's fleeting but I see it and his hand falls away from my cheek.

"I don't believe you."

"It's true."

"Like Cameron would hang around if you weren't having sex with him."

"Cameron and I are NOT together. So it would be strange if I was sleeping with him."

Xavier's head shakes, as if he doesn't believe what he's hearing. "But he... you said he was your partner."

"He's my *business* partner. We're not together." I repeat. I don't know why it's so important for him to know this, but I don't want him to get the wrong idea. I have never been with any man but him.

He takes a step back, still shaking his head. "No. Don't lie to me, Malynda. Just don't."

"I'm not, Xavier. I've never wanted anyone but you."

He looks at me, his pupils round and dilated, I can almost see the thoughts swirling in his mind.

"Fuck this, I've missed you so much."

In one movement, he sweeps an arm under my legs, my hand automatically coming up to loop around his neck, my mouth on his. I feel like air in his arms as he walks over to the bed and gently lays me down.

For just a moment, he looks down at me, his head haloed by the sun streaming through the windows.

"I have missed you every single day," he says, the words catching on his throat.

"I know," I say, running my fingertips down his bare chest. And he leans down, burying his face in my neck. I wrap my arms around him, holding him. Ignoring everything that tells me it's wrong.

"Make love to me, Xavier," I beg against his ear. "Please."

He doesn't say anything, his lips wet and warm against my neck as he moves his body on top of mine, guiding my legs apart.

I feel his hands tugging at the seam of my dress and I move my hips, helping him pull it over my head. I reach behind me and unhook my bra, and he pulls it away. For the first time in over a decade, I'm almost naked in front of a man. The only man who's ever seen me naked. I bite my tongue, my hands coming up to cover my breasts.

"No. Don't," he says, gently brushing my hands away.

He rocks back on his heels, looking down at me, running a finger from the tip of my chin, along my neck, down between my breasts, over my stomach to rest gently between my legs.

"You're more beautiful than I even remember."

The blush streaks up my neck and down my chest. "Really? I'm not eighteen anymore."

"No, you're a woman now. A gorgeous, sexy, irresistible woman."

He leans down, his beard tickling my stomach as he drops his lips over my right nipple.

His breath is searingly hot, and it sends a rush of heat from my nipple all the way down to the pit of my stomach.

"Oh..." the moan escapes my lips without my consent.

The sound seems to trigger something in him and his hand moves down, cupping me between my thighs, grinding the ball of his hand against me.

I feel my hips tilt to meet his hand, feeling my wetness grow.

Xavier pulls his mouth away from my nipple kissing down my stomach.

"So smooth..." he mutters, as his fingers hook into the sides of my panties, and slides them down my legs. I reach to pull the strap of my stiletto down and his hand follows, fingertips grazing my thigh. "No, leave them on," he whispers, and at this point, I'll do anything he says.

I'm not sure how keeping my shoes on makes me feel even more naked than I already am, but it does. Or maybe it's the way, Xavier is looking at me, his eyes sliding over every inch of me, like he's trying to brand it into his brain.

"Xavier," I say, and his eyes come up to meet mine. "It's been twelve years."

His face breaks into a grin and something in the mood shifts. He slides out of his track pants, and I see his cock spring out. Hard. Ready.

Ready to be inside me.

He leans over kissing up my body again. I can declare right now, that I could live my entire life with Xavier's mouth on me.

His tongue drags up my neck and a shiver trickles down my spine.

"Oh, Xave..."

"You need to stop moaning. Or else this is going to be faster than it already will be."

"The faster we finish, the faster we can do it again."

I take his hand and slide his finger into my mouth, sucking on it. He growls and his eyes turn dark. His hand disappears down my body and suddenly, he's touching me, sliding his finger around my wetness.

My breath catches, I try to remember what he used to do, but no blood is going to my brain.

Then his finger is inside me.

Deep.

"You are ready," he growls, and I dig my nails into his chest.

"Yes."

I lean back, his hands pushing my thighs apart, I feel him move, and there's a pause.

And then he's inside me.

Fast, hard, deep.

"Oh, Xavier."

His hands are gripping my thighs so hard, I know there will be a bruise later. But I don't care.

"Malynda... I have waited so fucking long for this. To be inside you again."

I push my hips down, taking him deeper, and he grunts.

He pulls back, and then thrusts forward, our bodies moving with the force.

"Oh!"

And he does it again.

And again.

My body slides over his slick cotton sheets, but he just grips my hips and pulls me towards him again, impaling me on his hardness.

I can barely breathe. I wrap my legs around his waist, and he leans over, flicking his tongue over my nipple. Stars burst in front of my eyes.

"God, Malynda, you are so hot," he growls, "I've missed being inside you."

I can only moan in response.

Our movements are faster, more erratic, there's no rhythm, just him driving himself in and out of me, each time pushing me closer to the edge.

His pubic bone grazes against mine, his body hard and strong on top of me.

"Make me come, Xavier," I beg him.

And he knows how.

He pulls back, the tip of his cock still inside me, but his thumb on my most sensitive spot.

"Oh, fuck!" I yell, as he circles, smaller and smaller circles until it feels like a constant torrent of caresses on my clit.

"Yes... yes... yes..." I mumble and he moves his hand faster, harder.

And just as I feel the wave crash over me, he drives his cock into me.

I come. I come so hard I barely notice him joining me.

I feel myself squeeze him, as my back arches and I gasp for breath, my hands, digging into his shoulders.

He falls on me, and I feel my legs fall open, to the side, exhausted.

"Malynda..." he murmurs, and I just move my hand to the side of his face and stroke his cheek in response.

And we stay there until we meet again in our dreams.

EIGHTEEN

Him

She's sleeping.

Her face completely relaxed, her hair splayed all over my pillow, like a golden fan. And she's completely naked. Well, except for her heels. I grin a little at how sexy she looks in them.

And how fucking hot she looked while I slid myself into her. Her body curving and soft and wanting. I can't help comparing her to the girl I knew. All the sweetness is there, but she's grown into this woman who no man can resist.

I wonder how she's been able to hold them back all this time. To save herself for me.

I just know I'm glad I saved myself for her. Nothing will ever compare to being with her. Inside her.

I curl my body around hers, trying not to wake her.

Because I never want this moment to end.

***

"You don't snore." It's the first thing she says when my eyes open.

"You don't either." I reach out to touch the tip of her nose, maybe to reassure myself that she's real, that's she's really here.

"I don't care if I do," she says as she shrugs. "Keeps the pests away."

"What pests? Men? I thought you don't sleep with men."

"Bears!"

"You can take the girl out of Maine but..."

I get a swift punch to the arm. That's another thing that hasn't changed.

"There aren't any bears in Manhattan, sweetheart."

She scrunches up her nose, but lays back down, laying her head on my chest, her fingertips drawing circles on my stomach.

"I've missed you, Xavier," she says.

I run my hand through her hair, twirling the strands between my fingers.

"I've loved you since the first time I saw you, Malynda."

She props herself up on her elbow and looks up at me. I love the way she looks, hair disheveled, lipstick smeared, her skin glowing.

"And when was that, the first time you saw me."

"You don't know?"

"You never said."

"That day... at the ice cream parlor. It was really busy and they had me at the counter. It was crowded and loud and hot and hellish, high schoolers everywhere. And then there was a ding of the bell and you walked in. And, I'd never seen anything so beautiful in my life." I smile and cup her face with my hand. It looks so delicate. "Until now."

"My friends said you were staring. But I didn't care."

"I didn't care either. Even if it did get me pummeled." I try not to let the cringe of the memory show on my face. But she knows me too well.

"Bad memory?"

"Not the best."

"I'm sorry. Mostly because it happened because of me. They were such assholes," she looks sheepish. Apologetic about something she had no control over.

"No, the bad memory is because I hated that you would think I was weak... and that I couldn't protect you. Those lanky arms weren't worth much back then."

"Is that why you've got all this now?" She pokes me in the stomach and then shakes her hand, pretending it's hurt. "Not that I mind," she gives me a wink, tickling my abdomen with her nails, sending sparks down to my cock.

"Is that so?" I growl, and roll her over onto her back, and the giggle is crushed against her lips as I kiss her hard. She moans in that way that makes me lose my mind and I crawl down her body, wasting no time to kiss her skin on the way.

Her knees spread out on either side of me, and I stop for just a moment to look at her, laid out in front of me.

Completely naked. Completely vulnerable. Completely mine.

I run a fingertip to open her up, running my tongue along the length of her, tasting her wetness. Sweet and salty in the perfect ratio. I glance up for a second and see her hands coming up to cup her breasts, fingers flicking at her nipples, as she watches me.

"You are going to come so hard in about two minutes," I tell her, and she bites her bottom lip, ready.

I press my face against her and slide my tongue as deep as it will go inside her.

She moans again. And I have to block it out, or else she'll be coming on my cock and not my tongue. And I want it to be on my tongue. Want to taste her gush into my mouth. I slide my tongue out, I flick the tip of it over her clit, and she whimpers. I do it again, another whimper.

I know she's waiting for me to do it again. So I don't.

I was lying about her coming in two minutes.

I'm going to play with her until she begs me to fuck her.

And I will.

But not just yet.

My tongue moves down to circle the rim of her pussy, her hips push down, wanting more. So sensual. So fucking sexy. The soft tip of my index finger rubs around the base of her clit, not quite touching it. She doesn't like that, and growls, her knees coming up to clamp around my head.

"Hold on there, sweetheart," I say, pulling away, letting her calm down before I continue. The last twelve years have been me waiting for her. She can wait for me for a few more minutes.

She lays back down, and I lower myself down to her, my face barely inches from her, my breath hot against her. She smells like pure sex. Still her, but something wanting and wanton. I can't hold back much longer.

I press my tongue flat against her clit, hard.

"Oh, fuck," she moans, her hands reaching down to press on the back of my head.

I grind my tongue harder against her, feeling her clit pulse, my finger coming up to slide inside her.

She's slick and hot. And I'm trying so hard not to remember how she felt wrapped around my cock.

Soon, Xavier, soon, I promise myself.

I pull away so it's my tongue tip on her clit now, flicking fast. Her breath is loud and fast, her head thrown back, her back arched deep, her legs lifting her hips off the ground.

I stop. Letting her breath slow for a moment, before I move my tongue down to her pussy, and drive it into her, my thumb and index finger pinching lightly around her clit.

"XAVIER!" she screams, and I could stay drunk on that sound for the rest of my life.

I pull my tongue out, and then cram it back into her, flicking the very tip of her clit with my finger, feeling her body jerk with each movement.

"Xavier..."

"What?" I say, stopping everything.

"No... god, don't stop. Please."

"Please what?"

"Just... please."

"I don't know what to do if you don't say it, Malynda."

"Make me come, you fucking bastard!"

"Oh, that. Okay."

I slide two fingers into her, feeling her gasp and squeeze around me as my lips close around her clit. I suck and suck and suck, fucking her pussy with my fingers until I hear her scream, her hips lifting off the ground and her knees clamping around my head.

And I keep going. Flicking her clit with my tongue as my fingers curl up, grazing the inside of her walls, making her feel every movement.

"Oh my god, oh my god," she moans, her fingers grabbing the hair on the side of my head and grinding her pelvis against my face.

I give her what she wants, moving my lips back over her clit and sucking hard, plunging my fingers deep into her.

She comes, her body tensing for a moment before she bucks on the bed, her legs kicking out as she groans my name. I have to concentrate to keep my mouth on her, pushing her orgasm as far and as long as it will go.

"Stop... god... oh fuck..." she murmurs, even as I see her tense, feeling another wave wash over her.

Finally, her legs stop kicking, and I release her clit, flicking over it gently with the tip of my tongue, making her whole body jump. I pull my fingers from her, and climb up her body, pressing my lips against hers.

She barely kisses me back, limp on the bed.

"Hey," I say, and she opens her eyes a little and smiles.

"That was fun," she mumbles.

"No kidding," I can't help but chuckle. She's an angel. I want to drown in the sweetness of her. "Want to do it again?" I ask her, winking.

"In a minute." She wraps her arms around me, and I lay my face against her chest. Listening to her heartbeat start to slow.

I kiss her chest and she sighs.

We lay there like it's the only place we were ever meant to be.

"Minute's up," she jokes a few minutes later and giggles.

"Yes, ma'am!" I say, sliding down her body to do it all again. She doesn't say no.

***

"Hmmmm, is that mine or yours?" I wake up saying a few hours later to the sound of a cell phone going off.

There's no answer, so I reach out and find my phone buzzing on the floor next to my bed.

"What?" I growl into the phone.

"What's up your ass?" Kaine responds.

I lay back down. "Sorry, you woke me up."

"It's 3 in the afternoon."

"Exactly, nap time."

"Where've you been? You missed our 2 o'clock."

"Shit, sorry. I er... got held up." I sit up on the bed. Alone. She's not here.

"OK, no problem. Just wanted to make sure you're okay, I can't remember last time you missed a meeting."

I get up and look around. Her clothes are gone as well. "Um, sorry, I just lost track of time." And Malynda, apparently. Again. Fuck.

"Fine. Jade wants you to come over for dinner tonight."

"Yeah, um, sure."

"And by-"

I hang up on him, pulling on my track pants as I walk to the bathroom.

"Babe?"

There's no answer.

And no note.

I dial her number as I turn on the shower.

No answer.

The water is scalding hot when I step into it.

But it doesn't take the sting away in my chest.

NINETEEN

Her

"You can't go in there!" I hear our receptionist yell and I look up to see Xavier storm into my office. I wave her off just as he slams the door closed.

"Don't," he says, slamming his hands down on the side of my desk. "Don't you dare fucking disappear on me."

The breath catches in my throat as I see his eyes staring back at me, his eyes as dark as I've ever seen them. "Xave-..."

He stops me before I can say anything else.

"No. Do not get up out of my bed after making love to me all day and just fucking leave. Do not do that to me."

He continues to stare at me, dead center in the eyes. I stare back, and it takes a moment, but something flickers in the depths of his pupils, and I realize, it's fear. It seems like anger, but it's fear. And I put it there.

I get up from behind my desk and put a hand on his forearm. He doesn't move but I can feel the muscle tremble under my fingertips. And it feels like it's emitting the same ache that I hold inside me.

"Xavier," I say, softly. He doesn't say anything and his chest heaves with deep breaths. "Xavier," I say again and this time he drops his shoulders, pushing up from the desk and stands up straight, looking down at me. "I didn't just leave..." I start to say.

"Well, you weren't fucking there when I got up," he interrupts.

"Wait. Let me finish. I mean, I didn't disappear. I... I wouldn't do that..." He gives me a look that tears at me. There's so much hurt in him. "Again." I add, not that it matters. "I left you a note."

"You didn't!"

I take a deep breath and hope he mirrors it, but he doesn't.

"I did," I say, as calmly as I can. "I left you a note in the kitchen."

His brow crinkles and then he sighs.

"Well... I haven't been in my kitchen for over a week."

"But don't you walk past it to get to the elevator. That's why I left it there."

"Yeah, but, I don't look IN it."

"Well, look IN it the next time you're home," I smile softly, trying to break the tension. "There's a note saying I had a meeting I couldn't miss and I would call you tonight."

He sits down on the loveseat, sinking deep into it, rubbing his palms roughly up and down his face and then grabs at his own hair.

"Fuck! Malynda. This is fucked up. I'm so fucked up."

"I'm sorry," I say. Scared to get too close, to see him this raw.

"It's okay," he waves a hand, dismissing my apology. "You left a note."

"No..." I wince, his frustration twisting in my gut like a red-hot dagger. "I mean. For... the other time I left. For fucking you up."

He sighs and shakes his head, then rests it on his fist, tilting it to the side to look at me. "You need to tell me what happened, Malynda. I need to understand. I can't keep going on like this."

It's my turn to shake my head. "No. Not yet. Just... please. Not yet."

"But if it's something I did, I need to know. I need to know what it was that made you disappear, that tore us apart."

"It wasn't you. I promise. You never did a thing wrong."

"Then what was it? Why couldn't you tell me? And why can't you tell me now?!"

I sink down onto the seat next to him, laying my head on his shoulder. I know this can't go on forever. But I can't let him go just yet.

"Xavier. I will tell you. Soon. It's only fair, I know that. But, please, just let us... be like this for a little while longer, okay? Please?"

He sighs and pulls me against him. He feels so warm and strong and comforting. Like a house. A home. My home. How did I survive all this time without him? I open my mouth, almost ready to tell him everything. But then the image of him knowing... the look on his face. The disappointment, the judgment. The humiliation. The hate. Things will never be the same.

He turns his head and kisses me gently on the temple, and like magic, nothing else matters, just him and me in this room.

I nuzzle my face against his neck. His hair is wet, probably from a shower, and his cologne is warm and sweet and spicy. It's intoxicating. My tongue slides out and licks his jaw before I can stop myself.

He looks at me, amused but doesn't say anything. I breathe him in again.

Something in my body feeling hot and in need.

Of him.

This is insane.

I haven't had sex for so long and now I can't stop thinking about it.

I stand up and take his hand. He follows me as I pull him towards the desk.

My eyes lock on his as I pull the hem of my dress up to my hips and slide onto the edge of the desk. I grab the front of his shirt and yank him forward.

He lets out a small laugh as his body bangs up against me before I pull his head down to meet mine, kissing him so hard my lips ache.

"Fuck me," I whisper into his ear, and I feel a growl rumble in the pit of his chest.

"Here?"

I nod. "Now. I want you, Xavier." I reach down, pulling down the zipper to his pants, my hand grazing over his growing hardness.

He reaches between my legs, and finds I'm panty-less.

He grins, his eyebrow raising.

"If you'd looked more closely, you would've found I left you more than a note," I lean in and whisper. "They're under your pillow. I wanted my scent to make you dream of us fucking, like we're about to do right now."

"You grew quite the mouth, didn't you, young lady?" he growls, his teeth grazing along my neck.

I grin and spread my legs wider, as he unbuttons his pants and releases himself.

He pushes me back against the desk, pulling my legs around his waist, and I can feel the tip of his cock nudge against me.

"Say it again," he tells me, his voice low and dark, thick with want.

"Fuck me, Xavier," I obey, staring into his eyes.

And they stay there, even as he leans forward, sliding his cock into me.

"Ohhhh," I gasp. I can't believe how this feels, having him inside me, his eyes on mine as we fuck.

"God, Malynda. Yes… squeeze me tighter, baby. Milk me," he pants, grinding his hips into me, his pubic bone grazing my clit, driving me wild. "I can't get enough of you, sweetheart."

"Then take me, Xavier. I'm yours. I was always yours."

Something in my words triggers him and he stands up, gripping my hips with his hands as he slams into me. Hard. Bruising me in a way I'll never forget. And never get enough of. Exquisitely painful.

"Oh god…" I moan, not caring that I'm in my office, not caring if the whole world hears me come on Xavier's cock.

He drives himself into me one last time, and I feel him tense just as I fall off the edge, moaning his name, pulling him with me.

"Fuck. What are you doing to me?" he whispers after we regain our breath.

"What do you mean?" I ask, my tongue catching a drop of sweat trickling down his neck as he gently lowers my legs from his waist.

"I go from a self-imposed monk to not being able to stop fucking you," he growls, and a shiver streaks up my spine. I know the feeling, the exact feeling.

"I'm not doing anything," I say, reaching down to run a finger along the wetness between my legs and bringing it up to my mouth.

He watches me wrap my lips around the tip of my finger, tasting our joint orgasm.

"Is that what you've been doing? Spending the last decade practicing how to be a temptress?" he asks, sighing as he reaches down to fix his clothes.

"Ha! Yeah, me in my flannel pajamas watching Gilmore Girls over and over. No. I guess you just bring it out in me."

He leans forward and kisses me gently.

And I sigh.

I don't know how I could've forgotten what it was like to be with him.

How totally and completely right it felt.

I can only wonder how I am going to survive once he is gone again.

The intercom buzzes.

"Leave it," Xavier growls, his kisses already growing deeper even though it's barely been two minutes since he came inside me, his finger lingering between my legs.

I don't stop kissing him, but I reach across the desk to press the answer button.

"Iz. Are you there? Just checking you're okay, heard something going on in your office. Iz?"

"MMmI'mfinehmmm," I mumble against Xavier's mouth.

"What?"

I pull away to Xavier's annoyance. I press a finger to his lips, and whisper, "If I don't answer, he'll come in here."

"Then fucking answer him, you don't want him coming in here to see what's about to happen!" He drops to his knees in front of me and runs his tongue along the length of my pussy.

"Ohhh," a moan falls from my lips before I can stop it.

"Iz?"

"Yeah... sorry... um, I'm fine... talk later." I switch the intercom off, and lie back, letting Xavier make up for lost time.

***

"I'm so hungry, what's taking so long?" I look around the cafe, trying to find our waitress, so I can give her a pointed glare.

"It's been three minutes," Xavier says, still looking down at his phone.

"Why aren't you hungrier?! You were the one doing most of the work," I say, winking at him. But he's still not looking at me. "Hey!" I run my foot up the inside of his leg, wondering how far I should take it.

He finally looks up, his eyebrow cocked.

"You don't want to do that," he says. And there's a powerfulness about him that makes me feel weak.

"Why?"

"Because you're hungry and if you do that, I'm going to have to take us back to my apartment right now. No food for you."

I grin and move my foot higher by an inch, our eyes still locked. But then I pull away, I've seen enough of this new Xavier to know that he has every intention of fulfilling his threat. Not that I can say I'd mind too much. I can't imagine anything better in the world, than being in Xavier's bed.

"I shouldn't even be eating now," I say, looking at the time. "I have to go out for dinner tonight."

"So, I'm not going to see you tonight?" I get a thrill at the thought that he still wants more of me.

"I would think you've seen enough of me today."

"It will never be enough. So, anyway, what did you tell Preppy about the noise from your office?" Xavier says, and I roll my eyes at his nickname for Cameron.

"I told Cameron that I was just laughing at a funny video on my phone."

"And he believed you?"

I shrug, "Don't see why not."

"It didn't sound like laughing from where I was standing."

"Well, you had a front row seat. Better acoustics. "

"And... he wants one."

"He doesn't, we're just friends. Best friends. He's been there for me for a long time, Xavier." I don't like the thought that there is any animosity between the two of them. It will make my life too difficult. Xavier doesn't reply, just moves his cutlery around a bit before looking up at me. His stare makes me feel nervous. "I told you, he's my business partner. Not... anything else partner."

"Doesn't mean he doesn't want to be." And I don't tell him the thought may have crossed my mind once or twice in the past.

"Well, if that were true, which it isn't, that would be his problem, not mine, and definitely not yours."

"Might be mine."

"It's not."

He reaches over and takes my hand in his, turning it over and then lifting it to press a kiss to my palm.

"Whatever's your problem IS my problem. You said it, you're mine. That's what being mine means."

Trust my own words to come back to haunt me. I did say that because it's true. Whatever is going to happen, I'm his. I've always been his.

TWENTY

Him

I walk Malynda back to her office but don't go up. I've spent so much of my time focusing on her since she's come back into my life, I've neglected a lot of my work. My walk back to Ash Industries is spent on the phone following up some loose ends for Kaine and planning some meetings for the rest of the week.

I step off the elevator on my office floor. "Patti, can I have th-..."

"On your desk," she says, her hands moving over her keyboard so fast I can barely see them, her eyes locked on the

163

computer screen. It's her "don't bother me" mode, and I know better than to disobey.

The file is on my desk, just as she said, and I sit back, flicking through.

What I'm looking for, I'm not sure. I guess I'll know it when I see it.

By the time I look up from my desk after working through the absolute urgent list of tasks for the day, the sun is level with my eye. I glance at my cell. Almost 7:30. And there's a list of texts.

I scroll through them, stopping when I see her name.

"What cologne do you wear? I can't stop smelling you on my skin. I'm turning myself on."

"Fine, don't tell me. Keep your sexy man scent to yourself."

"Just in case you're wondering, MY scent is Vanilla and Jasmine. Wait, don't tell me, you already knew that."

I tap reply and thumb in my response.

"It's not cologne, it's just the smell of my skin."

The reply comes back before I can even exit out of the screen.

"Don't believe you."

"Come over, I'll let you smell me to prove it."

"I can't. Busy, remember?"

"No." Yes, of course I do.

"Yes, you do."

"Fine, I'm busy too anyway. I just remembered I made plans."

"Smell ya later?"

"You can count on it."

I change into a fresh shirt and jog out the door, shouting, "Go home, Patti!" to my assistant as I step into the elevator.

***

B.B King is filtering through the speakers when I step out into Kaine's apartment fifteen minutes later. I can hear the sound of Jade's laughter before I step into the living area, the smell of something delicious making me salivate. I tease Kaine about putting on the pounds since Jade moved in, but he was always a pretty good cook anyway. I wonder who is on chef duty tonight considering Jade has been busy juggling the baby and her new roles with the foundation and I saw Kaine barely an hour ago at the office.

"Hey," Kaine greets me as I turn the corner into his foyer. He hands me a glass and the ice inside it clinks against the crystal. "Just in time for our toast," he says, stepping back to the drinks trolley.

"What are we toasting?" I ask.

"Me," replies a familiar voice. I spin around and Malynda is there, drink in hand.

My heart jumps and I feel my body tense and soften at once. I'm still not used to seeing her after all this time.

"Oh, hey," I say, wandering over to her and dropping a kiss to her cheek, lingering for a moment as I take a deep breath. Yup, vanilla and jasmine. "And why are we toasting you, exactly?"

"Because she told us, if we visit you now, there's somewhere for all four of us to sit," Jade yells across the room from the couch. She's stretched out, her bare feet dangling off the side. I laugh as I walk over and lean down, giving her a kiss, purposely lingering longer than I should.

"Hey. Enough," comes the expected gruff command from her husband and I pull away and give her a conspiratorial wink.

"Oh, leave him alone," Jade says to Kaine, "this tired old married mother needs some male attention now and again."

Kaine doesn't say anything, just swirls his glass and stares at his wife.

"Just kidding, I got plenty of male attention last night," Jade pretend whispers behind her hand and wiggles her eyebrows at Malynda, who giggles. I make a point not to look at her in case I give us away. It seems both ladies here have not been lacking in male attention lately.

Kaine clicks his tongue and walks over to the dining area, sitting down and staring out the window.

He and I bought our apartment building because of how it was structurally similar to this one. Wall to ceiling windows, strong concrete pillars, open plans. We both like our views, the open skyline in front of us. It's how we think, using that space to unclutter the thoughts in our head. It's why we work, why we're brothers in business and in life.

Why he's the only person who could've saved me when I was flailing at rock bottom.

I sit down at the table opposite him, looking at his focused gaze on the Manhattan horizon. I know a thousand things are running through his head. And judging by the way his jaw is tensing, I'm probably one of them.

"Hey," I say, breaking his train of thought. He doesn't reply, just takes a sip from his glass and turns to me. "What's going on?" He just lifts an eyebrow. He's going to give me nothing. But I can play at that game. We've spent whole days together barely saying a word and yet still getting more done than most people in a month. "I sent the contracts to Masterson. I expect he's going to quibble about the 12-month trial period but he'll sign. He needs this."

Kaine just nods.

"Also, I'm going to hire another assistant, take some of the grunt work off Patti's desk. She's probably still at the office."

"Sure," comes the one-word reply.

"And I've booked you in for an appointment with Dr. Peters." He frowns but waits for the punchline he knows is coming. "He's going to see if your tongue-tiedness is because there's something physically wrong with you or you're just being an ass."

He inhales sharply and opens his mouth, "Xave-..."

"Dinner's ready!" Jade shouts out and I look over to see Malynda helping her to her feet as they approach the table. I shrug at Kaine and his eyes narrow.

"Later," he says and I have no doubt he'll remember.

"Where should I sit?" Malynda asks Jade who just waves her hand over the table. "Wherever you damn well want. We're not very fussy."

I see her bite her bottom lip and come over and sit down at the table setting next to me, leaving Jade in the seat next to Kaine. Picking up the napkin I scan the table.

166

"Um. I see empty plates and smell deliciousness but there's no food. What are you playing at Ashleys?"

"It's coming," Jade says, waving her hand. Just as she finishes shushing me I see Jaxon Sinclair emerge from the kitchen carrying a large tray, filled with plates.

"Jax! Fancy seeing you here."

"Well, it's my night off, so what else have I got to do but cook for my landlords?" he grins as the server behind him helps to lay the food out onto the table. Once the tray is empty, Jaxon reaches over and takes my hand, giving it a good pump.

"No mac and cheese tonight," he says, winking to Malynda. "But it might just be a new addition to my happy hour menu, since my kitchen loved it so much. I'll call it 'Malynda's Mac and Cheese'," he says before jogging back to the kitchen.

"But... what? Her name's Isabella," Jade pipes up.

Malynda, Kaine and I exchange an awkward look. He hasn't told Jade. Probably for the best.

"Hey, let's dig in," Kaine says, probably to distract his wife.

"Er, yeah, this looks delicious. We're pretty spoiled to get Jaxon to cook for us here. He likes to try stuff out on us before he serves it at the restaurant, so it's usually his craziest inventions," I say, taking Malynda's plate and heaping it with something that looks like grilled quail and a strawberry and quinoa salad.

We all go quiet for a moment, enjoying the food and wine.

"I call dibs on leftovers," Malynda sighs after five minutes of silence and Jade grins, happy that her guest is satisfied. "Or maybe we should save it for Xavier, since he never goes into that kitchen of his." She gives me a pointed look and I remember there's an unread note waiting for me somewhere in that unused kitchen of mine. "Hell, I don't even know if his stove is real, maybe it's made of cardboard."

Kaine chokes on his food and takes a sip of his wine.

"Hey, most of my nights are spent at work dinners and the other half, well, someone has to keep Uber Eats delivery guys in work," I argue, though there's really no point.

"At least he's eating now. I think the first six months I knew him, the only thing I saw him put in his mouth were cigarettes and Scotch."

I feel rather than see Malynda turn her head and stare at me. It takes some effort but I continue eating, refusing to look at her.

"Oh, really?" Jade asks her husband, and unfortunately, she's too far away for me to kick her under the table.

"Yeah. Not really sure what he lived on, it's not like he was sleeping much either."

"Why weren't you sleeping?" Jade asks the question that I can hear is churning in Malynda's brain.

"Um, I dunno. I was young," I shrug.

"How old were you?"

"Eighteen."

"Wow, I just realized I don't know about how you ended up here. If it's anything like Kaine's story, it's pretty wild."

"Wilder," comes Kaine's one-word answer.

"Care to share, Xavier?" Jade presses.

"Not really. Nothing wild or special about it," I say, finally locking my eyes with Malynda's. "Typical guy meets girl, girl breaks guy's heart, guy spends his youth trolling the streets of New York looking for her type story. That kinda thing."

"Sounds pretty special to me," Jade muses. "How does the story end?"

I lift my eyebrows, daring Malynda to answer. Darkness creeps into her eyes and she looks away, lifting her wine glass to her lips.

"To be decided," I finally answer Jade.

"Curiouser and curiouser!"

Kaine ignores my glare and turns to his wife, giving her a soft kiss on her cheek and she beams at him, lifting a hand to stroke his scarred cheek, everything else in the world forgotten.

"So, um, Jade, I had an idea for the center," Malynda finally speaks up.

"Oh! I'd love to hear it."

"The gym that we're building in the back, do you think we could maybe add a wall of mirrors and a barre?

"Oh... like, for ballet or dance classes?

"Um, yeah, I know you guys think that sports are really important to teenagers, so the gym will cover basketball and indoor soccer and all that, but, maybe some of the kids would like to try something different. It wouldn't cost much, we could probably get one of the local stores to donate the mirrors or even use scraps. That's what my parents did when I was little.

"You dance?" Jade asks, her eyes lighting up.

I hold my breath, waiting for her answer.

"Oh. Um. I did. When I was a kid. Well, up until just after high school."

"Were you any good?"

I want to jump up and yell, "Yes! She was amazing, she could make you feel with a simple arabesque, tell a story with just the life of her arm."

But I don't. I don't know how I stop myself, but I do.

"I was okay. I loved it, I guess that's the important thing."

"Why did you stop?"

Now it's my turn to turn and stare at her.

"I... er," she shrugs, keeping her focus on Jade. "I just wanted to try something different. I liked art too. So I went into interior design."

No new information for me.

"Well, you're very good at the interior design," Kaine says. "And we are very grateful to you for donating your services to the center. But more importantly, to Xavier's apartment. I'd like to have a place to sit when I go over there."

Malynda laughs, the sound echoing around the apartment. It makes me smile.

"Yeah, sometimes the hardest thing is getting a client to let go of some of their old furniture. Not a problem with Xavier."

No. In my case, it's my emotional baggage that's holding me back.

TWENTY-ONE

Her

The evening at Jade and Kaine's place is one of the best I've had in a long time. Barring my birthday dinner on the roof, of course.

Kaine doesn't talk much, but he's always there, listening, present.

Jade is a complete and utter delight, spending half her time gushing about her husband and the other half relentlessly roasting him. I wonder how they found each other, and I remind myself to ask Xavier what's so wild about Kaine's story. The scars on his face tell me that life hasn't been kind to him, but it seems it's done nothing but imbue him with a generous heart.

It's hard to keep my hands off Xavier all night.

I take the lead from him, to see just how much he wants his friends to know about us. But it seems he doesn't really know either. After the few tense moments at the dinner table, the wine did its job and we spent the rest of the evening laughing and sharing ideas about the center. He gave me a few looks that told me I wouldn't be getting much sleep tonight and it was hard not to just stand up and ask for us to be excused for a few minutes.

But by ten o'clock the day has caught up with me, and after catching me yawning for the third time, Xavier takes over.

"Well, guys, since I'm expected back in the office in..." Xavier stands up and glances at his watch, "seven hours, I think it's time for me to say good night." He gives me a quick wink while Kaine helps Jade to her feet.

"Oh my gosh, is that the time, I'm so sorry we've kept you up!" I jump to my feet, pulling on my jacket.

"No, no! It was great! You've been such good company for me these last few days. It's nice to talk to someone who isn't looking at me like I'm breakfast, lunch and dinner," Jade says, reaching over to give me a hug.

"Hey. What about me?" Kaine says.

"I was talking about you," Jade quips, poking her tongue out at him.

"Well, my hours are pretty flexible, call me anytime you need adult conversation," I say smiling at her and meaning every word.

"Xavier, can you make sure Isabella gets home okay?" Jade asks, offering her cheek to him for a kiss.

"Oh, do I have to?" he whines, and I can see him biting his tongue trying not to laugh.

"Honey, I don't think we have to worry about her with Xavier," Kaine says. "Though I'm not sure if the opposite is true," I think I hear under his breath, but I'm not sure.

Xavier's smile freezes on his face for a moment before he recovers. "Goodnight, boss and boss wife."

I give them another wave and follow him to leave.

He doesn't say anything and I wait until we get into elevator before I speak.

"What... what does Kaine know... about us?"

He still doesn't say anything even when the doors open and we walk through the expansive foyer and out into the chilly New York night.

I turn to look for a cab, but his hand is suddenly hot on the small of my back and he leads me to a car waiting at the curb.

A man jumps out from the driver's seat and opens the back seat door. "Good evening, Mr. Kent."

"Sorry to have you out this late, Henry," Xavier says, as he helps me into the car. The car door closes behind him and the city's noise is completely filtered out.

"How..?"

"It's Kaine's car. He probably called for it while we were in the elevator."

"How do you know?"

"Because I know my best friend."

It seems like the perfect segue.

"And… how well does he know you?" I say, remembering Kaine's comments scattered throughout the night that he might know more about me than I know about him.

"You have to understand, Malynda, he literally scooped me up out of the gutter."

"You didn't answer my question."

"He knows everything."

"So everything he said was true? Were you… were you really that much of a wreck?"

"What did you think? That I was just going to let you go? I meant my promises to you, Malynda. Every single one. One letter wasn't going to change that. So yes, everything he said was true. He knows everything."

"Including we being together now?"

"I didn't tell him but I'm guessing he's caught on."

"He doesn't seem too pleased about it."

Xavier doesn't reply, just squeezes my hand and leans over, brushing his lips against mine. I forget everything for a moment, falling into his arms, remembering how I'm already becoming addicted to the comfort it brings me.

I swivel around on the leather seat and lean back against his chest. It's warm and blooms against my body as he takes deep breaths.

All these years I've lived a life of my own creation. My real name, my past, locked behind a door in my mind. I didn't think I was ever going to be confronted by it again.

But here it is.

The implication that Xavier wasn't safe with me stings like a drop of acid down my sternum. But he's right.

And I know I should end this, before we fall too far.

But I can't.

"Mmmm," Xavier mumbles low into my ear and I turn to see his eyes fluttering closed as his head bobs forward, his cheek against my forehead.

I pull his arm tighter around me, and let myself dream. Just one more day.

***

"Wake up, sweetheart. Wake up, it's just a dream!"

"Don't go!" I hear myself scream. My mouth is bone dry, almost cracking at the corners where I've opened my mouth to scream.

"What? Go where?"

"Just... don't go," I plead, wrapping my arms around his neck, burying my face in the sweaty crook of his neck.

"Shhhhh, it's okay. I'm not going anywhere."

"You promise?" I ask him, even though I know it's unfair of me.

"A hundred times. I promise it a hundred times," he whispers, running his fingers up and down my spine.

I forget how many times I ask him to say it again, but it's still there, soft in my ears, as I finally fall back asleep, taking him with me into my dreams.

TWENTY-TWO

Him

"Mr. Kent, where should I take this?" A lanky teenager in a hard hat and hi-visibility vest rolls a rusty wheelbarrow filled with broken glass over to me.

"Firstly, if you call me 'mister' anything again, that hard hat isn't going to save you," I scowl. He just grins and doesn't look the tiniest bit afraid of me. Ah, to have the confidence of a 16-year-old. "Secondly, ask Gabriel over there. He knows better what's going on. I'm just here for the muscle." I flex my bicep and he laughs as he goes. "And hey, I'll give you $5 to call him 'Mr. Sinclair' though!" I call after him.

I watch as the kid rolls the wheelbarrow over and says something to Gabriel who then looks up sharply at me and throws me the finger.

I chuckle and return the favor, before returning to the pile of bricks in front of me that need moving to the giant bin parked out front. The construction is well past half-way and at the rate we're going we shouldn't have any trouble being ready for our grand opening a few weeks from now. It should coincide with the new school year, a perfect time to provide a safe space for the kids.

To keep the labor costs down as much as possible, Kaine and I come down whenever we can to help out. It also means we can keep an eye on what's going on, and get a work out in the interim. Truth is, when the place is up and running, I think it's going to be hard to keep us away from this place. I can already feel myself attached to it, my breath embedding in the walls.

"Seriously? Your pile has barely moved at all!" My boss yells at me as he rolls his wheelbarrow past me for the third time since I've been here. Like me, he's left the Armani suit home for the day and is dressed in just jeans. Unlike me, he's wearing a hoodie while I'm in a plain white T-shirt.

"Wha? I have delicate hands. I'm not a peasant like you!" I yell after him.

"And does Mr. Delicate Hands have time for a quick lunch break?" A sweet female voice asks behind me.

"Well, that all depends on what the lunch includes? And whether it wants the hands to be delicate or rough." I say even before turning around and seeing Malynda's face.

She's holding a picnic basket in her hands, and I can see the champagne bottle's neck poking out from under the blanket. "Hi."

"Hi," she says back, a smile stretching from ear to ear.

"What are you doing here?"

"I had to drop off some plans for Jade so I thought I'd bring a picnic and you could watch me eat it."

"Wow, what an offer. But I think you're bluffing, I bet you're really here to watch me." I make a show of picking up some bricks, flexing every muscle I have, straining with the effort.

"Wow, I don't think I've ever seen you look so...manly. Maybe I should just sit back and watch you pour water all over yourself." She wiggles her eyebrows and it's so cute I can't help but laugh.

"Your wish is my command. But it's much more fun to pour water over you when you're wearing a white T-shirt," I flirt back, enjoying the banter. It's been over a week since the dinner at Kaine's house and she seems to have stopped worrying too much about the revelations of my life in the time we were apart. We were supposed to spend the day apart and get some work done, but I'm glad she couldn't stay away. I'd been planning to sneak away and steal some time with her anyway.

I lean down to kiss her but before our lips meet, there's a sound of tires screeching on the street outside the shelter and then a large bang and clanging. I hear a glass window shatter and then the tires screech again, fading into the distance. Kaine, Gabriel and I throw a quick look at each other before we drop everything and run toward the entrance.

"Tell everyone else to stay inside!" I call over my shoulder. She nods and puts the basket down and I can hear her try to reassure everyone as we run out the door.

There's no one out there.

No sign of who was here and no other bystanders, which I'm glad for.

The path is littered in trash; about three metal bins lay on their side, rocking back and forth. Rotten food and candy wrappers and empty drink containers are strewn all over the street in front of us. Kaine walks over to the shattered window and reached down to pick up a brick.

"Fuck off. We don't want your shelter here. We're trying to take OUT the trash, not bring more in," he reads off it.

"What the fuck?" Gabriel shouts, taking the brick from Kaine and examining it. "Who the fuck do you think did is?"

I shake my head. "I dunno, but I can take a guess." Kaine nods, agreeing without even needing me to say it. "What are we going to do?"

"*You* aren't going to do anything. I can't trust you to keep your head dealing with these fucktards. Gabriel and I will think of something."

"But…"

"Go. She's waiting for you," he says, and I know there's no point in arguing.

But just because he isn't sending me to take care of this doesn't mean I can't send myself.

TWENTY-THREE

Her

I'm close, but I'm tensing every muscle in my body not to fall over the cliff. My eyes focus on my hands stretched out in front of me, my knuckles bone white as I grab fistfuls of the Egyptian cotton bedsheet while Xavier drives himself into me from behind.

"Ohhh, God. Fuck..." I groan as he pulls back and then slams his hips forward again, completely filling me up with his hardness. His breath is hard and ragged in my ears; his hands hot as they grab at my hips, pulling me back onto him.

I'm even closer now.

"Oh, sweetheart, fuck. Fuck." His moans mirror mine and I know we're both about to come.

My bottom lip finds itself between my teeth as I try to hold back, but there's no point.

Xavier's cock is inside me and I'm going to come on it.

Just as he slides into me one more time, his hand reaches under me and an index finger finds the hood of my clit.

And everything explodes into stars.

"Oh god. Xavier. Oh my god," I think I scream as a white-hot orgasm rips through me, draining my cells of every last ounce of oxygen.

I feel my body pushed forward as Xavier slams into me again, his own orgasm making him growl my name over and over and over until there's nothing left and we collapse on the bed, spent.

I'm not sure how long we sleep but the sun is bright in my eyes when I wake up again, Xavier's head still on my back, my limbs spread out like a starfish on his bed.

"Uhhhhh," is my first word.

"Hmmmm?" is his reply.

It's several more minutes before either of us makes any sense.

"Eggs?" he asks.

My head moves half an inch up and down. Eggs actually sound great. As long as I don't have to make them.

Apparently, he feels the same way as he makes no attempt to move.

But it's okay, I could lie like this here with him forever.

Ding Dong, the doorbell sounds, right on cue, as if to make a mockery of my thoughts of forever.

"Hmmm?"

"Eggs," Xavier replies, before he groans and drags his body off mine. There's a big sigh and then I feel him pull himself off the bed and shuffle to the elevator, pulling on a pair of shorts over his naked body.

Shame. I like completely clothes-less Xavier.

I pull a pillow over my head to block out the light. I don't know what time it is, but it's okay, I don't have any appointments today and have no rush to get to the office.

I could wait for eggs.

And more naked Xavier.

"Eggs!" he exclaims a minute later, suddenly more awake. The pillow is dragged off my head and he's holding out a plate to me.

"What the..? How?"

He grins and pushes the plate forward and I take it, sitting up, crossing my legs under me. I stare down at my plate filled with piping hot eggs on toast and my mouth fills with saliva; I didn't realize how hungry I was. Frequent sex equals an increased appetite, I guess.

Xavier comes back with another plate and cup of coffee in his hand that he lays on the nightstand next to me before joining me back on the bed.

There's no grace to the way I lift a forkful of scrambled eggs into my mouth. They're soft and fluffy, perfectly seasoned.

"Mmmm, eggs," I sigh and he grins at me, nodding, his own mouth full.

"Do you have a magic wand? Where did these come from?" I mumble between bites.

"I do have a magic wand," he winks at me and I roll my eyes. "I meant this, pervert!" He laughs and waves his iPhone at me. "The magic wand of Uber Eats."

"When did you do that? I thought you were asleep!"

"Oh, my sweet, I can work much magic while you think I'm asleep."

"Oh, I remember." I giggle, thinking back to how I was woken up during the night. "Makes me wish you were asleep again right now."

He drops his jaw and clutches at imaginary pearls before leaning over and kissing me gently.

It takes everything I have not to sigh like a lovesick teenager, clasping my hands to my bare chest and swooning.

But it's exactly how I feel.

Like a lovesick teenager. Because the last time I felt like this, I was a lovesick teenager, and my whole life was ahead of me.

"What's your day like?" Xavier asks, and I take a sip of the delicious coffee before I answer.

"Pretty free, actually, why?"

"Like you have to ask," he looks at me, and the intensity in his pupils makes me shiver. It amazes me how he can shift from playful to spine-shivering intensity in the blink of an eye.
I thought we could spend the day together. If you don't have any plans."

"I don't but don't you have to work? I can't imagine you have a lot of free time." I've heard enough about Ash Industries from Cam to know that their daily operations are no joke.

"I have my magic wand, remember. I can do most things from that today," he says, moving our empty plates away and pulling me into his arms. "Don't you want to?" he whispers against my ear.

I simply sigh in response, feeling my body completely relax into his. We stare out the window for a moment, watching the sun move to hide for a moment behind an early morning cloud, watching a section of Manhattan darken in shadows as the cloud passes by.

"You know, you should really let me choose some curtains. Pink ones. Fluffy." I suggest.

"Nope, no curtains."

"You're going to be visited sometime soon by the police for indecent exposure."

"Totally worth it. I want the whole world to see me ravaging your naked body," he growls against my neck, and I can feel his body coming alive. Wanting me.

"You're not jealous?"

"I said "see," I didn't say they could touch. That's just for me." He runs his tongue along the length of my neck.

The ring of a cellphone is harsh against our eyes, and we both grunt our disapproval at the interruption.

"You should turn that bloody thing off."

"It's not mine, doofus. It's yours." I point to the flashing screen of his iPhone at the foot of the bed.

"Oh."

"Yeah, oh!" I say, hitting him over the head with the pillow as he yelps ducking away from my assault as he reaches for the phone.

I watch as his forehead furrows and he taps on the screen. "Hello?" he answers, turning his back to me.

"Oh, okay. Um, don't worry. Don't touch anything. I'll be right there."

He hangs up and springs to his feet, jogging to the bathroom, barely turning to look at me,

"Sorry, babe. I've gotta go," he says over his shoulder as he disappears.

I sit back, hugging the pillow to my chest, a chill suddenly falling around me.

I'm not a part of his life. I gave up that right. I have no right to feel like this. I push myself up off the bed, reaching my dress on the floor.

"Hey." I look up, he's standing there, naked, towel over his shoulder. "There's something I have to do. Wanna come with?"

I feel myself nod. "But I need to shower first."

He grins and holds his hand out to me.

"Your wish is my command."

***

I don't recognize the apartment building we arrive at thirty minutes later, or the apartment number on the door that Xavier knocks on.

"Where are we?" I ask for the countless time. He just ignores me and pulls a key out of his pocket and slides it into the lock.

"Hello? It's me," he calls out as he pushes the door open.

"Xavier?" A woman's voice answers.

"Yes, where are you?" he says, pulling on my arm and closing the door behind me.

"Whose apartment is this?" I mouth and he just smiles and takes my hand.

"Come on," he says, walking down the empty hallway.

It opens up into a large living area and I see an older woman perched on the sofa in the middle of the room, her leg propped up on the coffee table in front of her.

"Mom! What happened?" Xavier lets go of my hand and walks over to her, leaning over to give her a kiss on the cheek.

"What are you doing here?" she says to him, while eyeing me up and down. I'm speechless. I heard so much about her when Xavier and I were together in Maine, but I never met her. I never knew if he was keeping her from me or me from her. Either way, I try not to stare, but he looks just like her. How strange. "Who's this?" she asks, once Xavier straightens up.

"Oh, Mom, this is, er..." he looks over, conflicted.

"Malynda," I hear myself say, and it surprises me almost as much as Xavier, going by the way his eyes widen. "I'm Malynda," I repeat, walking over and holding my hand out to her. I try not to admit to myself it's because I want to see if she recognizes me by name.

Something flickers in her eyes, the same deep green eyes as the man's standing next to her, and she takes my hand shaking it once. "I'm Denise. Denise Kent," she says and drops my hand, but doesn't stop staring at me.

I think I feel a chill, but I must be imagining it. It's not cold in here.

Xavier is oblivious to it all as he scans the room.

"Mom! What happened?" he asks again, circling the coffee table, taking in the scattered broken glass and water and flowers strewn on the rug.

"Ugh, it's nothing, I was moving this vase of flowers your brother sent me and trying to talk to him on the phone at the same time, but my ankle twisted and I dropped the vase on the floor. I'm fine. I was just going to rest for a bit longer before I cleaned it up." Her eyes continue to bore into me even as she speaks.

"Mom. Don't worry about that, just sit."

"I'll... I'll get a mop," I say, as ridiculous as it sounds. I don't know where the mop is. I just need to get away from her probing eyes.

"There's one in the closet in the hallway," Xavier calls after me.

"How did you even know I fell, honey?" Denise's voice follows me as I leave the room.

"Michael called me. He said he was on the phone with you, but then you yelled and he heard a big crash and then he said you just said you had to go and hung up."

"Oh geez, I didn't realize I raised a bunch of drama queens. I was fine. I just didn't want him hearing me swear as I hobbled over to the couch. You know, in case he overreacted and called you or something," she scoffs.

"He did the right thing, Mom. Are you sure you're okay, did you want me to call the doctor?" Xavier says as I come back into the room with the mop and dustpan in my hand.

"Will you tell my son I'm fine, Malynda?" she says, and I almost drop the mop in surprise at her directly addressing me.

"Well, um, I'm not sure I can tell your son anything he doesn't want to hear."

This makes her laugh, and I feel a little more relaxed as she seems to warm to me.

Xavier fusses over her while I help him pick up the debris, mopping up the water and gathering up the broken glass. He teases her and she returns the jabs two-fold, and I realize how strange it is to see the relationship in person.

It isn't how I envisioned her.

I remember him telling me how tired she always was, how drained, how she resembled a wrung-out dishrag, alternating between long days at work, and restless nights worrying about money.

Whoever that was, it seems to be a distant memory.

This woman is full of life. She gets up from her seat and hobbles around after Xavier, moving things that he touches, telling him off when he tries to help her back to the couch.

"I can do it myself, Xavier!"

"I know, mom, we're just helping, geez. Who knew you liked sweeping so much. Maybe I should get you one of those miniature Japanese zen gardens for you to rake back and forth."

"No way, I'd fling that across the room in a minute."

"Well, then you could sweep up the sand from that as well." She rolls her eyes and sinks into a recliner with a moan. "Mom?"

"It's fine. That was an old lady moan, not a broken bone moan."

He looks over at me and makes a show of throwing his hands in the air and sighing.

"She's unbelievable!"

"So I see... where you get it from."

"Hey!" They both yell in unison and we all fail in not bursting into laughter.

Xavier's phone rings and cuts through the laughter. He pulls it out of his pocket and glances at the screen before excusing himself and disappearing down the hallway.

"Malynda? Why don't you come sit over here," Denise says, and I put the dustpan down and settle on the couch next to her.

She turns to me, her eyes boring into me again. Those eyes, they must be made from some sort of alien space rock. They're unnerving. Bottomless.

"So, you're the girl," she finally says, and the shiver up my spine comes back.

"I'm sorry?"

"You're the girl, the reason. The reason he left Maine. The reason he almost died."

I feel my face freeze. She says it so matter-of-factly. Like it's nothing. Or, like it's something she's had a decade to process. But for me, it's all new.

"You broke his heart. He went from the happiest I ever saw him that summer, to a shell of a human. It was you, wasn't it? He never told me your name. But a mother knows. Only love could've made him that happy. And only the loss of that love could break a boy like Xavier."

"I... I don't..."

"You don't have to say anything. That look in his eyes right now? I've seen it before. And I don't mean when he was happy that summer. I mean the fear. I've seen that in his eyes before, just before he left me a note and disappeared off to New York. To find you. And finally, after all these years, he's found you." She takes a deep breath. "Well, that's too bad." She clicks her tongue and finally breaks the eye contact.

"I... didn't come looking for him." I don't know why I say that.

She turns back to me, "That's the only right thing you've done. If his life has been any good it's been achieved despite you. He is who he is now because of his brain, his ambition, his dedication. Because of Kaine."

"I- I know. He's done great. He's... an amazing man. He works very hard."

"No thanks to you, dear girl. After you left him, he was nothing. All he wanted, cared about, was finding you. And when he couldn't, he was trying to get himself killed. He's been doing that ever since. Still. He works hard? Don't think he's being a hero. He's just trying to find an excuse to work himself to an early grave. All because of you. I could've told him that love was never going to bring anything but heartache. But he's too much like me to have listened anyway."

I can barely process the words I'm hearing. "He almost... died?"

"In some way or another, he's been trying to die since you left. At first it was roaming the streets looking for you. Then it was the fighting. Now it's working until his body has no choice but to give out. He's too proud to ever take his own life, or maybe he doesn't even know he's doing it. But my sweet, beautiful Xavier. He always felt everything so strongly. I should've known it would be his downfall. And now that he's made some money, taken care of me, his brothers, he doesn't think he has a reason to live. That left when you did."

She shakes her head again and stares out the window.

I can't believe what I've heard.

Again.

From his best friend and now his mother.

Xavier. Oh, Xavier, what did I do to you?

I can't breathe. I need to air. I need to get out of here.

"I'm... I have to go. Please tell, Xavier," I say.

"Go. Don't worry about Xavier. He's used to you leaving," she says, twisting the knife, and I almost retch at the bitterness in her voice.

My head is spinning and I can barely walk as I stumble down the strange hallway, bumping into Xavier as I go.

"I... I have to go," I stutter, trying to feel my way along the way.

"Malynda! Where are you going?" he says, covering the mouthpiece on his phone.

"Just... I have to go..." I say, throwing the door open and flinging my way out of the airless apartment.

All this time, I had thought that I was the one who's suffered more. Having to give him up, give up my own identity. I thought there couldn't have been anything worse. Sure, I knew he would've missed me, but I never thought... I thought I'd done the right thing. I really did think he would eventually move on. I had hoped.

"Malynda!" I hear him come running after me. I can't wait for the elevator so I race for the stairs, running down them, my face drenched with tears. Tears for him. For my Xavier. For the sweet boy I kissed by the lake, who gave me his heart. And for the man who still holds mine. Who I hurt. Who I almost killed.

"Don't follow me!" I yell over my shoulder, as I turn to see him almost catch up to me.

"Where are you going? What's wrong?" he gasps.

I reach the bottom of the stairs and he jumps the last few steps and grabs me around the waist, spinning me around to face him.

"Malynda! What's going on?"

"I'm sorry! Oh my god, Xavier! I'm sorry, I'm so sorry!" I sob, barely able to recognize his features through the blur of the downpour of saltwater from my eyes.

"What are you talking about? Tell me!" he says, shaking me, panicked.

"I'm so sorry I left. I should never have left Maine. I should've stayed... forever!"

"What are you saying?"

"I ruined everything when I left! I shouldn't have gone. I was stupid, I was so stupid!"

"No, no, honey! You had to leave, we BOTH had to leave! Our lives weren't meant to be confined to that small town! You were destined for bigger things. My beautiful dancer girl," he says, desperately, pushing back my hair, holding my face in his hands.

"But it ruined everything! Everything! I should've stayed and waited for you to come with me," I scream, almost hysterical.

He doesn't say anything and pulls me against him. The sobs wrack through my body so strong I feel like my bones are rattling.

"Shhhh, baby girl, shhhh," he whispers, trying to calm me.

But I can't be calmed.

"I'm so sorry, I'm so sorry," I sob against his chest. Over and over and over.

"It's okay, we're here together now. It took a little longer than expected. But I found you."

I pull away and look at him and I see it. I see what his mother was talking about.

The fear.

The fear that I put there.

That I can't do anything to take away.

I sniff and wipe my eyes on the back of my hand, trying to control my breath.

"I... I need to go home." I say, my body suddenly so tired I can barely stand.

"Come on, I'll take you." I can't even argue, I just let him lead me out the front entrance, leaning against him as he gestures to the doorman for a cab.

Closing my eyes, I lean my head on his shoulder, listening to his breath and matching it with my own. At some point, I feel him guide me into a car and slide in next to me. He mumbles something to the driver and we slide into traffic, the momentum rocking me against him, my head against his chest, his hand on my back, soothing me.

"What happened? What triggered this?" he asks and I can barely answer.

"Your mother... said..." I struggle to say.

He sighs, deep. "Ah. I shouldn't have brought you there. I thought... I thought she'd be happy to meet you. To know I found you."

"She said... you..."

"Shhh... don't listen to her. She is just very protective of me. She thinks she understands what happened, but she doesn't."

I shuffle back so I can look up at him.

"Xavier... did you... were you really trying to die?" His breath is sharp, surprised; then lips tighten for a moment while he contemplates his response. "Tell me the truth."

"Malynda, trying to die and not having a reason to live, are two different things." Now it's my turn to gasp. "Wait, listen to me. Yes, I went through a time when I was just going through the motions. And I... didn't want to be here. It hurt, Malynda. It hurt with every breath, to not know where you were, what you were doing, what happened to you. But there finally came a time I just got used to the idea, that I wasn't going to have the same kind of life other men do. I wasn't going to fall in love with another woman, have a family. That part of me was dead. So, I live a life most people don't understand. But that doesn't mean it doesn't have meaning. Because it does. It just doesn't look like what other people expect when they examine their own lives. And hey, Kaine's life was just the same. And look at what he eventually found."

"Do you... do you think fate brought them together?" I ask though I'm not sure I want to know what the answer is. I'm not sure I believe in fate. Mine has done me no favors.

"I don't know. Maybe. Or maybe sometimes, people defy the fate that was meant for them." He looks down at me, and brushes a hair from my cheek.

"I love you, Xavier. I never stopped loving you."

"I know."

"How do you know? After everything I did. After all that time apart."

"Some things transcend time and space, Malynda."

I sigh and melt into him. His fate for having me in his life is even worse than mine.

TWENTY-FOUR

Him

She feels like a rag-doll in my arms as I lead her down the hallway to her apartment. I know this building, I pass it almost every day on the way to work. And here she's been all this time. I guess I wasn't as alert as I thought I'd been. I thought I'd committed to memory every face that I'd seen in Manhattan these last twelve years, and in ways I have. I see people in restaurants I remember passing in a Barnes and Noble three years ago. I see women with new husbands, children turn into adults, widows with old flames all the time. I see them all. But I never saw her.

Maybe it was fate.

We come to a stop outside her apartment, and she hands me the key, her face almost white from bloodlessness. I don't know what my mother said exactly, but it shocked the very life out of her.

I slide the key into the lock, but there's no need. It's not locked.

"Malynda, did you lock the door last time you left?"

She lifts her head off my shoulder. "Yes, of course. I always do. Why?" The hackles on the back of my neck spring to life. Something's not right.

"Wait here," I say, and she nods, confused.

I push the door open.

To complete and utter destruction.

"Oh my god!" she gasps behind me, her hands over her mouth, her eyes wide, scared.

The apartment is completely trashed. A bookcase in the foyer as you walk into her home is lying on the ground, its contents scattered all over the floor. Furniture is turned over, drawers pulled out and emptied. Broken glass and ornaments shattered and strewn everywhere.

Whatever they were looking for, they were very thorough. My hand is on my phone ready to call the police, but I need to make sure she's okay first.

"Oh my god," she gasps again. "What happened..?" She steps in behind me, her hand clutching at my arm, looking around at the wreckage of her home. "I've been robbed?"

"I... think so. Is anything missing?" I say, spotting the TV knocked onto the ground, its screen smashed. TVs aren't the commodity they used to be, and it might be hard to carry one out of here without being noticed.

"I... I can't even tell."

She stumbles deeper into the apartment and I follow her. It's a large apartment for Manhattan. Not as large as mine, but decent. We pass something that looks like a guest room and then into a master suite. Her bedroom. This room hasn't fared well either. It looks like the entire contents of her closet have been dragged onto the bed and floor of her bedroom. The curtains pulled from their rods and left piled on the floor. She points to the nightstand and her jewelry box is open and empty.

"I... I had a lot of jewelry in there," she says, and then sobs. "They took my grandmother's ring."

I feel something crack in my heart. I know how much she loved that ring. She's been wearing it since I met her. "I so sorry, sweetheart. So your jewelry is gone, anything else?"

She just shakes her head, her mouth gaping open, trying to take everything in.

"I... I don't know. I can't tell," her voice catches on her throat.

"It's okay, just sit down. I'm going to call the police. Don't worry, we'll get to the bottom of this, okay?"

She just nods and I clear a spot for her to sit on the side of her bed, trying to breathe through the fury. Who the fuck would do this? Mess with her? They must have been watching for some time, knowing that she wasn't spending the night here last night. I'm almost relieved. Relieved that she had been with me and not here. Who knows what might have happened to her if she had been here.

The dial tone barely loops once before I hear her choke on a scream. I turn and see her throw something clear across the room, her face blazing red, her eyes wide, terrified. I hang up the phone and reach out to her,

"What's wrong? What is it?"

She just shakes her head, her eyes growing wilder and wilder.

"Malynda!" I yell, shaking her.

It only momentarily shocks her out of her trance and she points to the object laying on the floor.

Running over, I pick it up off the ground.

It's a ballet shoe. Worn. I turn it over and recognize the handwriting on the sole. It says, "Malynda ..." Her name. And attached to the ribbon is a note.

"I'm back. Did you miss me?" And it's signed "DR."

What does this mean?

"Malynda." I read off the slipper again. And something clicks in my brain.

I sit down next to her, pulling her into my arms, squeezing her hand and giving her a moment to breathe. When her breath is steady, I tell her once and for all.

"I think it's time you told me what happened twelve years ago."

TWENTY-FIVE

Her

"It started the moment I got to New York. The moment I stepped into my freshman contemporary dance class. The moment he saw me. I thought at first it was just the way he looked at everyone, all the students, girls and boys, sizing them up from the start, picking his favorites, his prodigies. I was so stupid. I thought he liked me for my dancing."

Her voice is quiet but steady. She stares out the window as she speaks, her hands clasped in her lap, eyes lost in the memory. I tell myself I won't interrupt until she's done. I don't want to spook her, stop her. I need to know it all.

"He never really said anything that I thought was out of the ordinary. It was just the looking, the staring. But that's what dance teachers do, I told myself, they watch your every movement. I was used to it. I should've listened to my instincts. It didn't feel the same. But I'd worked my whole life to be there, I wasn't going to ruin my chance. No, I wanted to make the most of it, no matter what." She nods, as if her past was reminding her of her reasons.

"About a month in, the looking moved onto touching. Again, it wasn't anything I could pinpoint, instructors touch us all the time, helping our angles, our turn out, making sure our positions are correct. Even a ten-degree difference in the turn of your hips sets the good dancers from the best. I wanted to learn it all. I almost welcomed the touches, because I knew I was improving with each one. Then he started singling me out, picking me for demonstrations in front of the class, praising me in front of everybody. The other girls both loved me and hated me in equal turn. I didn't really have any friends. I would spend my mornings in dance class, my afternoons studying and my night time writing letters to you. I missed you so much, Xavier, so much. It was almost unbearable."

193

Her rhythm breaks for a moment and she turns to me, her eyes sad. I give her a gentle nod, encouraging her to continue. She gives me a tight smile and then turns back to the film running through her brain.

"He asked to see me once, after class. It sounded like just an opportunity to talk about my future. I was the last one to leave one day and he came up and asked me if I had thought about what kind of dance company I wanted to work with. I told him I would work with any that would take me. I just wanted to be given a chance to perform. He told me not to be small-minded and that if I worked hard, I could pick and choose who I could work for. And then he told me to come by the studio later that night and we would talk about some of my options. I didn't really think anything of it. I showed up that night and we didn't talk for very long. There were a few stragglers training with one of the other instructors, so he just handed me a few brochures for local dance companies and told me we'd talk another time. But after that, the uneasiness I felt at the start was growing. So I put it off for a while. He didn't seem too bothered by it, so I thought maybe I was just imagining it."

She shrugs and then takes a deep breath. I can sense that whatever's coming next is hard for her. Hard to say, hard to remember. I look down and notice her hands that were laying still on her lap are now wringing themselves. Her fingers nervously tugging on each other as she struggles with her story.

"Go on, sweetheart," I urge her gently and she just nods.

"About six weeks into the semester, we were getting ready for a performance exam. I was having trouble with it, my pas de deux partner wasn't very good and I felt like he wasn't doing the lift right, which affected my own performance. *He* came up to me at the end of class and said, 'This first exam is very important, it's going to set the tone for the rest of your time here. The way you're going, you might not even pass. If you want help, I only have tonight to help you. All the other girls have booked up my other one-on-one sessions.' I panicked. As I said, I'd worked hard to be there. If the person who was going to be grading me didn't think I was going to do well then I was going to get all the help I could."

194

She takes one long, deep breath.

"I showed up that night, and he was alone. He was... strangely quiet. He kind of just murmured a hello and then we warmed up together, but he didn't talk much. Once we were done, he pointed to the barre and he followed behind me as I walked over. Then, I caught him in the mirror, one second too late. He ran up and grabbed me pushing me up against the barre, hard. I can still feel it digging hard against my ribs, bruising me. He pushed his mouth against mine and started kissing me really roughly. I was so surprised, I didn't even know how to react. I tried to push him away, but I couldn't. He was too strong. I screamed. But nobody heard me. He didn't say anything, he just kept running his hands all over me, trying to pull down my tights. I just kept kicking my legs, and struggling, trying to break free."

Her voice grows louder, shaking. Her hands tearing at each other, her skin rubbed raw. But I know I can't stop her. I close my eyes and try to swallow the bile rising up my throat. I don't want to hear this, but I know I have to. This is why. This is why our lives turned out the way it did.

"I kept trying to scream, I remember he slapped me. It was so hard. I saw stars. His mouth was all over my face, my neck, even while he tried to... tried to pull my tights down. I did everything I could to just keep moving, struggling, kicking my feet out, freeing my arms. I think I even tried to bite him. One of my kicks finally connected with his shin or something and he let go, just for a moment and I manage to break free."

My heart leaps in my chest, as if I'm there watching it.

"I ran as fast as I could but he chased me. I didn't think I could make it to the door before he'd reach me so I picked up one of my slippers I saw laying on the floor and flung it at him. It hit him on the side of his head but it didn't really slow him down. He grabbed me from behind and threw me down onto the ground."

I almost throw up in my mouth. I want her to stop. Tell me it's all just a bad dream. This never happened. She's making it up. The thoughts swirl in my head so fast I can barely process them. No, I can, I can see them, they're just buried under the one clear thought that is flashing clearer than anything else; I'm going to kill him. I'm going to find him and I'm going to fucking kill him.

"He... started to kneel down, to straddle over me, I can still see his face, he was sweating, not even looking at me, like he was in some sort of haze and... I'm not sure how but I lifted up my knee and it... it hit him in the groin. He doubled over and I... got up and ran to the door. I could hear him yelling after me that he was going to kill me if I ever told anyone about what just happened. That he knew everything about me. And to never come back to his class. I... I never did."

She stops.

But she doesn't move.

I want to feel relief, that that's all that happened. But I know there's more. I know how it ended. With us apart. There had to be more.

"Malynda," I say, after she's quiet for almost a minute. The sound of her name triggers something, and she turns to me, shaking her head. "You can tell me. Nothing you will say will change the way I feel about you."

She sighs, her shoulders dropping after the tension from the story.

"If only that were true, Xavier." She says and leans over and presses a kiss against my lips. "One last kiss," she whispers.

Then she sits up and tells me the rest of the story.

TWENTY-SIX

Her

"I never went back to class. I went to my dorm, packed up my things and left that night. I couldn't tell anyone. I was so scared. I didn't think anyone was going to believe me if I said anything, and I... I believed his threats. I believed he would hurt me. I'd seen that emptiness in his eyes that told me he would kill me if he had the chance. So I just left. I packed up everything I had into a bag and left. I didn't have a lot of money. I couldn't tell my parents what had happened so I couldn't ask them for money. I stayed in a cheap motel for about a week and spent almost all my savings."

"Why... why didn't you tell me?" Xavier asks.

"What could you have done?" I ask him. "You were just an eighteen-year-old boy as well. What would you have done?"

He doesn't say anything, and it hurts too much to watch how he's going to react to this next part so I return to my stare out the window.

"One night, with only a few dollars left in my pocket and knowing I would have to leave the motel the next day, I was walking around, looking for a place I could afford with the last of my money when I saw a flyer. It was for a club downtown, looking for dancers. I thought it was the best luck, that it was fate." I stop, laughing at my own naivete. "Yes, they wanted dancers. Not for any kind of dancing I had done before, but I didn't know that. Not until I got there. $100 a night, the club manager promised me after she looked me up and down for a minute. It was $100 I didn't have and desperately needed."

He doesn't say anything. And I can't blame him.

197

"I told myself, I'd just do it for the night and if it was really too bad, I could quit and no one would ever need to know. And I'd have $100, and that could get me through another day or two." The years fall away, and it's like I'm right there, staring at that darkened stage for the first time. The fear. The shame. The hopelessness.

"That first night, was one of the worse nights of my life." I have to stop for a moment, swallowing down the shame that comes with the memory. "I had no idea what I was doing and, I had no idea what to expect. I didn't know the rules and... when some of the customers touched me, I - I didn't know that I could say no. So I just let them. It wasn't until some of the bouncers caught on and kicked them out, that I realized I'd fucked up. Some of the other girls thought I'd let them do it on purpose for better tips and none of them would talk to me. That night I went back to the motel and cried in the shower for about three hours. And that's when I sat down and wrote you that letter, Xavier. I thought I could never face you again. I never ever wanted you to know the things that had happened to me, and the things that I'd done. I wrote you so many letters. Somewhere I told you everything and begged you to come to New York as soon as possible. But I threw them all away. I couldn't do it to you. I couldn't do it to myself. Because even though the thought of never seeing you again was worse than death, it was better than you knowing what I'd become. What had happened to me. I never wanted you to know, Xavier, I never ever wanted you to know. So, I wrote what I thought would be the only thing that would keep you away. That I was happy. And to let me go."

"Oh, Malynda," I hear him whisper my name. And already, it sounds different.

I just look at him and shrug.

"After I sent the letter, I felt like my life was ending so I just went back to the club. The manager agreed to keep me on a week by week basis. It got... a little bit better after that first night. They didn't expect too much from the new girl, and there were one or two girls who were nice to me once they realized what position I was in. They taught me to dance... the way they did. And the tips were good. And what else was I going to do with my life? I couldn't go home. I couldn't go back to school. I couldn't go back to you."

He doesn't say anything, just sits there, frozen. So I just go on.

"But anything can happen... bad things, at any given night. And I might've been lucky, but not everyone was. It eats at you. Leeches on your soul. And your self-worth. Not the dancing itself. That was the best and worst part about it. On a good night, I could get up on the stage and pretend I was doing exactly what I wanted to do. I was dancing. Maybe not ballet or jazz, but it was still moving to music. On a good night, I could ignore the eyes. More, always wanting more. And telling myself, I had nothing left to give."

"It's not what you think it is. There's nothing sexy or glamorous about it, at least where I worked. You don't know, until you've been there. Some girls love it. And some girls don't care. But I wasn't one of them. I... wish I could've been, but I just wasn't one of them. And I hated myself. I... knew, I could never go back to you. There was no chance I could ever look you in the eye after what I'd done." I feel myself sob and my hands come up to cover my face. I can't look at him. I don't want to see that look in his eyes, that look I've been running from for twelve long years. That look of disgust and disappointment. I would've gone my whole life not seeing him again to not have to see it. But it's too late now. I'll never be that sweet girl to him anymore.

"So, that's it. That's... what happened. Everything."

He clears his throat, I brace myself for his first question since I started talking. "How... how long...?"

"Um, not too long. Long enough, but not too long. There was... there was this one guy. He came in for a drink or two a few times a week. He was different. He wasn't a sleaze, he never bought private lap dances, he always tipped well and was polite. We never could figure out what he was doing there. We wondered if it was just the closest place to get a drink on his way home from work. He'd sit and talk with us sometimes when it was quiet. He was nice. To all of us. He actually knew a lot about art, which was a bit of a change from the other guys, so we shared that. I hadn't talked to anyone about how much I'd loved color except for you, everyone was so used to just looking at me the dancer. Anyway, one night... um, a fight broke out in the club, and I was there, um, on stage. He... er, he pulled me off the stage and made sure I was okay. I was a little shaken up and he offered to take me home. Normally, I probably wouldn't have, he was still a patron, even though I never really saw him that way. He felt more like a friend. He took me home and he spent the night."

There's a flicker of something, jealousy maybe, across Xavier's face, and for a moment, I feel a jolt of hope. That maybe, just maybe, there is hope for us. But it passes and he bites his lip and stared straight ahead, waiting for the end of my story.

"We stayed up talking, and I told him... everything. It was such a relief to get it off my chest. He didn't know anything about my past here in Maine, or anyone that I knew. And I really needed a friend. So I told him. Everything. And when I woke up the next morning he was gone. But when I went by the club that night, he was waiting outside and told me that he had a proposition for me. He would help me get back on my feet, if I helped him start his interior design business. I told him I knew nothing about interior design, and he said all I needed was an eye for color and shapes, and I had that. So... I agreed. I couldn't stand doing what I was doing for much longer. And that was my last night."

"Cameron," he says, his lips tight against his teeth.

"Yes, that was Cameron. He saved me, Xavier."

"I get it."

"I know you do."

He gets up, hands stuffed in his pockets as he looks at the mess around us.

"And... the..."

He can't bring himself to say it. I can barely say it either.

"The guy who attacked me? I don't know. I didn't keep in touch with anyone at the school. As far as they know, 'Malynda' dropped off the face of the planet. But... I read somewhere that he left the school shortly after I did. Opened up a studio or something upstate. I haven't heard anything about him since." Except for in my dreams, my head reminds me. "Until now."

Xavier's head whips around.

"The slipper," I gesture to the shoe I'd thrown across the room. "That's the shoe I threw at him that night. He's the only one who could've had it."

"How...? How does he know where you live?"

"I don't know. I changed my name. Maybe... maybe he saw my picture somewhere. I don't know." The shiver that's been creeping up my spine spreads over every pore of my skin, raising goosebumps that make me wrap my arms around myself. "He must recognize me from a picture, it's not like I'm that easy to find by my old name."

"Don't I know that," Xavier mumbles under his breath.

Suddenly, any energy I have left in my body is gone. I feel my body sway and I fall back against my headboard.

"Malynda!" I hear him call my name, but I can barely open my eyes. I haven't thought, *really thought*, about that night in years. Having to live through it all again, telling the one person I never wanted to know, it's taken everything out of me.

"I'm okay. I just... I just want to sleep. Please."

"Malynda..." he calls me again, but this time, it's like through a wind tunnel. And his voice, his face, everything is fading into air.

"Xavier..." I try to say, and it's the last thing I hear before everything does quiet.

***

"You fucking bitch! Don't you fucking dare tell anyone about this or I will kill you. I will find you and kill you! Don't you ever set foot into my dance studio again!"

I'm shaking my head as I run. The only thing giving me relief is his voice getting quieter the further I run. He's not behind me.

But he's always there; everywhere I turn, I can see his face.

"I'm back!" His voice is taunting me.

My ballet shoes appear in front of me, a hundred, no, a thousand of them scattered all over the floor.

"I will find you and I will kill you."

His voice is getting louder now.
"No!! Leave me alone!!!" I scream, so loud my throat burns.

"Shhh. You're okay.... you're safe, I promise, you're okay," I hear a soft female voice say and something cool and wet on my forehead. It instantly soothes me and quiets the voice and images in my head and I feel myself grow calm. "Get some more sleep, I'll be right here," the sweet voice says again. I obey, and feel myself fall back into the quiet darkness.

***

I'm not sure where I am and what time of day it is when I open my eyes. My head is throbbing and I rub my temple for a moment as I try to figure out where I am. I don't recognize the place. It's dark though and warm. I feel comfortable in this strange bed. And safe. And really, really thirsty.

I notice a glass of water on the table by the side of the bed and turn on the light as I sit up and reach for it. The first sip of water feels like a crystal-clear lake trickling through my brain. Bliss. There's a knock on the door and I freeze.

"Um, yes? Hello?" I say, hesitantly.

"It's Jade, can I come in?"

The sense of relief that floods my body is almost enough to ease the pounding in my head.

"Yes, of course, please."

The door opens slowly and Jade's friendly face appears through the gap.

"I don't want to bother you, I just wanted to see how you're doing."

"Come in, please," I say, patting the bed. I actually prefer her company to being alone right now.

"Okay," she says and comes to sit by the side of the bed. "How are you feeling?"

"I'm... okay, confused." I laugh a little, but it jars my head and my hand involuntarily comes up to cradle my left temple.

"Oh, you have a headache. I'll go get you some Tylenol." She starts to move but I reach out, touching her arm.

"No, please, stay. I'll be okay. Where am I?"

"Oh! I'm sorry, you probably haven't seen this room. This is the guest room in our apartment."

"Yours?"

"Yes. We used to have two but we converted one into a nursery. My brother, Gabriel, spends some nights a week here so it's his stuff in that closet. Is there anything you need? Another pillow? Are you warm enough?"

Something in the way she sounds, it's so sincere, I instantly burst into tears.

"Oh my God! Are you okay?" she says, startled at my sudden sobs.

"I'm okay," I say, hiccupping through the tears. "You're just being so nice to me. I'm sorry, I must be feeling really emotional. What am I even doing here?"

"Well, Xavier called me and brought you over here. He told me about your apartment and wanted to make sure you had a safe place to stay while he called the police and tried to sort out what happened."

"Xavier?"

"Yeah, he and Kaine went over to your apartment. I'm sure they'll call when there's some information. You must be so scared. Xave told me what happened."

I look up, startled, surely he hadn't shared everything. He and I hadn't even really had a chance to talk about it. "He did? What did he say?"

"Well, he said that he had taken you home and the place was an utter mess, like someone had gone through all of your things. He said you were really upset, so he didn't want to leave you alone while he dealt with the police. So he brought you here."

"Oh." Maybe, hopefully, that's all he said.

"You must be so devastated, I can't imagine being violated like that. I love my home, if anyone ever came into it, I don't know what I'd do." Her words make me remember the state of my home and it causes a new rush of tears. "Oh, I'm so sorry, I didn't mean to upset you."

"No, no, I'm just... I'm feeling a little emotional." I try to wipe away the influx of new tears.

"Totally understandable! Do you want something to eat?"

"Um, I think... if you don't mind, I'm going to try to sleep some more."

"Of course, I'll let you rest. If you need anything, I'll be right outside." She looks at me for a moment, and then reaches over and pulls me into a hug. It's tight and warm and reassuring, and exactly what I need at this moment. I wait until she pulls away.

"Thank you, Jade. I'm sorry to be a burden like this."

"Nonsense. Hey, when you feel better, I'll tell you about my own experience with being brought to this room by Xavier. It's a good story." She winks and grins and I smile for the first time since this all happened.

"And, um, can you... um, if Xavier calls or comes here, please wake me up. I want to see him."

The smile freezes on her face, but she quickly recovers. "Of course I will. I'm sure he's worried about you too. But they could be busy for a while."

The cold starts to set in again and I just nod and slide back down into the bed, pulling the covers right up to my chin.

Worried about me, she said, about Xavier.

I'm worried about me, too.

I'm not sure how I'm supposed to go on without him.

TWENTY-SEVEN

Him

"Hey, Xavier, how are you doing, man?"

I ignore the guy at the front desk and continue walking past the machines to the back of the training area. My jacket lands on the floor where I throw it, and I kick my shoes off, looking around the gym.

"Hey. You. Wanna spar?" I say to a young guy doing burpees on the mat.

"Me?" he says, patting his chest.

"Yeah, I'm looking at you, aren't I? What? Scared I'll kick your ass? You've got forty pounds on me."

He snorts and jumps to his feet. I was wrong, he's got at least sixty pounds on me, and six inches. "No, old man, I'm not afraid of you. I'm afraid FOR you."

"Don't waste your breath on the trash talk. Just put your money where your meathead is." I slide under the ropes and into the ring.

"You wanna stretch a little first?"

"Let's just do this." I don't need to warm up. The walk here from Malynda's apartment was warm up enough. I need something to help me cool the fuck off.

"Don't say I didn't warn you," he says, joining me in the ring.

"Rules?"

"No fucking rules," I say and swing my left arm.

He ducks out of the way, light on his feet for such a big guy.

"Your funeral," he says, shrugging.

I can only hope.

He's fast. I can barely keep up just trying to duck and weave out of the way of his fists. His long arms make it hard. My breath is ragged already. I'm not really dressed for this. My suit pants aren't conducive to the high kicks, so I'm going to be aiming for his fucking knees instead. Even though they're almost the height of my waist.

He punches and I lunge forward, hoping to catch his arm in a hold. He shakes me off like I'm an annoying bug that landed on his wrist. I trip as I land, awkwardly, but manage to get up onto my feet before he pins me down.

I attack this time with a barrage of strikes and land a hit on the side of his face. He growls and spins, his foot connecting with my hip with a back kick that knocks the air out of me.

We both retreat to our corners to catch our breath, shaking the pain from our bodies.

He lifts his arm to wipe the sweat off his brow and I take this chance to charge him, ramming my shoulder into his stomach.

"Ah!" he grunts as he doubles over but he doesn't fall; instead, he moves his arm to hook around my neck and slams me to the ground. I fall on my back, and he straddles over me, his eyes burning red. He lifts an arm and his closed fist comes down to slam against the side of my face. I almost choke from the impact, I've never been punched so hard.

I barely have time to recover before I feel him lift his arm ready for another punch.

"Give up?" he growls.

"Fuck you," I spit and he responds, striking against the other side of my face. Fuck.

I punch my arm up out of habit and make contact with his chest. Not that it matters. It's hard as steel.

"Is... that all you've got?" I taunt him, as I feel him move to get off me.

He snorts and looms over me again, I stare at him, daring him. He bares his teeth and swings again, his knuckles slamming against my face so hard I feel something tear and crack.

"Again," I rasp, and he grins lifting his arm again.

"What the fuck?! Stop! Marcel!" a familiar voice yells out, and Meathead stops his fist mid-swing, looking up.

"Get the fuck off him," I hear Ram say. Fucking hell.

"Dude, I warned him," Meathead says, getting up off me.

206

"Just shut up and go work out somewhere else."

I lay there, head-spinning, a streak of wetness leaking from my mouth.

"What the fuck is wrong with you?" I hear my friend ask, as I feel him kneel by the side of my head. "You trying to get yourself killed?"

I almost laugh.

He pulls on my arm, helping me up. My head feels like it's been run over by a snow plow, and my mouth like I've been hooked by a marlin fisherman.

"You're a fucking mess, man."

"I'm fine." And I am, I feel better than I have in hours. I'll take this over the red-hot iron poker skewering a hole from my gut all the way to my fucking heart any day. "Jesus, I'm fine!" I yell, as he tries to turn me over, checking for wounds.

"What the fuck is going on with you? I haven't seen you this bad since... since I first fucking met you."

"Huh, that sorry sap had it fucking good," I sneer.

I push myself up but the ground shakes under me and I fall back onto the mat.

"Whoa, steady, man." Ram catches my arm and I shake him off.

"I said, I'm okay! Geez, like I've never taken a punch before. I've taken plenty of YOURS in the past."

"I was pulling them, dickhead. Now, are you going to tell me what the hell is going on?"

"Nothing, just blowing off some steam, it's been a hard week."

"Problem with the girl?"

I feel my head whip around, and it just makes him appear in front of me in double.

"What? What girl?"

"Shut up, I'm not an idiot. I've seen this all before."

I can't argue. He has. I take a deep breath, letting it out slowly, until there's nothing left in my lungs before I inhale again.

"I found her. Well, she found me. Or, I dunno. Fate found us. Or Lucifer."

"The girl?"

"Yeah."

"Holy fuck, man."

"Yeah."

"And?"

"And what?"

"It's not sunshine and rainbows, dancing around in each other's arms singing 'la dee daa'?" He purses his lips together and makes a kissy noise.

"Can you please not ever do that ever again? I'm in enough pain."

"You asked for it," he shrugs.

Yeah. I'd have happily taken more if he hadn't stuck his fucking nose into my business.

"No. It's not... all la dee rainbows," I wave my hand at him. "It..." The memory of her telling me suddenly floods my brain. The images. Her fear, palpable. Her voice cracking. Her eyes filling with shame, sadness, hopelessness. "Oh god, Ram." My heart feels like it's tearing itself open in my chest. I struggle to breathe.

It's my fault. It's all my fault.

I should never have let her go alone.

I should have dropped everything and told her I'd go with her to the ends of the earth, wherever she wanted, whenever.

But I didn't. I sent her here, alone.

Again and again and again... I've failed her. I have never been able to protect her, not even from me. What kind of man was I that she thought she had to protect me from her shame?

Not just then, but now. Had I not changed enough, grown up enough, that even now, it took her home being broken into, her life being threatened, before she felt like she could tell me?

"Breathe, man, breathe," I hear Ram's voice remind me.

All I can do is shake my head.

The person I loved most in the world, I failed.

I drop my head into my hands, and there's a deafening pounding in my skull. I couldn't save her from the past, but I'll be fucking damned if I ever let anything happen to her from here on out.

I push myself up, this time I couldn't care less that the world under my feet is crumbling. I've going to make this right.

"Where are you going, man?" Ram shouts after me.

To the past, buddy. To the past.

TWENTY-EIGHT

Him

She looks so peaceful.

Just the soft hue from the moonlight filtering through the blinds, washing over her. Watching over her.

I know she's safe here in Kaine's apartment. He's about as paranoid as they come and his place is a fortress. I know there's nowhere else in the world I feel would be safer for Malynda right now.

Not even with me.

Her breathing is slow but steady in her deep sleep. I reach over and brush a hair off her cheek, and she doesn't even stir.

My sweet, beautiful girl.

She looks so peaceful, but all I can see is the trauma she's been through.

My breath catches in my throat as the image replays in my mind of her terrified, fighting the assault, running for her life.

And the shame, the shame that followed.

She was in trouble.

And I wasn't there to save her.

Yes, I know all about shame.

I lean over and brush a kiss on her forehead. This time, her breath quickens and her eyelashes flutter against her cheek, then still.

"I'm sorry, my love," I whisper. I tiptoe out of the room and close the door silently behind me.

TWENTY-NINE

Her

It's definitely morning the next time I open my eyes. And my stomach rumbles.

The water jug by the side of my bed is magically full again, and I smile; Jade really is the perfect hostess. My arms lift themselves high up into the air and my spine cracks a little as I stretch, feeling my muscle fibers spark into life after almost a day of hibernation.

My legs swing off the bed and I stand up, a little wobbly.

I feel okay. I needed the sleep, but now I need to get on with my life, whatever that means, and with whom.

I peek out the door, and a waft of sizzling bacon almost knocks me off my feet. I follow the scent like a cartoon character, my nose twitching, a white swirl of delicious smell leading me into the kitchen.

Where a giant is standing towering over the stove.

I freeze.

Fight or flight?

He turns and I don't have time to make a choice.

"Oh, you're up. Great," he says, waving a greasy spatula at me, before turning his attention back to the sizzling pan, one that looks like a toy in his hands.

"Um, hi."

"Sit down. Juice or coffee?"

I don't know why, but I obey, sitting down at the stool on the kitchen island. Okay, I do know why, it's because I don't think it would take much for him to turn me into a sausage link cooking on that frying pan of his.

"Um, coffee, please."

He spins around, and it's only then that I notice he's wearing an apron. One of Jade's aprons specifically, judging by the thin ruffle and lily pattern. It barely covers a third of his front and the ties dangle on the sides, unable to meet around his waist. He stares at me for a moment and pours a glass of orange juice from the jug and slides it across the island to me.

"Um, I'm sorry, I said coffee."

"I know," he says, and continues staring at me.

Weird.

Even weirder, I feel like I should be afraid of him, but I'm not.

"Drink," he says, finally breaking his stare to fill up two plates with the food he's cooked and come around to sit down next to me, a plate of bacon and fried eggs in front of each of us.

I drink. The cool tart juice feels good sliding down my throat and I can feel the vitamins being absorbed into my body. There's something... different in the juice, earthy and spicy. I feel instantly more alert.

"It's ginger, " the giant says, without my even asking, as he shovels an entire egg into his mouth. "Way better for you than coffee. Stop drinking that junk."

"Then why did you offer it?"

"Test," he mumbles through a mouthful of food.

I pick up a piece of bacon and take a bite. It's hot and salty and crispy and delicious. I'm not usually big on bacon but my body is craving energy. Nothing like sizzling pork fat to provide it. The sustenance builds up my courage.

"So, um, are you going to tell me who you are and what you're doing at Kaine and Jade's place?"

"I'm Ram."

Ram. The name sounds familiar. I take another sip of the juice, hoping to shock my brain into remembering. Ram.

"I'm Xavier's friend."

Ah. Yes. The bouncer.

"Oh, okay, yes, he's told me about you."

"Probably not as much as he's told me about you." His eyebrow twitches, but he doesn't volunteer any more information.

"Oh, okay. But that doesn't explain what you're doing here."

"Xavier asked me to make sure you get around okay today. I'm here to take you wherever you need to go."

212

The mention of Xavier again turns the pit of my stomach into a centrifuge, spinning until the bottom threatens to fall out. We haven't spoken since yesterday at my apartment. I have no idea what he's thinking, about me, about what I told him, about our past or our future.

"Xavier?" I say, surprised there isn't more of a tremble in my voice. "Um, where... where is he?"

"He'd be here himself but... um, he's taking care of some business. I'm sure he'll get in touch with you soon."

"Oh okay," I say, but I really want to grab him by his mountainous shoulders and shake him and make him tell me everything he knows. "Well, I don't need you to babysit me, I can take care of myself."

"Sure, whatever you say," comes the answer. "Just let me know whenever you're ready to go," he grunts as he pushes himself off his stool, carrying his empty plate to the sink.

"I... ugh, are you always so bossy?" I whine.

"Yes."

"Ram!" I yell out of frustration.

"Look. If you're thinking that either Xavier or I will let you go back to your apartment alone after what happened, then you're even stupider than I give you credit for."

My eyes narrow at him, but he has a point.

"What do you know, Ram?"

"I know everything, *Malynda*. Now finish your breakfast. Take your time. I have nothing else to do today but keep you safe."

He turns on the sink and drowns out any protestation I might have made.

***

There's a strip of yellow tape outside my apartment door. Crime scene. It seems over the top, but I remember that Xavier was here, talking to the police. So, I guess I shouldn't expect anything less. He organized a bald 7-foot middle-aged babysitter for me, after all.

213

I take a breath before I go inside.

Jade is right.

This is a violation. I know I can never go back to living here now.

All I can see are his fingerprints over everything he touched. Tainting it. The air is poisoned with his breath. I catch myself holding mine as I walk through the apartment, careful not to touch anything he's touched.

"I won't be long, I just need to grab some clothes," I say to Ram. He just nods, his lips stretched tightly over his teeth, his jaw twitching as he takes in the scene.

They did a really good job of destroying this place. They. Huh. *Him.*

I feel my stomach turn and I swallow the reflex to retch, as I always do in the handful of times I've allowed myself to think about the attack since it happened.

"Focus," I say to myself. "Grab a bag and some clothes and let's got out of here as fast as we can." I make a mental note of some other things I will need that I will send my assistant to get. I don't want to be here a second longer than I have to.

Ram is waiting for me outside when I emerge from the apartment, cellphone to his ear.

"She's okay, do you want to talk to her?" I hear him ask the person on the other end. I hold my breath, but then he just taps the phone and slides it into his pocket.

"Oh," he says, finally seeing me standing there with my suitcase. "Um, that was Xavier, he was just checking up on you. He... er, he had to go into a meeting."

I just nod.

I never expected anything different.

"Where to next?" Ram says, with a forced smile.

"Work, it's time to get back to work."

And onto a new chapter of my life.

***

"Isabella! Where have you been? You look a wreck!" Cameron exclaims as soon as I step into our office floor. The sight of his familiar and friendly face breaks through the last layer of bravado I have, and I fall into his arms, the tears bursting from my eyes like a broken hydrant.

I can feel Ram looking behind me and I turn to him. "I'll be fine here. You don't have to stay."

He just nods and drops the suitcase on the floor and heads back to the elevator. Something tells me he won't be far though, and I have to admit that it gives me some comfort.

"Oh, sweetheart, what's wrong?" Cameron says, taking my hand and leading me to my office, closing the door behind us. "Why haven't you answered any of my calls, I almost sent the police to your apartment!"

Something about the image of the police showing up and seeing the crime scene tape makes me laugh through my tears, and it comes out in an unattractive snort.

"Oh my god, isn't that always the way? Police showing up when it's too late."

I catch a flicker of confusion ripple across Cameron's forehead.

"What are you talking about?"

I just look up at him, the full impact of what is happening crashing down on me, the sobs returning and I can't breathe.

"Shhh, I got you, I got you, Iz," he coos as I fall back into his arms, the vibrations in his chest comforting me.

It's almost ten minutes before I can finally speak.

"He… he's back, Cam."

"Who? Who is back, honey?"

"Him… the… my dance teacher."

"What?" Cameron jumps to his feet, he knows. He knows what this means to me. "How… how do you know?"

"Yesterday, we went to my apartment…"

"Wait, who is 'we'?"

"Xavier. Xavier was with me. He took me to… um, pick up some things from my apartment and when we got there, everything

215

was trashed. It... my apartment's just... just a mess, Cameron."
Relaying it to him is making me walk through it again. I need to get
through this fast.

"Oh, Iz. That's horrible."

"Yeah, I thought... I thought it was a robbery at first but, then I
found... he left a message." I have to take a breath, reliving the
shock of seeing an object from that night in my hand after all these
years.

"A message? What did it say?"

"It said, 'I'm back, did you miss me?'" I shudder, just saying
the words. "I'm scared, Cam. I don't ever want to go back to my
apartment again."

"I know, don't worry. I'm going to keep you safe. You'll stay
with me until... well, until we figure out what we need to do."

"I'm... staying with Jade for the moment."

"Well, that's very nice but... I've been here with you before,
remember?"

I nod. I remember. Life is making it hard to forget.

Cam reaches out to squeeze my hand, and in that moment I'm
grateful for him, more than I ever have been. He opens his mouth
to say something, but a loud shout interrupts him.

"I'm sorry, sir!! I need you to wait outside while I call her! Sir!"

The door flings open, and suddenly Kaine is standing in my
office, Ram looming behind him.

He nods at Cameron, before turning to me.

"I need to know everything that's going on. Right now."

Cameron jumps to his feet, hands out in front.

"Hey, you can't just barge in here and tell us what to do,
man."

Kaine brushes past him and stands over me.

"Malyn-er,... Isa... fuck it. Malynda, you need to tell me what
Xavier knows about what happened with the break-in at your
apartment. And we don't have a lot of time."

"What, why?"

"Because... Ram, tell 'em."

"Ram?"

"Um, Xavier just called me and told me… he told me to tell you that he's sorry. And that he loves you."

The message sends a chill down my spine. Nothing ever ends well with that message.

Kaine sits down on the couch next to me.

"Malynda, I need to know. Remember what I said to you at my house the other night? About the lengths he will go to? I think he knows something about what happened to your apartment that he's not telling me. But you need to help me and tell me. To help him."

Kaine's words echo in my brain. And his mother's words. Surely, he's not still looking for a way to die? Not now that we're finally back in each other's lives?

I look into Kaine's eyes and I know. I would trade my shame for Xavier's life, any second.

"Twelve years ago, I was almost raped. The guy is back. And Xavier knows about it."

Kaine springs to his feet and takes my hand.

"Come on, we'll need to work fast then. We'll talk more in the car."

THIRTY

Him

It's funny the information you can find when you know what you're looking for.

She changed her name. That was the problem, all this time. She changed her fucking name and was lost in the sea of new people coming every day to this godforsaken town, and I couldn't find her.

Malynda. I'd been looking for Malynda. But my Malynda had died in a sea of shame and emerged as Isabella.

But she'll still always be Malynda to me.

At least she was smart enough to change her name.

It wasn't that hard to find her attacker's name, even twelve years after the fact. Not that hard to bribe the admissions officer at the dance school to look up her name and what classes she took and who taught them. And who wasn't around come the next semester.

And now here I am, in Albany, New York, standing outside a glass door with his fucking name carved into it.

Damien Romanski Studios.

It's funny the information you can find, when you know what you're looking for. And have a wad of cash to bribe whoever needs bribing to get it.

I push on the door. The wind follows me in as I'm greeted with music muffled by walls.

"Can I help you?" a young woman perched on a stool in front of the front counter asks me.

"I'm looking for Damien."

"He's um, actually, he's just in a training session. Can you wait for about ten minutes? He doesn't like to be disturbed."

"He's in a class?"

"Well, yes. It's a one on one."

The hackles on the back of my neck spring up as if on command, and it feels like an ice cube is sliding down the middle of my back. I push away from the counter and head toward the music, ignoring the protests of the woman.

It leads me up a narrow staircase and to a closed door on the second floor.

I take a breath and push it open.

Two figures in the middle of the room spring apart. And I know instantly, it's him.

"Who the fuck are you?" he growls at me.

"Are you okay?" I say to the girl, ignoring him. She just shrugs. "Good, then I'm going to give you five seconds to collect your things and leave. You're not going to want to be here for this."

"Hey! Who the fuck do you think you are?" he says again, grabbing onto the girl's arm.

I steel myself. Not yet. "I suggest you let her go. Right now. You're not going to want a witness for what's about to happen."

Something in my words makes him drop his hand from her forearm and she hesitates, looking at each of us in turn.

"GO!" I yell and she jumps, her hands coming up to her blushing face as she runs past me and out the door.

He takes a step toward me, chest puffed in an involuntarily display of his masculinity. "I'm going to ask you one last time. Who the fuck are you, and where do you get off coming into my dance studio and telling my students what to do?"

"And that bothers you? Because you're the only one that likes to tell young girls what to do?"

"What the fuck are you talking about?"

I turn toward him, square on. I want him to hear every word I'm about to say. "I'm talking about Malynda. I'm talking about you trying to rape her. And I'm talking about how I'm not going to let that happen to any of your students ever again."

His face is instantly white.

Yes, you motherfucker. Be scared.

I roll up the sleeves of my shirt, slowly, meticulously, up one arm and then the other, feeling his breath grow shallow as he watches and listens.

"Malynda was an eighteen-year-old girl. All she wanted to do was dance and create beauty. She was a light in the world, and because you couldn't just go home and tug on your own cock one night, you stamped out that light. And despite everything, she managed to make something of her life, and now, now you think you can come back and take it all away from her again? No, not if I have anything to do with it."

I walk toward him, and he reacts to each of my steps by stumbling one step backwards.

"I... I don't know what you're talking about. I haven't... I haven't seen her since that night," he stutters.

"You're not ever going to see her again. This ends here."

I push off from my back leg and lunge toward him. He turns and runs toward the back wall, lined by mirrors. I reach him in three steps, grabbing the back of his wife-beater and pushing him hard against the barre. He braces with his arms, but I'm on him, slamming my body against his, crushing him against the hard-wooden rail.

"Ahhhh," he grunts, winded.

"Does that feel good, you fuck?" I yell, pushing his face hard against the mirror until it's almost disfigured. "How's it feel to know you can't do anything to get away?"

He struggles under me; he's strong, but I'm stronger. I press harder against the side of his head, watching his breath fog up the mirror against his face.

Kicking back with his leg, I jump out of reach, letting him go. He takes the chance to tear himself off the mirror and runs toward the middle of the room.

I charge toward him, giving him no time to recover. I swing my fist and it connects with his face. I revel in the crunch of my knuckles against his cheekbone, his whole body feeling the impact as he stumbles to stay upright. I sweep a foot under his leg and he

220

crumples to the ground. I stamp a foot down on his back and he cries out in pain, but I can barely hear it.

All I see is red.

Like a crazed bull charging for the moving cape. All I want is to destroy it.

"You complete and utter piece of shit," I say, as I deliver another kick to the side of his body, ignoring the hands coming up to shield himself. "What made you think you could put your hands on her, and get away with it?"

"I'm sorry! I... I haven't! Please! Stop!" he whimpers as I drop to the ground, turning him over to look at his pathetic face.

"Oh, yes. You are going to be very sorry." I say, slamming my fist down on his face, feeling the skin tear on his mouth as well as my knuckles.

It just urges me on.

I want his pain.

I want to hear him beg.

As if every time he cries, it will erase one of hers. And I'll keep hurting him until there's nothing left of him to give, and she can be reborn.

"Stop! Please!" He pleads, the sound gurgling in his chest.

I stand up and pull him to his feet, staring him dead in the eye, ignoring the streak of red across his mouth.

Dragging him by his arm, I slam him against the wall. He sways once and then I push him against it again, so he can stare into his own pupils in the mirror.

"Did you stop when she begged you to?" I snarl against his neck, so he can hear every single word.

"N-n-no."

"Then what the fuck makes you think I should?" I say, pulling his head back by the hair and then slamming it up against the glass.

It shatters and he falls to the ground, body limp, eyes closed.

"Get up!" I yell at him, nudging him with my foot.

He groans but barely moves.

"I'm not done with you yet, you shitfuck!" I say, my leg digging hard into his side.

He's just a warm bag of sand to me at this point. A pinata that I want to bust. His salvation paid to Malynda in blood.

I drop to the ground next to him, the sweat stinging my eyes, as I slap him hard across the face.

"Wake up, asshole!" I didn't know it, but I've been training my whole life for this moment. "Don't you pussy out on me now."

I stand up, nudging his side with my foot. He moans and opens his eyes, turning on his side and pushing himself up. He already looks a mess.

Good.

"Ready?" I say. "Come on, put your fucking hands up and fight."

He sways, but lifts one hand up, covering his face. "I'm sorry," he whimpers.

"It's too late for that. You shouldn't have come back. You should've jumped off a cliff or in front of a fucking bus but you should never have come back."

"I didn't... I don't know what... I swear," he stammers between pants, a lying fuckwit to the end.

"I'm not really one for believing would-be rapists."

"I made a mistake..." he says. And it sounds so pathetic, I almost pity him. Almost. Until I remember how frightened she looked as she told me the story. And the utter shame that has followed for her whole life.

That tore us apart.

"Yes, you did. And now you're going to pay." I lunge at him, ramming my shoulder into his sternum. I feel the air escape from his lungs and his body crumples against me and onto the floor, I pull my leg back, and take a breath. Ready to deal the last kick. One he'll remember for the rest of his life. If he remembers anything ever again.

"NO!!!" A yell echoes around the room from behind me.

I turn to see Malynda run into the room, I barely have time to pull my leg back before she pushes against my side with both of her hands, and I stumble three steps back, surprised by the attack. And for a split second, something about this moment reminds of the first day we met and her intervening into my fight. Except this time, I'm the one she's trying to stop. I catch the sight of Kaine and Ram coming in behind her in a reflection of the mirrors, but I'm focused only on her.

Her.

Here.

"What the fuck are you doing here?" I shout at her, but she doesn't even flinch.

"What the fuck... what the fuck am *I* doing here? What the fuck are *you* doing here?"

Her head moves from me to him and back to me, eyes wild, her mouth dropped open.

Is she kidding me? What did she think was going to happen once I found out what had happened?

"I came to... make sure he never hurts you, again, Malynda."

"I don't know what he's talking about..." Damien stutters as he tries to sit up, his hands cradling the side of his waist, his face smeared with his own blood.

"Shut the fuck up. I am not done with you," I growl at him.

"Xavier! Stop!" Malynda yells and I turn back to face her. "I didn't ask you to do ANYTHING! There are other ways to do this!"

I can't help but guffaw.

"Other ways? What other ways?" I challenge her with a look.

"Other ways that don't include you beating the crap out of him! Or worse, getting the crap beat out of you."

"Those other ways don't work, Malynda." I step over to him, grabbing him by the shoulder as he tries to stumble away. "You fucking scumbag, are you ever going to bother her again?"

"N-no. No," he stammers, his eyes avoiding hers. "Never. I promise."

I snigger at his response.

"See? This was the best fucking way, Malynda."

"You've lost your mind, Xavier," she says, her head still shaking from side to side.

"No. I'm finally seeing more clearly than I have for a long time. I know where you are. I know why you left me. I know who's to blame." I push him to the side, suddenly feeling the sick rise up when I realize who I'm touching.

"Xavier, let's go."

"I'm not done with him yet."

"Yes. Yes, you are. You should never have come here! I can't believe this."

She takes one last look at me and runs out of the studio.

"Malynda!" I yell and chase after.

"Xavier. Careful," I hear Kaine say as I run past him, but I ignore him, just as I know he expects me to.

She's barely at the bottom of the stairs when I catch up with her, grabbing her wrist and swinging her around to face me.

The tears on her cheek shock me, almost as much as the way she's looking at me. Not... anger. Disappointment. It finally sinks in, she's upset at me for being here, for trying to protect her, from trying to avenge her.

"Where are you going?" I shout at her, and she doesn't even flinch. She's seen worse from me today.

"I can't... be here. Where he is," she shakes her head, hand gesturing upstairs.

"I never wanted you to come here, Malynda."

"Not as much as I never wanted you to come here, Xavier."

"But I came here for you!" I yell, trying to make her understand.

Her breath hisses through her teeth. "No, Xavier, you're doing this for you."

I can't believe she would think that. "He tried to rape you, Malynda."

"Don't!" She throws up her hand to stop me. "Do *not* tell me about what I've been living with every single day of my life. I don't need you to tell me what he did. I was there. *You* were not."

Exactly. I wasn't.

"You can't let him get away with it, Malynda. That's why I'm here."

She shakes her head at me. "No. That's not why you're here."

"What are you talking about?"

"You're not here to *avenge* me, you're here to avenge *yourself*. Punish him for what he did."

"To *you*," I say, reaching out for her, but she steps away from my touch.

"No, you're here because of what he did to *us*. This isn't about me. This is about *you*," she repeats, each word like an accusation.

I stagger a step back. Is that really what she thinks? Is she right?

"No. Sweetheart, you're wrong."

She sighs, "I'm right, Xavier. And you know it. You're here because of some fucked up vendetta you have against your own ego. Because of some pent-up feelings of inadequacy, about not being able to protect me."

"He wouldn't have done it if I'd been here, Malynda."

"Maybe, maybe not. We'll never know, Xavier. What we do know, is that... you're not much fucking better."

"What?"

"I saw you. I saw you, Xavier. You were out of control! If I hadn't stopped you... you, you were probably going to kill him. And that scares me more than anything any stranger could do to me. I don't even know who you are. I don't know who you've become. I might've changed my name, but you changed who you are."

Her eyes lift to mine, and they're wet but I can see my reflection in them. And worse, I can see how she sees me. A violent monster. Worse than her actual attacker. A stranger.

"Oh, Malynda..."

"I've gotta go. I... I can't be here. I have to go."

Her front teeth dig into her bottom lip, stopping it from trembling, and she holds my look for one more second before she turns and walks away.

I want to run after her.

I want to tell her, she's wrong. It was for her, everything, it was always for her.

225

I want to tell her I'm the same Xavier she knew and loved back then.

But my feet won't move. My lungs can barely drag in air.

Maybe it was all for nothing. The moment she left on that bus to come to New York, it ended then, and I've been chasing a dream ever since.

"Xave?" I hear Kaine's voice say, low and quiet.

"She's gone. She left."

"Go." I hear him say quietly, and I feel Ram push past me and then out the door.

"Ram will take care of her, don't worry," he says, and I feel his hand, warm but firm on my shoulder.

"She's gone," I say again.

"I know. Come on. We need to get out of here." His hand squeezes.

I turn, looking back up the staircase. "I need to..."

"No, that's done."

"I'm not done, Kaine. He's still..."

He cuts me off. "It's done. You heard him, he won't be bothering her again."

"But he..."

"I know. She told me."

"Everything?" I search his eyes.

"Yes."

"Then how can I leave? When he can still walk out of here."

He sighs and shrugs. "Because it's what she wants. You're going to have to live with that."

I shake my head. "She doesn't know what she wants. She's terrified of him."

"And yet she came here. To stop you from making the biggest mistake of your life."

"And now she's terrified of me."

He doesn't lie and say she doesn't. He wouldn't. "You can change that."

"Maybe it's too late."

"Maybe. And you'll have to learn to live with that as well."

"No, I don't, Kaine." I brush his hand off and walk out the door.

I don't have to learn to live at all.

***

"Xavier, what are you doing here?" my mom asks when I show up at her door three hours and a bottle of scotch later.

"I... I came to check up on you, your knee," I say, swaying down the hallway and collapsing on the couch.

"You mean my ankle?"

"Yup, that too."

She hobbles over to me, "You've been drinking again?"

"Yup. You want some?" I drag myself up off the couch and over to the small drinks bar.

"No thanks. I'm fine."

"Good, more for me."

"Are you going to tell me what's going on?"

"Nothing, mom. Just same old same old."

I stagger into the guest room and fall into the dark.

THIRTY-ONE

Her

It's quiet in the building when Ram follows me up the elevator and into my office. The world outside has quieted with the setting of the sun, and the darkness has drawn a cloak around my mood. The ride back to the city was done in complete silence. I couldn't even tell you if I breathed, except that I'm still here, alive.

Replaying the scene over and over in my brain, watching Xavier pummel Damien, the way he pulled his leg back, ready to slam into his head.

In my mind, in some of the replays, he follows through.

Sometimes I want him to. Sometimes I don't.

The times I want to watch his foot smash Damien's head in two, I want him to, for me.

The times he stops, I want him to, for him.

It's not something I want him reliving, realizing what he's done, once he's out of his revenge trance. Even though I said that he was doing it for him and not for me, I don't truly believe it. I said it because it's what I thought would shake him back into himself, wake him up, because that man, that vicious, violent, angry man, is not Xavier.

I won't have him make a mistake that could ruin his life because of me. Not twelve years ago, not now.

There's a soft light at the end of the hallway, from Cameron's office, and I check the time on my watch.

Almost seven p.m. What's he still doing here?

"Isabella?" he calls out.

"Yeah," I answer quietly, turning into my office. I don't want to see him right now, don't want to see anyone. Ram stops and pulls back into the shadows, but I know he won't be going anywhere. I wonder if Xavier knows that even though he felt he'd

228

lost me, the friends he gained are worth more to him than I ever should.

The couch is soft and familiar under me as I sink into it.

"Hey, everything okay? You guys just kinda ran out of here," Cam says, appearing at my door. The light from his office casts a soft glow around his form, but I can barely make out his face. He reaches for the light.

"No. Please, leave it off. I... I have a migraine."

"Oh, no. Can I get you something?" He perches on the arm of the couch and presses his palm to my forehead. "Hey, hey. You're burning up. Are you sure it's just a migraine? Want me to grab a Tylenol from my office?"

"No. I'm okay. Do you mind staying?"

"No, sure, of course."

I give him a soft smile before I close my eyes and lay my head back.

He might have Ram and Kaine. But I have Cameron.

And maybe, maybe that's what we'll have to be happy having, for the rest of our lives.

I knew I should never have told him.

But it turns out, neither of us has ever been really good at protecting the other.

THIRTY-TWO

Him

"Hey. Dickwad."

The giant turns, slowly, from the waist, his biceps protruding like two baked hams from his shoulders, his forearms dangling by the elbows. I can't help but wonder how he can reach behind to wipe his own ass. He blocks most of the light from the main road into the back alley where I'm leaning against the paint-cracked wall.

"You better not be fucking talking to me," it growls, as it tries to place my face in the dark.

"I don't see any other dickwads around here, do you?" I push off the wall, the vibrating from the club music on the other side causing too much fuzz in my brain.

"No, but I see a little shit about to get his brains pounded out."

"Well, that definitely can't be you then."

He growls again, and I can see the rumble of the wide expanse of meat, muscle, and bone up his barn door of a chest as he takes a step toward me. There's a ripple across his reddening forehead that suggests he's a little surprised that I don't move back in response.

He wouldn't be surprised if he knew why I was here. And running away isn't a part of it.

"You got a death wish, you fuck?"

Yes. But that's beside the point.

"I heard you caused a bit of trouble for my guys at the construction site."

"What do you know about that?"

"I know I don't want anything getting in the way of that youth shelter being ready in a month."

His eyes narrow and I know he knows why I look familiar now. "Well, I don't want that bleeding heart tax write-off around the corner from my apartment building. Those little shits are going to cause trouble. Let them go litter the streets with their overdosed stinking corpses somewhere else."

There's a pounding behind my eye that mirrors the pounding I want to give him.

Not yet, Xave. Not yet. I tell myself.

"Wow, you're a real gem of a human, aren't you?"

"Yeah, you bet I fucking am. I'm not trying to lower anybody's real estate value just so I can sleep at night. Don't you stand there in your fucking Armani and Rolex and lecture me about charity, what the fuck do you know about being on the streets? Give me a break, fucking savior complex. You and your buddy and that blonde whore strutting around Harlem like you're God's gift to the poor."

He spits straight ahead. And I've got to give it to him, it takes some balls to do that without even feeling the need to turn his head. His phlegm lands about a foot from me, and the repulsion quickly replaces the grudging credit I might have given him if he wasn't a complete fuckbag.

My hands pull out of my pockets as I walk up to him. He smells just like I imagine, a combination of over-sprayed cologne, testosterone, and bourbon.

I walk up to him, and I don't stop until I can count the number of clogged pores on his nose.

"Stay. The Fuck. Away from my employees. And away from my youth center."

He snickers, and the bourbon fumes almost knock me off my feet.

"Or what?"

"You don't wanna know."

"Too bad. I'm a curious fella. Come to think of that, that blonde, she is a cute one, isn't she? Why don't you send her to do your negotiations next time? At least there's something from her I want. Or maybe I can just take it."

He barely finishes his sentence before my fist connects with his face. Experience tells me, I should feel the burn of my knuckle-skin tearing and the jarring of my whole arm, but I feel nothing. In slow motion all I see is his face turning back toward me, blood already dripping from his nose, the startled look on his face already turning to something like bloodlust.

If he wants my blood, he can have it. But not without paying with his own first.

I pull my hand back and swing it toward him again before he can react. This time it rams into his chin and he barely stumbles to the side before I feel a giant fist slam into my diaphragm. Every ounce of air in my body leaves me, and I feel the bile push up into my esophagus.

Before I can steady myself, I feel my arms pulled backward, two hands around each wrist, like vices.

Fuck. He wasn't alone.

"What? You can't handle me on your own, you gotta bring your goons in on this?" I taunt him, trying to struggle against them, but there's no point. It's three giants against me now.

He just grins, nostrils flaring at the pheromones seeping from his own sweaty skin as he pushes the sleeves of his shirt up as far as they can up his baked ham forearms. He walks up to me, his rough sausage fingers gripping my chin as he bares his teeth.

"It's going to be such a shame to fuck up this pretty face. Your little blonde isn't going to recognize you once I'm done with you," he pants.

"Still going to be prettier than that overcooked meatloaf you've got on top of your shoulders." And this time it's my turn to spit straight at him.

His eyes narrow and his lips tighten against his top row of yellow teeth. It'd be almost comical if I wasn't thinking about how it's going to be the last thing I ever see. He draws his fist back and slams it into my stomach, and it feels like a truck driving into my guts.

I try to double over, but they hold my broken body up.

I'm wrong, the last thing I'm going to see is stars.

And the last thing I'll say is her name.

THIRTY-THREE

Her

My phone is ringing. It's ringing and I have no idea where it is. Or where I am. I open my eyes, and I don't recognize the sheets on the bed, the pillow under my head, or the clock on the nightstand next to me. I drag myself up, patting the mattress around me for my phone, my eyes focusing on the window to my left. Those curtains. Those curtains I do recognize. I bought them. For Cameron.

I'm in Cameron's bed.

The realization dawns just as my hand closes around the flat, smooth shape of my iPhone. Jade, the name flashes at me.

"Jade?" I rasp into the phone.

"Isabella," she says. And I know. Something is wrong. "It's Xavier."

"What's wrong?"

"Just go downstairs, Kaine has a car for you, it's going to take you to the hospital."

"The what?" I spring to my feet. I'm relieved to see I'm still dressed in my underwear, my dress slung on the back of the chair in the corner.

"Just come. Hurry." She hangs up the phone with a click and I freeze for a moment, trying to decide between calling her back and running the fuck out of here.

Then the sound of her voice saying "hurry" replays in my head and I throw my dress over my head, running for the door.

"Woah! Where are you going? I brought you coffee!" Cameron almost slams into me, as I rush down the hallway.

"I... I gotta go. Can't talk! Sorry!" I don't even have time to feel guilty for running out on him like this as I grab my bag and run out the door, my partner calling after me.

The ride down the elevator gives me time to straighten my clothes but I ignore my reflection in the glass. Then it dawns on me, how did Kaine know to send the car here. Two minutes ago, I didn't even remember I was here.

The answer is there when I arrive at the street to see Ram holding the car door open for me. I can't meet his eyes, I just mumble hello and slide into the back seat of the town car. He closes the door behind me and settles into the passenger seat, giving the driver a nod.

I wait until we're in traffic before I ask, "Ram! What's wrong? What happened to Xavier?"

But it's silent all the way to the hospital.

***

Jade is the first person I see as I rush into the ER. I'm relieved to see her, even though her hair is falling like a bird's nest around her face, and she's dressed in what looks like Kaine's suit coats over her pajamas. I've never seen her look anything but completely put together.

"Isabella!" She jumps up out of her seat and runs up to me, throwing her arms around me. I hold onto her a moment longer even when she pulls away. I don't know who is comforting whom.

"What happened?" I ask, biting the inside of my lip to keep from yelling from the acidic fear burning in the pit of my stomach.

"He... Xavier... they found him..." Her red-rimmed eyes fill instantly with tears and she stops, trying to catch her breath. I just want to shake her to get the information out, but I can see this isn't easier for her than it is for me.

Not for the first time, I can't help but think how lucky he has been to have found such friends.

"He's in bad shape," Kaine says as he comes up behind his wife, touching her softly on the shoulder. "He was being beaten up by some guys in a back alley near the Cotton Club. Some people walking past saw it and they intervened. Lucky because... as it is..."

"W-w-what... how bad is it?"

I'm too scared to look at Jade again, who lets out a sob, and Kaine leads her over to the row of seats before coming back. He

234

gestures with his head and I follow him to a quiet spot down the hall.

"He's in surgery right now."

"Oh my god!"

Kaine waits for a beat while I process before he continues. "He has at least three fractured ribs and a broken cheekbone."

I gasp, but he's not done yet.

"But what the doctors are most worried about is that he might have some internal bleeding. They... they beat him up pretty badly."

I don't know what to say; I just stare up at him. He's pulled his hoodie back, his face completely exposed. But instead of feeling uneasy, I find something comforting about his scars. Or that he trusts me with them.

"We'll know more soon. I've got the best doctors on it, you know that."

I nod. I know.

"Why... what? Why did this happen?"

"I'm... I'm not sure. We're still looking into it."

There's a twitch of his jaw, and I know there's more than what he's telling me. But I'm too busy worried about Xavier's current state to dwell on it too much.

"Can... can I do anything?"

"I think being here is the best thing you can do. I know he'd want you to be here."

"I don't know. We... we had a fight at the..."

Kaine reaches out and squeezes my hand. "No. He'd want you to be here. No matter what," he says, his voice soft but firm.

I just nod.

Down the hall, we hear Jade cough, and his head whips toward her, his eyes sharp but worried. It's an involuntary action that tells me everything I need to know about them. She wraps her arms around herself but doesn't cough again. I see his shoulders relax and he turns back toward me. The corners of his eyes crinkle a little when he realizes I was watching him.

"She's been a little tired lately, the baby's been keeping her up."

I shake my head, "No, don't apologize for worrying about your wife. It's really sweet."

He smiles at me and walks back to her, before stopping and saying over his shoulder, "You know, everyone cares and worries in different ways. Sometimes it's sweet. Sometimes it's destructive. And sometimes it's up to us to decide whether the way we show that love is right or wrong."

***

An hour later, I see Ram walk through the hospital entrance. Leaning against him is Xavier's mother. He helps her over to a chair before giving me a quick look, as if to ask if I'm okay. I shrug and give him a little wave. His chin drops in the slightest nod and then disappears back down the hall, his giant shoulders slumped, his head down.

We haven't heard anything from the doctors yet, and with each ticking minute the tension rises.

I do the only thing I know how to do in that moment. I get up and sit down in the empty chair next to his mother. She scowls at me, her eyes wet and red, her lips tight against her lips. I ignore it and simply reach over, take her hand and squeeze it tight, not letting go.

She looks at me for a moment and then turns her face away but doesn't pull her hand back.

We all care and worry in different ways.

***

The door swings open and the doctor walks toward us down the hallway. We all stand up spring-loaded ready for the news.

"There was some damage to his spleen, but not a lot and we were able to repair it. His broken ribs didn't puncture his lungs and that's what we were most worried about. He should make a full recovery. We're going to keep him sedated for a few more hours to make sure he gets the rest he needs. He's very lucky that the damage wasn't worse and he was found when he was," the doctor says, and gives us a small smile.

Xavier's mother bursts instantly into tears. I have to bite my lip to stop myself from joining her; instead, I watch as Jade runs over and puts her arm around her. I hear Kaine pull the doctor aside with questions as I face the wall and stare at a poster of a doctor explaining to a child about cancer, trying not to think about what could've been.

The hours tick by. Slowly. Torturously so.

Several nurses come by to tell us he won't be waking up any time soon and maybe we should go home and get some rest, but nobody moves. Eventually, they just stop trying.

I've felt time moving this slowly before.

Those first few days after I fled college following the attack, sitting in my hotel room, trying to sleep the day away. Watching the watch on my wrist tick second by second by second until midnight, when another day would pass. Another day I had survived without him. Another day I'd managed to stop myself calling him, writing him, begging him to come rescue me.

For the first time in my life, I'm questioning the choice I made then.

Had I made the right decision, not telling him?

It had taken me a long time, years, to get over the idea that I had only myself to blame for the attack. I'd never thought of myself as naïve, but knowing what I know now, would I ever have put myself in that position? I had felt uneasy with Damien before. But I still went to the studio that night. Because I thought dance was everything.

Turns out it wasn't. I was still able to live a life without it.

And Xavier? Would I still able to live a life without him?

Survive, yes. But in just the few weeks he's been back in my life, I've realized it wasn't much of a life I was living before.

The image of him in his pajamas and slippers in the middle of Manhattan flashes in my mind. And I can't help smiling.

He is many things: stubborn, uncommunicative, infuriatingly protective. But he's always been able to do one thing. Surprise me. Well, two things. Surprise me and make me smile.

And that hasn't changed after all these years.

Xavier, sweet Xavier. He's become everything I ever envisaged he would be, and more.

Everything about him, compared to how he was twelve years ago, is just… more.

More passionate, more confident, more thoughtful, more gentle and forceful all at the same time.

More generous.

He had so little back then, and yet he gave so much of himself. Now he has a fortune at his fingertips, and he works even harder to share as much of it as he can.

I was wrong. I made the wrong choice. I should've trusted him to understand. My shame was just that, mine. And I realize now, it wasn't that I thought he would not be able to handle it, it's because I didn't think I could.

Me. It was me all along.

The revelation makes me almost cry out, and I choke back a sob.

I did this to myself.

I did this to the both of us.

And it stops today.

"Um. Hey," I look up and Kaine is standing beside me.

"Yes?"

"He's awake."

THIRTY-FOUR

Her

I hang back, letting Jade help his mother in to see him first. As much as I want to run in there and tell him what I've realized, I know there will be time. We will have all the time in the world now.

They're only in there for a few minutes before they emerge, his mother sobbing as Kaine gently helps her to a seat. Jade gives me a small smile and hugs me for a second.

"He's really weak, but he's asking for you. I'm just warning you though, he doesn't look great."

His eyes are closed when I walk up to the side of the hospital bed. If I were here alone and looking for him, I would not recognize the person lying in front of me. His face is bruised, dark purple and swollen. A bandage loops around the circumference of his head, and I can see blood still caked on his scalp. It's dry, burgundy red.

I wipe away the tears streaming down my face. *He's okay*, I remind myself. *The doctor said he would be okay.*

I sniff, and the sound makes him open his eyes. Eye. One is swollen shut.

"Hey you," I say softly, running my finger along the hem of his hospital gown.

"Hey," he croaks.

"I hate to see what the other guy looks like," I try to joke, and his mouth tightens into a split-second smile.

"Yeah, he's a mess."

"The doctor said you're going to b-"

"I can't do this anymore, Malynda," he says, cutting me off.

I stop. I'm not sure I heard him right.

"What are you talking about, Xavier?"

He tries to turn his head to face me and winces.

"I mean, I can't do this anymore. Live like this. Or, almost die like this. I have to stop. I have to stop chasing you. I have to let you go."

His words crush the air from my body.

"Xavier, no. I'm sorry. I've... I've done this all wrong. From the beginning, I was wrong."

"No, you didn't know any other way. And I get that. I'm sorry I wasn't here to protect you. And you're right, I'm trying to make up for the past, but I'm just fucking up the future. It's time for me to realize that what we had is over."

"I... I don't understand," I say, and I can feel my head shaking.

"I just don't know what you want from me."

"All I ever wanted was for you to be happy. Are you happy?"

"Does it look like it? And you? Are you happy?"

"Me? Worried that you're going to go off and kill someone, or worse, get yourself killed? No. That doesn't make me happy."

"Then what am I doing in your life? I have no role. I don't want to be the one who makes you look like this."

"Like what?"

"Like you don't have any tears left to cry."

"Oh, Xavier. I was so worried."

"I know. And that's not fair on you. But I don't know any other way to be right now. I can't help feeling like I never was, and have never been, good enough."

"What are you talking about?"

"There's only so much chasing I can do, Malynda. I waited, searched for you, for twelve long years. All I wanted was to show you how much I loved you. How much I wanted to be with you. I put my life on hold. And then I found you. And I loved you even more than I did before. And my life finally started moving forward. And it still wasn't enough. But this time, I'm thirty, not eighteen. And maybe I can read signs I couldn't before. That sometimes the person you love, isn't the same as the person who is right for you. If I'm making you cry like this, I'm not the person for you, Malynda. And if you felt like you couldn't tell me what happened, then I'm not the person you should be with."

"Xavier!"

"I'm sorry. I think this is best."

"But I love you."

"You will never love me as much as I loved and love you. Don't you ever forget that."

"But Xavier!"

There's a beeping from the machine on his left and a nurse runs in, pushing me to the side.

"He needs his rest, you should wait outside, miss."

"No! I need to..."

"Go," he says, turning his head from me. "It's better this way."

I feel a hand circling my wrist and pulling me from the room.

"Come on," Jade's voice gently says to me. "I'll take you home."

How do I tell her the only home I ever had just left me?

***

Him

It's quiet in here, just the sound of my own breath and the beeping of a machine telling me I'm still alive. Even if I wish I weren't.

"Hey," says the voice at the door.

"Hey back," I say. What else is there to say?

His voice is low and I can barely hear it through the bandage and the machines. "Jade took her home."

It takes more strength than I knew I had to just lay still and not rip the tubes from me and run after her. "Okay. Thanks."

"I can bring her back when you're ready..."

"No. That won't be necessary."

"You sure?"

"Yeah. I think I've said what needed to be said."

"For you or for her?"

"For her."

"And what about you?"

"Don't you get it? What's best for her is what's best for me."

"Have you ever considered that what is best for you is best for her?"

He leaves before I can respond. Bastard.

THIRTY-FIVE

Her

He always says he waited, searched for me for twelve years. But I spent twelve years trying not to be found. I never realized how much that shaped how I lived, what choices I made.

Those first few years, changing my name, how I looked. I became someone new.

I shed the girl I had grown up with for eighteen years, and evolved into someone who lived a life I didn't think could be traced to someone I wanted to forget.

But nothing really changed.

The very essence of me, my love for art and color stayed.

And it brought me back to him. The one who'd lured that love out of me in the first place.

As much as I was hiding from him, I'd made my life a tribute to him. Living vicariously through my memories. Too afraid to give him a chance.

I never realized that until now.

Now that it's too late.

He's right. We weren't good for each other.

If I was driving him to the brink of death to try to right some wrongs of the past, then I shouldn't be a part of his life.

How can I stand by watching him kill himself, in the name of trying to protect me?

But if I could, I would change it all.

I would show him that he was enough, that I trusted him, that I needed him. That nothing would ever be the same without him.

"What do you want for lunch?" Cameron's voice makes me jump. We've spent the last week packing up my apartment. There's no way I can stay here, after what happened. In a way, it almost feels like a relief to have something to focus on, something to wipe the slate clean. Something to mark a new phase in my life.

"Um, I'm not really hungry."

"You've gotta eat something! How 'bout I go grab something from Donali's."

I smile at my friend and business partner. He's been here for me from the moment Jade brought me home from the hospital.

We talked about what happened the night before I woke up in his bed, and while I know it was innocent and he was just there to comfort me, I can't help feeling that maybe he feels like it was the start of something new. But I'm not ready for that. And I may never be.

"Um, yeah, that sounds great. Thank you."

"Sure, I'll be right back, okay?" He drops the box he's packing and gives me a wink as he heads for the door. I wait until I hear his footsteps down the hallway before I run over and pull the chain across.

I can never feel safe here again.

THIRTY-SIX

Him

"I don't need your help! I can walk to my own bedroom," I snap, and regret it almost immediately. Almost.

"Fine, fall over and break another rib. See if I care," Kaine says, stepping back and ignoring my sway to the side.

"Passive aggression is not a good color on you, boss. Stick to grey hoodies and pinstripe suits," I hiss, my breath ragged after only a few steps.

"You're cranky when you're not beating up other people."

"You could volunteer as a punching bag and help out your loyal friend."

"No thanks, my face is scarred enough," he jokes.

I laugh and then my ribs make me regret it. "You did that on purpose, you sadistic fucker," I groan as I ease myself into my recliner, staring out into the grey.

"Have you heard from her?"

"Who?"

My friend's eyes roll far back into his head. "Now who's being passive-aggressive?"

"I have no choice, doctors said if I was *aggressive* aggressive I could tear my stitches."

"So all I had to do to get you to listen to me was get a medical degree?"

"Yeah. Why don't you get on that? See you in seven years."

"Eh, I'll just buy one." He shrugs.

I can't help but laugh again, and then wince as something pulls tight and throbs inside my torso. Gotta stop doing that.

"So, what are you going to do with your time off?" Kaine asks, pouring himself a drink.

"What time off? I'm not taking any time off! I'll be in the office tomorrow." I reach out my hand for a glass and he ignores me as he sips on his drink, the ice clinking against the sides.

"Yeah, no thanks. I don't want you scaring the other employees."

"You just don't want me usurping your role."

"Exactly, can't have their fear shared between the two of us."

"Pfft. Whatever. I'll work from home." I shift in my seat trying to get comfortable. In vain.

"You'll *rest* from home."

"I'm not taking time off, Kaine. We have too much work."

"Last I looked it was Ash on the side of the building, not Kent."

"This is horse shit, man!"

He grins and for a moment I'm glad to see him smile. I haven't given him much reason to recently. "Horse shit might actually be good for you. Go sit on a farm somewhere and breathe in the fresh air."

"If I go down and sniff the manure mounds from the horse carriages down at the park, will you let me get back to work?"

"Sure. But only if you take a selfie."

"Kaine."

"Shut up, you idiot. Your head's not in the right space. I don't want you fucking up any of our projects while you're like this. So get yourself sorted out. Take the car, take the plane, take whatever you need. But sort yourself out. The work will be there when you get back. I don't intend on going belly up any time soon."

"You might if I'm not there."

"Too bad they didn't inflate your ego instead of your spleen."

"You're a real asshole, you know?"

"I have you to remind me every day, Xave. Stay alive for that if nothing else."

"Fuck off."

"I'm serious. Try to stay alive. You still owe me $20 from last week's card game."

"It was Go Fish, and I was half-conscious."

246

"Not my fault you didn't check the fine print. Jade will be by later to fuss over you."

"I'll make sure I need a sponge bath then!" I yell at his back as he chuckles on his way to the elevator.

I wait until I hear the door close behind him before I let out my breath, groaning at the pain in my chest.

That has nothing to do with my injuries.

THIRTY-SEVEN

Her

"Who are these from?" I ask, as Cameron carries a large bouquet of flowers into my office. I try to bite back the hope that the card will be signed with an X.

"From me," he replies, with a smile, setting the vase on my desk.

I hope he doesn't see the disappointment on my face.

"Oh, they're beautiful, Cam. What's the occasion?" I pull a rose from the bunch and bring it to my nose. Not much of a fragrance, which is why I like flowers in the first place, but still beautiful.

"Do I need an occasion? How about, just a reminder of how much I appreciate you being my partner, and that I'm excited about our future."

"This is very sweet, Cameron. But you didn't have to do that. You've done so much for me these last few weeks."

"It will never be enough, Isabella." He winks and walks out the door, whistling down the hallway as he goes to his own office.

Something about the way he says my name causes a scrunching inside my chest. It's been three weeks since anyone has called me anything but Isabella, but day by day, I'm feeling more distanced from the adopted name.

There's nothing wrong with Isabella. But I miss Malynda. And the life she was supposed to have lived. I shake my head and focus back on the designs in front of me. The youth shelter has almost finished its renovations and hopefully, in a few days, I can start moving things in. I only have about ten days to get everything ready for the grand opening. I scan my list of furniture that still needs to be ordered and try to estimate how much labor will be needed for the painting and fixtures installations.

I don't realize how long I've been working on it until I look up and the sky outside the window is a soft pink, sinking into night.

The office is almost empty and my neck cracks as I stretch it to the side.

For the first time in weeks, I feel so tired I might actually be able to get some sleep.

I shove my laptop into my bag and flick the light off. I can see Cameron on the phone in his office and I give him a wave as I make my way out.

The building's foyer is empty except for the security guard and I smile at the doorman as he wishes me goodnight. I step out into the cooling air and stop dead in my tracks.

It's him.

Here.

Damien.

I freeze, my entire body cold and hot all at once.

And then I turn to run.

"Please! Stop!" He reaches out, his hand circling around my wrist, stopping me. I shake him off so hard that my shoulder almost pops out of the socket.

"No! Don't you fucking touch me." I yell, all the rage of twelve years built up inside me, drenched with fear.

He throws his hands up into the air.

"I'm sorry, I'm sorry! I'm not going to touch you. Or hurt you."

"Too late!" I yell again. I can see rather than feel my lip quivering, and I try to relax, counting to five under my breath. "What are you doing here?"

"I-..."

"No." I hold a hand up to cover my eyes from the sight of his face. "I don't care. Don't ever come near me again. I dropped the charges from you breaking into my apartment because I didn't want to drag... anyone else into this. So *you* trashed my apartment, *he* bashed you. Let's call it even. But I'm warning you, don't ever come near me again."

I spin around and start to walk away.

"It wasn't me! You have to know, it wasn't me!" He shouts, a desperation in his voice I can't place. I stop, even though I know I shouldn't. But something... something makes me stop. "I swear, it wasn't me who trashed your apartment."

I turn and face him. I stare into the face that has kept me up for twelve long years. Into the eyes that color my nightmares and turns my blood cold. He doesn't look away. And he says it again.

"I thought, I owed you at least that. To promise you I didn't break into your apartment. That's what the police and that guy who bashed me said, that I had broken into your apartment and trashed it. It wasn't me. I swear on everything that it wasn't."

I shake my head. The nerve of this man. "You're just saying that to get off the hook. I found the ballet slipper you left, you sick fuck!"

His forehead creases. "I don't know what slipper you're talking about. I came here because you find out who did do it. You have to know I didn't want to come here. I never wanted to see you again either. If he found out, I don't know what will happen. But that night, I can't tell you why I acted like that, but it wasn't who I am and I'm sorry. I'm so sorry."

The eyes I'm staring into fill with tears, and he looks away.

"What did you say?"

"I said, I'm sorry. I don't know what came over me that night. I promise you, it had never happened before and hasn't happened since."

"No. Not that. If 'he found out' you came here? Who is 'he'?"

He shakes his head. "It's nothing. I came to say, I'm so sorry. And you might never believe me about that, but please, believe me when I tell you. It wasn't me who broke into your apartment. I mean, I don't even know where you live."

"Then how...?" I start to ask.

"Hey, what's going on here?" We both turn at the sound of Cameron's voice.

I'm relieved until I see his face.

It's scrunched in anger.

"What the fuck are you doing here?" he growls at Damien, moving his arm to shield me. "Get the fuck away from her right now!"

Damien's face scrunches up, like he wants to say one last thing, decides against it and starts to run down the street.

I push Cameron's arm away and shout after him. "Wait! How did you even find me?"

For a second it doesn't look like he's going to stop. But then he does and yells back at me, "Ask him. Ask Cameron. And remember what I said." Then he dashes across the street and is lost in the crowd before I can ask him one last question.

I don't realize I'm shaking until Cameron wraps his arms around me.

"Hey, Isa," he whispers. "You're okay. He's gone now."

I take a moment to let my breath and body settle, the words spiraling in my mind making me dizzy.

"Cameron?" I pull away and look up at him.

"Yeah?"

"What did he mean, 'ask Cameron'?" As I wait for his answer, something occurs to me, "And how do you even know who he is?"

He doesn't answer immediately but I know him so well, I can see his brain formulating an answer. But I don't want a formulated answer. I want the truth. All of it.

"Cameron!"

"Look, it's nothing. Um, well, you told me about him when we first met, remember?" I just nod; of course I remember. But I'd never told Cameron his name or showed him what he looked like and yet Cameron had recognized him on sight. "Well, I figured out who he was from what you'd told me. So, er, I went by the dance school one day and he and I had a talk."

I can't believe it. "Oh my god! Why didn't you ever tell me this?! What happened when you went to talk to him?"

"Isa! Does any of this matter? It was so long ago! And everything worked out for the best. Come on, let's go back inside."

"No, Cameron, I am not leaving this spot until you tell me what happened!"

"Look, I just wanted to help you. So I just offered him some money to leave New York. He could leave and never ever come back here to bother you ever again and I wouldn't report him to the police for attacking you."

"Oh my god! That's why he left! Because of you!"

"Yes, but he obviously didn't listen or else he wouldn't be back here."

I shake my head, speechless. And then the thoughts start to filter through. "Wait. That's how he found me. That's how he knew I would be here tonight. He found me through you. He couldn't have found me as Isabella Fountaine. He only knew me as Malynda before." My head is pounding as my past appears in front of me completely jumbled. Cameron and Damien? Talking? Making deals?

"I'm sorry. I'll... I'll make sure he gets a reminder about our deal," Cameron says, totally oblivious to what I'm thinking.

"No! Don't! I never wanted you to do that!"

"I know. I did it for you anyway."

"And I don't think he was here to hurt me." I say the words before I think them.

"Come on, Isabella! Grow up. Then why was he here?"

It takes me a moment to remember. And then I do.

"He said... he wasn't the one who broke into my apartment."

"Pfft, and you believe him? He's probably just covering his tracks."

"No. I believe him." Again, the words come out of my mouth even before I can process them in my mind.

"You're just in shock at seeing him again. I'll take you home and you'll feel better in a bit." He moves to take my hand but I take a step back.

I look up at my best friend, my partner. "Did you really pay him off?"

He nods, "Yes."

"Why?"

"To protect you."

"But you barely knew me then."

"I knew enough to…" his voice trails off just as a car horn blasts, drowning him out.

"To what?" I prompt him.

"Iz, are we really having this conversation now?" he asks, running a hand through his blonde hair.

"Just tell me, Cameron."

"I knew enough to know, okay?"

"To know what?"

"That I loved you. And I would do anything to protect you."

"Oh, Cameron." I wish he hadn't said it. There's no going back from here.

"You know it's true," he whispers.

And I do. Just as he has always known that I have never returned those feelings.

"It's okay. You don't have to say anything. I can wait."

I just shake my head. No more. I don't want anyone waiting for me anymore. I can't take that responsibility.

"No, Cameron. I need you to understand. I'm not going to change my mind. Ever."

He just smirks and I feel a sudden urge to wipe it from his face. I've tolerated his arrogance because it made him a good business partner, but I don't want him feeling that about me.

"I'm here for you. I've always been here. I was here when your life came crashing down around you. I was here when your attacker broke into your home and stole your grandmother's ring. And I'll be here when all this settles down and you realize that I'm the only person you've ever been able to rely on. Not Xavier. Me."

He drapes his coat around my shoulders as I stand there, thinking about his words.

"Come on, I'll take you home. One more night in that apartment and you can stay with me tomorrow until you find a new place. I'll have the guest room made up."

"Wait. Cameron."

"Hmm?"

"I didn't tell you that my grandmother's ring was stolen."

"What?"

253

"I said, I didn't tell you that my grandmother's ring was stolen. Only Xavier knew that." This doesn't make sense.

"I'm sure you did, maybe you just forgot," he says, waving my words away.

"I didn't forget! I know I didn't. I didn't tell the police either. That ring was worth nothing. It was just some costume jewelry. I didn't list it on the insurance either. But you. You knew that was my grandmother's ring. So how did you know it was stolen?"

His face freezes, then he just shrugs. "You were upset, I can't remember when you told me. We've talked a lot in the last few weeks, Iz. You probably just don't remember!"

"No! Oh my God. Cameron. How did you know?"

"I..."

I back away. There's only one way. "No. Please. No."

"Isabella."

"Oh my God. The slipper!" My head aches with the revelation. "You went to Damien's dance studio when you went to bribe him to go away. That's where I left it. And that's where you got it. Oh my god. You're the one who broke in and... put the slipper in my apartment. You were trying to frame him."

"Isabella, wait no. You have it all wrong."

I feel so sick I can barely stand straight. The feeling of walking into my trashed apartment comes hurtling back to the front of my mind. The way I felt seeing my ballet slipper again, reliving the worst moment of my life. My stomach turns and I bend over and retch into the gutter. I push him away as he tries to help me.

"It was you. It was you?"

His face tells me everything I need to know.

"Isabella."

"Why? WHY?"

The anguish is etched deep on his face as he stumbles for the right words. But there are none. "I was just trying to help you. Remind you, that I'm here for you. That I've always been here for you."

"That's not what love is, Cameron! Scaring me into your arms?! Do you have any idea how utterly *fucked up* that is?!" The betrayal is so colossal, I can't even comprehend it.

"Then what IS love then? I have been here for you all this time, Isabella. I stepped in, got rid of that piece of shit, and he hasn't bothered you until now! That is love, Iz. Not some teenage puppy love you didn't even trust enough with your secret."

And it all becomes clear. "Oh my god, is that what this was all about? Xavier?"

"No! It's about us. It's always been about us. Isabella, please understand why I did this!"

He reaches out and grabs my wrist. I have no energy to shake him off. I don't have the energy to process what my life is, has been.

"Let go of me, Cameron." His touch disgusts me so much, I almost retch again.

"No, Isabella-..."

"She said 'let go.'"

We both whip our heads around at the sound of the voice. Xavier.

How? I don't care.

"Get lost, you fucking creep." Cameron spits.

"Now, I'm saying it. Let go of her," Xavier says. He doesn't move, just stands there, his hands in his pockets, staring Cameron down. But something in his voice makes Cameron obey and he drops my hand and takes a step back.

"Xavier!" I cry and run over to him.

He doesn't say anything, just takes one tiny step to move his body in front of me. "You okay?" he says, and I just nod. I am. He is here.

"Everything is fine. She doesn't want you here," Cameron scoffs.

"I think I'll let her speak for herself."

"I'm okay. Can you take me home, please?" I beg Xavier gently. He pulls off his jacket and throws it around my shoulders.

"Isabella! Wait!" Cameron yells out as I walk away. The sound of his voice makes my body shudder.

I force myself to stop and address him once and for all. "No. I can't believe that I'm saying this to you. After everything. But no. Don't you ever come near me again. I don't know who you are anymore, Cameron. Maybe I've never known."

He storms toward me, but Xavier blocks him, a hand against his chest.

"You heard her."

"What, you're going to smash my face in? Is that all you know how to do?" Cameron smirks. And in that moment I feel like I hate him more than I've ever hated anyone.

"No. I know when someone's not even worth touching," Xavier says.

I look at my former friend one last time and turn to walk away.

"Isabella!" he yells.

"Forget Isabella. That fucking name you convinced me to take. My name is Malynda. But you should forget that too."

***

By the time we reach my front door, I'm so tired the hallway echoes with the sound of my feet dragging one behind the other. Xavier props me up against the door and rummages inside my purse until he finds the keys. Unlocking the door, he swings it open and then pulls my arm around my neck as he tucks one arm under my legs and carries me into the apartment.

It's almost completely bare. All my belongings packed in boxes stacked in the hallway, ready for my new life.

A life I have no vision of right now. And a past that lies in ruins.

He lays me gently on the bed, and I only let go because I have to.

He slips my shoes off my feet.

"What were you doing there?"

"I was watching you."

"How long have you been doing that?"

He just shrugs.

"It's a hard habit to break."

"Did you see Damien?"

"Yes."

"And did you hear Cameron?"

"Yes."

"I wouldn't have let either of them hurt you. I didn't step in until I thought you might actually be in danger."

"I know."

"But that's not my job anymore, is it?"

"No."

"You get some rest." He leans over and kisses me gently on the forehead.

"Xavier?"

"Can you just stay for tonight? Please?"

"Malynda."

"Please. I miss you. Just stay. For tonight."

He sighs, and then I watch as he pulls off his jacket and throws it onto the foot of the bed, sliding off his shoes before sliding into bed next to me.

I roll over and I'm in his arms.

"Just for tonight," he whispers, his lips in my hair.

My hand falls onto his chest, and I watch it rise and fall, rise and fall with his breath. My fingertips play with the buttons and I push one through the hole. And then another. And another until his shirt is completely undone. The two sides fall apart and I run my nails up his taut stomach, feeling the hot skin stretched over muscle.

I try to ignore the purple and yellowing marks, but I can't. They're there because of me. I roll over and press a kiss to the wounds on his chest. His heartbeat races under my lips and I move my body until I'm straddling over him, gently kissing up the bruises on his sternum, his neck until my lips are on his.

I feel his whole body close around me, his legs hooking around mine, his arms around my back as the kiss deepens.

I know what I want, what I need in this moment. Xavier, wholly and completely. I reach between us, fumbling with his zipper.

"Malynda," he whispers and I shush him with another kiss.

"Just for tonight. Please."

He sighs, and lies back, watching me as I shake my head, my hair falling over us.

He pushes my hands away and frees himself as I slide my panties down my legs.

He reaches up, his hands cupping my face like it's a precious chalice in his hands.

"I love you, Malynda. Whatever happens to us, I want you to remember, I will always love you."

My tears trickle down my face and onto his fingers.

If only I knew he would always be here to catch my tears.

I shift, positioning him under me, and then slide my body down, feeling him fill me up. Just as I wanted. Wholly. Completely.

He exhales and drops his hands down onto my hips, looking up at me, as we start to find a rhythm.

Our eyes lock and never leave each other's.

Not even when he lifts my dress off my body. Not when I reach down, bracing my hands on his chest. Not when I feel myself fall over the cliff, or when his whole body clenches and then releases inside me.

Not even then.

Only when my exhausted body falls against him, do we finally look away.

"What are you going to do now?" I whisper to him, when our breath is quiet.

"Try to figure out what my life is meant to be without you," he says, brushing my hair off my neck and dropping a kiss to the top of my head.

"You've done it for twelve years."

"No. There wasn't a day you weren't with me."

"And what am I supposed to do?" I ask him.

"Whatever it is you want. Without the weight of the past, without the fear of me finding out, without looking over your shoulder. Free from all that. Just to do whatever it is you were meant to do."

I slide up until my ear is just over his heart. "What if what I want is to be with you?"

"Then you'll figure out a way to do that too."

***

I'm not sure what time it is when I wake up, but the room is completely dark. I turn over onto my back and nothing stops me. I reach out my hand to touch the sheet and it's cold. He is gone but I still, strangely, feel safe as I slide out of bed pulling on the dressing gown I left on the chair next to my bed and walk through my empty apartment. There is no sign of him. There's barely a sign of me left in this empty space and I'll be glad to be gone from here tomorrow.

I hear a cough on the other side of the door and I freeze just for a moment before I realize what I'm hearing. I tiptoe to the door and peep through the eyehole, and there he is, sitting in the hallway outside of my apartment on the floor, his arms wrapped around his own body. His eyes staring straight ahead, waiting, watching, always protecting.

It takes everything I have not to throw the door open and run to him.

But I know, it's not our time.

I know that now.

I know that for me, I know that for him, and I know in the morning when I step outside he won't be waiting for me anymore. I push away from the door and slide to the floor, my back against the flat, cold wood, and cry over Xavier Kent one last time.

259

THIRTY-EIGHT

Him

"Are you going to tell me where you going? I mean, it's not that I don't like having you here but it's that I don't like having you here," Ram says. "You kind of cramp my style."

The laugh that bubbles out of my throat surprises even me. I haven't been in much of a laughing mood lately. "I was here ONE night. And please! What style? Your nightstand is literally a stack of Playboy magazines from the 1970s."

"Exactly. Porno chic," Ram retorts.

"Yeah, well, you needn't worry about people stealing it from you. Anyway, relax. I'll be gone by the time you get home tonight."

"Where are you going?"

"Away," I shrug.

There's a twitch of his left eyebrow, but he doesn't push it. "Is there anything you need me to do while you're gone," he asks, but he didn't need to ask.

"No," I say, even though we both know it's a lie. "You take care of your business and I'll take care of mine."

"Mate, that's always been the problem. Your business is my business."

Our smiles at each other soon turn into idiot grins.

"Should we hug it out?"

"Fuck, no. You'll just break my ribs again."

FORTY

Her

"Jade, I can't thank you enough for letting me stay here," I say, as she reaches into a moving box and pulls out a cushion and lays it on my bed.

"Are you kidding me? I am so happy to have a friend in the building. I'm thrilled this apartment became available just in time. And don't worry, you're far away enough not to hear my baby cry at four in the morning. Although five floors away isn't far enough from me not to come down and have a chat with you every night," Jade says, and then giggles, reaching over and squeezing my arm.

The truth is I can't thank her enough. I was supposed to move in with Cameron while I looked for a new place but even the mere thought of his name right now makes me shudder. I don't know if I'll ever be able to be in the same room with him again, but right now all I can think about is how he tried to manipulate me by committing one of the most heinous things I could ever imagine someone who calls themselves my friend could do. My life feels like it's fallen off a cliff, and there's nothing left for me to hold on to.

"Jade, about the youth center. Now that I'm not partners with Cameron anymore, do you still want me to finish the design work?"

Jade shifts closer to me on the bed and takes my hand in hers. "If I recall, we hired you, not your firm."

My firm. As much as I can't imagine ever working with Cameron again the thought of the business we worked so hard on together now lying in ruins breaks my heart.

"Hey. You'll work it out. And will be here to help you."

All I can do is nod. I'm sure she's had enough of my moping by now. I hadn't known how she and Kaine were going to treat me; it would've been understandable if they'd wanted to kept their distance from me considering how close they were to Xavier. But once again, they'd proven just what wonderful people they are. It's

261

only fair I try to repay them by doing the absolute best job on the youth center that I possibly can.

Jade cuts open another box and reaches inside.

"Hey, what's this?"

I look over as she turns a crumpled white envelope in her hand. Just seeing it turns my stomach upside down. I reach for it, turning it over in my hands, remembering.

"Just something from the past."

She smiles, "Looks like it's had an interesting life."

I nod.

"Actually, Jade? I've just had an idea I want to float by you," I say to her. And something about the thought suddenly brewing in my mind makes me smile for the first time in a long time. Apparently, it's contagious, because Jade grins and sits up straight, suddenly looking just as excited as I feel.

She gives me a wink and says, "I'm all ears. Float away."

FORTY-ONE

Him

Do you ever wonder what they mean when they say, you can never go home? Do they mean that home isn't really a place, a location, an X on a map? Maybe it's just a feeling you have in your heart that can't ever be recreated.

I never really thought about it, I guess, because I don't know where home is. I love Manhattan, I really do. The hustle and the bustle and the manic chaos and the anonymity while having nothing but a thin wall between you and your neighbor excites me, keeps me feeling alive. But home?

I don't know. I don't know what home is supposed to feel like.

But some places, home or not, are coded in your DNA forever.

That's how I feel as I step off the company jet onto the tarmac in Portland, Maine.

The last time I was here, I was eighteen, sitting on a bus, backpack stuffed with three days' worth of clothes, a crumpled letter in my hand and fear in my heart.

Scared but, I remember, I felt alive.

And oh, how alive I feel now.

A gust of wind kicks up as I walk to the car Patricia booked ahead for me, and blasts against my face. I close my eyes to shield them from the dust, while breathing in the scent of mown grass and sea air.

I throw my overnight bag into the back seat of the convertible and settle into the driver's seat, breathing lungful after lungful of nostalgia. And something inside me starts to heal over.

I plan for the drive to Langham to take me almost half an hour. Or it should only take me half an hour, but I can't help constantly stopping along the way. Every few miles I pull over to take in the landscape of my childhood. We didn't take a lot of trips after my father left but in that short time when I remember having two parents, on lazy Sunday afternoons he would have us all jump in the car, then somebody would shout out a town name not too far but close enough for us to play several car games and off we would go. Off to Gray, off to Auburn, off to Reid State Park we would go, the six of us crammed into his old Buick with so much excitement sometimes I think the car ran solely on our energy.

Somehow, everything looks the same and yet everything looks different. The road signs are different, the fields of wildflowers have been leveled for farmland, the old lobster shack that you could see from the road with its red roof is faded and covered in spiderwebs. Every few miles I stop and take it all in, readjusting the images in my head of what Maine looks like now. It's almost two hours after I land when I finally turn off the exit into Langham. I try to pretend I don't know where I'm going but my internal navigation system steers me to the place that I've been longing to return to.

I turn into the half-full parking lot and the sign tells me they're still open for the summer season. The sign still says Dairy Joy but it's faded, the menus on the windows have changed to typed and laminated, a far cry from the owner's messy scribbles on the chalkboard. The door is closed probably to lock in the cold air. Two kids laugh as they race their way out of the ice cream parlor to a bench under the shade, multicolored ribbons of ice cream already trickling down their arms. I slide through the closing door and the aroma that wafts into my nostrils instantly takes me back.

Takes me back twelve years to the first time I saw her. I was standing at the counter handing out some samples which she walked in the door. Something about the ding of the bell sounding different from the thousands of times before and I looked up just as she swept in, her curtain of blonde hair messy after a long day of high school but still shimmering in the afternoon light. Her face glowed with a smile, seemingly about nothing in particular, and in that moment I didn't know it but she had stolen my heart forever.

"Can I help you?" says the man standing behind the counter, drawing me out of my reverie. It only takes a moment for the question in his eyes to linger, but then it clicks. "Xavier? Is that really you?" He shakes his head, as if to combine the image of me in his head with the person standing in front of him. He holds out his hand to me, awkwardly. It's funny what the passage of time can do. Last time he saw me I was just eighteen. And he was my boss. Hardly the type of person he'd be offering his hand to. But times have changed and he knows why I am here.

"Hi Mr. Horsham, how are you doing?" I ask, taking his hand and giving his a good shake, then following up with a grin.

"I'm doing okay, Xavier, I'm doing good." He hasn't let go of my hand yet and I have no reason to pull away.

"That's good, I'm glad to hear it." There is another ding of the bell as a family comes in behind me. "I'll get out of your way. I just wanted to come and see how you are doing."

"No, please, stay for a minute. Can I get you something?"

"Sure, how about one of your famous banana splits. And don't cheap out on the whipped cream," I say giving him a wink remembering the hundreds of times he would tell me off for being too generous.

He laughs and steps over to the serving station. Someone comes from out back to serve the other customers while I stand there taking in the sights and sounds of my high school summers working here. It takes him less than a minute to put my sundae together and he gestures for me to follow him outside. It is still warm considering that the summer is in its very last days and the tips of the leaves are starting to turn. I let a mouthful of ice cream melts into a creamy puddle on my tongue before I swallow it.

"Xavier, I don't know how to thank you-" he starts.

"No. Please. You don't have to." I cut him off.

"No, it has to be said. If you hadn't given me that gift, that... loan, you know we wouldn't have been able to stay in business. I'm not even sure how you knew about our troubles. I tried to contact you but... you never returned any of my calls."

"It was the least I could do, Mr. Horsham. You helped me when I needed it most, and you taught me how much just one kind person can make a difference to your life. """

"You know, I still regret letting you go that day. It's just... those kids..." he says his voice dropping.

"No. It was the right thing to do. I know now how important it is to run a good business. And you always did. This place would not be the same without you. I did it just as much for me, for Langham, as for you, sir," I say. I mean every word.

***

Banana split in hand, I find myself starting to wander down the street, the rental car left behind. I don't think too much about where I want to go, just letting my feet take me where they wish. I walk down Main Street, taking in the new businesses that have spread out beyond the old skate park I used to take Brian to. There's growth here, but it's slow. Maybe that's okay. Not everywhere has to be Manhattan.

It's not long before I find myself away from the busiest part of town. The houses and buildings are more sparse, interspersed between empty land and trees.

In the distance I can hear the water crashing over the dam and I close my eyes and listen. There must've been some rainfall in the last few days. Even after all these years, I can tell what month it is just by the sound of the waterfall.

A car whizzes by and I open my eyes and continue on my walk. There's no doubt where my feet are taking me now. I don't fight it.

The trees grow thicker on either side of the road. There are bushes and branches I remember so well, I automatically duck to avoid the thorns as I pass them. The path is paved now though, no longer just dirt and pebbles and errant weeds under my feet.

It's not too far now, my destination.

My body turns into the gap in the trees even before I really realize where I am. It's more overgrown than I remember; I have to push aside some branches and my feet stamp down on the ankle-high weeds before I emerge in front of the lake.

But once I do, it's like I never left.

I gasp, just like that first time. Just like *her* first time seeing the lake from this very spot.

No matter what time of day it is, the reflection of the sky off the water's surface is breathtaking.

I sink to my feet and sit down in the long grass, looking out over the water. A bird chirps behind me, and I can almost hear the sound of Malynda's twinkling laughter as she used to sneak peeks into the nests to watch the baby birds grow.

The first night I slept here, it was right under the stars. My mother had come home after a double shift, the twins were screaming, and Brian had slammed the door and locked himself in his room. As soon as I could I disappeared out the back door and ran and ran and ran until I ended up here. The chaos in my head was still so loud I could barely hear the water over the buzzing. I'd dived under the water, and it was only under there that I found silence.

I'd loved my little sanctuary out here.

I'd thought it was because I liked being alone, and that maybe that's just the sort of person I am. A loner. A hermit. A romantic isolationist.

But then I brought her here.

Without knowing anything about her, without having ever really spoken to her, I brought her here. And I loved it even more after that. After all that time, I spent here before her, it's her ghost that now haunts this place.

I should've perished in New York. After I moved there, to find her. I shouldn't have lasted a week, a month, let alone all this time. And I wouldn't have if I was really the loner I thought I was back then. It turns out, however, I just hadn't met the right people. I think back to those who have been there for me all these years. And I wonder what I ever did to deserve friendships like those.

Eighteen-year-old Xavier was a fool. The self-imposed isolation only ever hurt me.

I sigh and I push myself up onto my feet.

One more place to go.

***

I can see the wall is covered in faded movie and concert posters even before I come up close. I'm not sure what I was hoping for, but it would've been unrealistic to hope that her mural would still be visible. But other than that, nothing about this place has changed. The basketball court lines are almost invisible after decades of sun and rain. The hoop has lost its original red tint but still stands tall and strong.

I walk up to the wall, eyes scanning the concert posters peeling at the corners, the dates barely readable. My eyes close and there she is. Dancing in front of me, arms and body and legs moving to the music inside her head as she arranges the paint swatches on her work of art.

I need to see it; I need to know what she was working on all those hours. I need to know what I'd inspired in her.

I start ripping at the posters, peeling them away from the wall, layer by layer, careful not to disturb what lies beneath. The adrenaline starts to course through my body as I feel myself getting closer and closer. I start to tear at the sheets of colored paper, tossing them on the ground, not caring when the wind kicks up and carries them away.

Yes!

There it is! I spot the first corner of a paint swatch, and I feel myself hurtled into the past. I'm careful again, pulling the last layer away, slowly exposing her work inch by inch by inch until there's nothing left covering it.

I take a deep breath and I stand back.

And see it for the very first time.

It's hard to take it all in at once, it's so big, but it's beautiful. Breathtaking.

It's unfinished, but there's no doubt what it's was meant to be.

And there's no doubt that it came from her.

The background stretches outward in an array of vibrant colors that surround the central image; one hand outstretched to another.

Me and her. Hers and mine.

I'm just not sure who is the one offering their hand and who is the one taking it.

In my mind, I always thought it was me.

All this time.

Even now.

I thought I was the one meant to be saving her.

But she had it right all along, we were meant to save each other.

Even by not telling me about what had happened with her attack, and then subsequently her shame about doing what she needed to survive, she wasn't protecting herself. She was protecting me.

All this time, I thought I was the one protecting her. I thought fighting over her was the same thing as fighting for her.

I was wrong.

Fuck. I've been so wrong!!

I stare at the unfinished mural, hidden under layers and layers of history.

Unfinished. Just like us.

No. We need to continue what we started. And something tells me, that starts with her finishing this mural.

I stand back, taking a mental picture with my mind.

Malynda, I will help you finish.

If it's the last thing I ever do for you.

To remind her who she was, and how the things that have happened don't change that, don't change who it is she can be now.

That she was put on this earth to make art like this.

FORTY-TWO

Him

"Can you drive any faster, man?"

The Uber driver just shrugs, but I feel the car lurch forward and knock me back into my seat.

"What's the hurry?" he asks over his shoulder.

"I need to see a girl. About something. Something long overdue."

"Ah. Well, we're almost there. You sure you know what you're going to say?"

"Yes. I just don't know how she's going to respond."

The youth center looms ahead and I point to it. "Over there! Just pull over!"

I jump out even before he's come to a complete stop.

Turning almost immediately back into traffic he yells, "Good luck, man!" out the rolled-down window, and merges into the throng of cars.

I spin around to face the building, eyeing the signs and banners announcing today as the grand opening. I don't have time to take in the finished construction before she comes walking around the corner.

"Malynda!" Her name comes spilling out from deep in my gut and onto my lips.

She instantly stops in her tracks, her hands full with a box of decorations, causing a chain reaction of people almost banging into her and each other. Someone curses as he jumps to the side to avoid her.

She doesn't say anything for a moment.

I don't say anything for a moment longer.

270

I thought I knew what I wanted to say. But seeing her in front of me right now makes all the declarations, all the revelations, all the promises seem unworthy of what I feel. Unworthy of her.

"I didn't know if you were going to come today," she finally says. And I nod. I can see why she might've thought that.

"I'm sorry I haven't been in touch, I was out of town. But I'm here now," I say, as if I need to convince her I'm real. Just as I had needed to convince myself over and over that she was real in those first few days she came back into my life. It was so much easier to think that she's been just an aberration. Memories are much easier to deal with than reality.

But now, we are both real and both here. Just where we're meant to be.

"Do they know?" she asks, her eyes giving nothing away. I feel more nervous than I ever have in my life. My fingers feel clammy and I shove them into my pockets to stop from fidgeting.

"Jade and Kaine?" I ask. She nods in reply. "Yes. They're the ones who told me what time you'd be here," I say before I think that that might come across as a betrayal to her.

"Where did you go?"

"Maine." My answer makes her eyebrows shoot up, but she doesn't respond.

I take a step closer, the letters slowly starting to form into words and sentences again in my head. And then I speak, and say all the things I should've said a long time ago.

"Malynda. I'm sorry. I'm so sorry. The things I said, the things I did. I was wrong. You're right, all this time I've been trying to pass it off as my need to protect you, but it was just my misguided machismo at having failed you all those years ago. I should've been here convincing you, showing you that the things that happened to you mean nothing in the scheme of how I see you, how I respect and admire you... how I love you. I was off nursing my own bruised ego, and getting more bloody bruised in the process. And then to blame it on you? I don't even know why you're still here listening to me. I don't deserve it. But I need you to know how sorry I am. The truth is, I've been in a state of suspended animation for so long. I thought I'd grown up, matured, when I've just been making excuses for my immature way of thinking. While I've been waiting and searching, I should've been working on making myself worthy of you, for the day you might come back. I realize that now. I also realize that my role was never to protect you; it's to support you. It's not to inspire you; it's to help you inspire yourself. And that I should never have put that burden on you, to be my reason for living. And I should've told you, there's nothing you can't do without me. You don't need me. I need you. Then, you might've known that there's nothing you should've been afraid to tell me. Because I would never have stopped loving you because of something that had happened to you, or something you had done. My love was never contingent on you staying the same. You were always meant to grow. I just wanted to get to watch it. It's still what I want." I take a deep breath and say the final thing I came here to say. I hold out my hand to her, outstretched, open. "Come with me. Please, I want to take you somewhere."

She doesn't answer me right away, just stands and stares at me for a moment.

She looks down at my hand and there's the slightest shake of her head.

"I can't, Xavier. It's - it's the youth center opening today. I have to be here. And so do you."

Her words slash through the breath I'm holding, and I feel every cell in my body convulse.

I had never thought about what would happen if she said no. If she wouldn't let me take her back to where it all happened. I had never thought about the fact that I could be too late. I drop my hand and take a few steps back, tripping over the curb behind me and stumble onto the street.

A car horn beeps and startles me out of my thoughts.

"Xavier!" She runs over and grabs my arm pulling me back onto the footpath. "You idiot!"

She lets go and looks me over, "Are you okay?"

I nod, the years ahead of me without her in my life arranging themselves in my head and weighing on my heart.

"Er, yeah. I'm fine. Don't worry about me. It's your day." I say.

She frowns. "No. It's *our* day. You've worked on this for much longer than I have. Don't let me ruin it for you. And anyway, I have something to show you." There's a twinkle in her eye and this time it's her reaching her hand out to me. "Are you game?" she asks.

And I say the only thing there is to say as I take her hand, "Fuck, yes."

I'm not sure what I'm expecting as I grip her hand and she pulls me through the entrance of the youth center. I haven't been here in two weeks, since I checked in one last time before I left for the airport and out of New York for the first time in twelve years. At that point, the construction was almost finished, but as most people know, that's when it can look the worst. There had still been debris everywhere, the partitions were erected by still bare drywall. The cement floor was covered in layers and decades of dust and the erratic pattern of footprints of the construction workers.

So when I step through the doors, and into the now bright and clean and modern space, it is unrecognizable as the warehouse that Kaine and I first saw, peering through a broken window one Thursday night all those months ago when we'd gone location scouting on a whim. We'd ignored the advice to go through a real estate agent, instead, hoofing it ourselves through the better part of Harlem until we'd found the place that called out to us.

Now it's here.

A literal dream come to life.

And I can hardly care less because my hand is in Malynda's hand, and the future as unknown as ever.

"Where are we going?" I say, staring at the back of her head as she leads me through the center.

"You'll see! So impatient. Have you always been this way?"

I stop and give her a look that even she can't help but laugh at in this strange and crazy moment.

"Come on! You'd think I was taking you to your public hanging."

"I'm not so sure it isn't."

"Be quiet."

The warehouse has never felt so big to me before, but it seems like it takes forever for her to drag me through it, passing the new kitchen and study rooms and offices in the back. We come to a small door and she winks at me before throwing it open.

She leads me into a full-size indoor basketball court, complete with hoops on either end. On one side of the room are racks with nets and poles for what looks like volleyball and badminton. The opposite wall is covered in a long mirror, and two long wooden barres stretching almost the length of the entire room. All the way on the back wall, is a blank sheet, hanging from ceiling to floor.

And in the middle of the court, standing and watching me, is Kaine, Jade, Ram, Gabriel, Harriet, everyone I know from Ash Foundation, my mom and my brothers and over fifty or sixty kids I recognize from the neighboring schools.

"Er. Wh... what's going on?" I whisper, suddenly self-conscious, trying to shield myself behind her tiny frame.

She laughs and moves out the way. "Today's the grand opening of the youth center... you know that!"

"Yes, but..."

"Well, we can't have the opening of The Ash Center without you."

Kaine steps forward from the group and hands me a microphone. "Go on, everyone's been waiting for you."

I cover the microphone, "Waiting for what?"

"To hear what you have to say, duh." He smirks and steps back to join the crowd.

Malynda has joined them, and I don't know what to say. I thought I was done with speeches for the day, and the result of the last one didn't fill me with confidence.

I clear my throat and wipe my hand on my suit before gripping the microphone in my hand.

"Um, hi everyone, thank you so much for coming out here today." Everyone is silent and the sound of my voice echoing through the speakers and around the gym is reminding me why I choose to be a contract lawyer and not a barrister. Paper and ink don't stare at you and expect you to make sense on the spot.

274

I take a breath and look around at the space. Even in this gymnasium, it looks like everything we envisioned and more. A space of hope and inspiration. Of inclusion, acceptance, guidance. Above the mirrored wall there's a collage of different figures dancing in different styles. Different races, different shapes, different abilities.

On the other wall, there are handwritten motivational quotes. That was a Gabriel idea. To get the kids to come up with their favorite sayings, not necessarily well known, but ones that they could relate to, that inspired them and that they thought might inspire others.

Everywhere I can see little touches that came from all of us. Things that speak to how this whole project came to life, a joint, community effort.

I'm overcome by what this place might achieve

I realize it's been sometime since I've spoken, and everyone is still looking at me, expectantly.

"This center has been a dream of mine since I knew that I had a right to dream. That hasn't always been the case, sometimes some of us have to fight for what others take for granted as given. But I'm here to tell you, we all have a right to want what we want for our own lives. Achieving it, however, it not a given. And not everyone has the same opportunities. That doesn't make your dream any less valid. It just means you might have to work harder. And the Ash Center is here to give you the support you need." I turn to the group of high school kids. "If you ever feel like you have a dream that is unreachable, remember me. Remember Kaine. Well, mostly Kaine, he's the one with his name on a building." There's a ripple of laughter and I feel more at ease. "Thank you for being here to help us remember this day. And for your part in making it come true." I search for her eyes and lock on them when I find them. "We could not have done it without you."

I clear my throat and the mic drops down and there's a spattering of applause as Malynda comes up and takes the microphone away from me.

"Not bad for being put on the spot," she says and gives me a wink.

I want to wink back but I can't. I can't act normal when I just made the declaration of my life and she rejected it. I need to get out of here.

"I gotta go," I say, leaning in.

"But I haven't shown you what I wanna show you yet!"

"This isn't it?" I say, gesturing to the gymnasium.

"You ain't seen nothing yet." She lifts her hand and gives Jade a thumbs up; Jade grins and gives her a thumbs-up back.

"Wha..."

"Just shut up for once and trust me, will ya?"

"I do trust you, Malynda. The question has always been, do you trust me?"

She gives me a look that has the butterflies in my stomach taking flight.

"Yes. I do, Xavier."

Before I can respond, there's a loud sound, like a sail catching in the wind, and I turn to see the giant sheet covering the wall fall to the ground.

And I gasp.

It's her mural.

Brilliant, alive, larger than life.

And finished.

"It's your mural."

She turns to me, mouth dropped open.

"How did you-...? You saw it in Maine?"

I nod, unable to take my eyes off it. It's twice as big as the wall at the basketball court, and this time she's used paint, but it's still the same image.

Somehow she's replicated it almost exactly; the colors are vibrant and stunning, the image larger than life, filling you with warmth and hope.

Two hands outstretched to each other.

To each other, not one taking the other.

And the image is circled by the words, "Never underestimate the effect of a single act of kindness."

She did it. My girl did it.

"I'm dying, tell me what you think?!!" she yells.

I force myself to look away and face her. Her eyes are as wide and bright as I've ever seen them, her cheeks flushed, her teeth sunken into her bottom lip.

I have no words, so I just cup her face in my hands and kiss her.

Kiss her until I feel like every emotion I have in this moment is made clear to her, how much I love her, admire her, am inspired by her, amazed by her. Kiss her until I have no breath left in my lungs.

And she kisses me back. Kisses me until I know that she's forgiven me.

"When did you decide to do this?" I say, as we pull apart, panting, ignoring the crowd of people cheering us on in the background.

"Something reminded me that you don't always respond so well to words," she grins and pulls a crumpled letter out of her pocket and slides it into my hand. The unopened letter. "So I decided to show you instead. That you've always been my inspiration, Xavier. That's what you've meant to me. Not my savior, my bodyguard, my protector. You were the one who helped me find myself."

"It took me a long time to realize that, I'm sorry," I tell her. "But I realize it now."

"And I'm sorry that I didn't trust you. I realize now that the only thing I ever needed to do was be honest with you. I trust you to be able to handle everything our lives have to throw at you."

I sigh. I didn't know I needed to hear that until I did. I trace the line of her face with my fingertip, a small gesture compared to the way my heart feels, dancing in my chest.

"How 'bout we start with breaking some secrets now?"

"Sure," she nods.

I take her hand and lift it to my lips, pressing a kiss to her palm. "Tell me - what's the secret ingredient in your mac and cheese?"

She throws her head back and laughs, gently punching me on the arm. "No fucking deal. That goes with me to the grave!"

I pull her still shaking body into my arms and kiss her again.

Until the whistles and cheers die down and I know even when I let go, she'll still be there.

The End

ABOUT THE AUTHOR

The first thing you should know about the author is, she hates writing these "About the Author" things.

But if you should run into her in a café in her hometown of Adelaide, Australia, then, for the price of a free smile, she'll tell you details you never needed to hear about another person.

Her husband can vouch for this. It's how they met. Kinda. But you'll hear about that when you run into her in a café in Adelaide.

She hopes you liked her book though. Like, really. It's pretty much all she's ever wanted to do. Write a book that you'd want to read.

Thanks for helping to fulfil that dream by reading this book.

Don't forget to subscribe to Daisy Allen's email newsletter to receive information on upcoming new releases and bonus offers just for subscribers!
Click here to subscribe or go to:
http://www.subscribepage.com/b3l2q9
You can also follow Daisy:
on Facebook for ramblings: **facebook.com/daibyday/**
or Instagram: **@daitvdowriter** for pictures of her morning coffee and baby elephant memes.

ALL BOOKS BY DAISY ALLEN

Available on Amazon and Kindle Unlimited and Audible

The Rock Chamber Boys Series
Play Me: Book one.
Strum Me: Book two.
Serenade Me: Book three
Rock Me: Book four

Men of Gotham Series
Kaine
Xavier
Gabriel (coming **mid-**2020)

An O'Reilly Clan Novel
Once Bitten

Subscribe to Daisy's newsletter for updates.